A PIRATE'S PROMISE

"Listen, Tsunami Blue, and listen well." Gabriel's voice was low, intense, frightening.

The sirens grew louder. The Runners were almost upon us. Terrified didn't begin to cover the emotions I was feeling.

"You will die at their hands, you know this?" Gabriel continued.

I nodded.

"I can't say what will happen or how long it will take to get rid of them, but if they find you, they will kill you."

"What do we do?" I asked.

He pulled back and looked at me with desperation in his eyes, something I hadn't seen before. And that scared me almost as much as the impending Runners. "Trust me," he whispered.

"I can't," I said back.

"Then try. If only for twenty-four hours. Just until we reach land. Try."

GAYLE ANN WILLIAMS

LOVE SPELL

NEW YORK CITY

For Hugh, my biggest fan. How I love you.

LOVE SPELL®

April 2010

Published by

Dorchester Publishing Co., Inc.
200 Madison Avenue
New York, NY 10016

ISBN 10: 0-505-52821-5
ISBN 13: 978-0-505-52821-6
E-ISBN: 978-1-4285-0840-8

Printed in the United States of America.

10 9 8 7 6 5 4 3 2 1

ACKNOWLEDGMENTS

As with any debut novel there are a lot of thank-yous. Here are mine:

A great many thanks to Leah Hultenschmidt, my editor. Thank you for your guidance and care with *Tsunami Blue*. Yes, you are my first editor, but I'm convinced you are the best editor in the entire world.

To my brilliant agent, Miriam Kriss, thank you for helping me navigate the mysterious waters of publishing. You are amazing.

Thank you to my beautiful sisters and my crazy brother, to my perfect nieces and nephews, and to my brothers-in-law and my sisters-in-law. Thank you to Ty and Ann, and Ash and David, I love you all so much.

Thank you to my beautiful Summer Girls, Bristol (Bristol Bay), Katie (Katie-did), Mollie (Moll-teenie), Desi (Desdemona), Lindsay (Lindsay Wagner), and Haley (Haley-Girl). Read close, girls, there may be a part of each of you in Kathryn "Blue" O'Malley.

Thank you to the beautiful and talented, Stella Cameron. A writer who gives from her heart both on the written page and to the community around her. You are a treasure.

To Caroline Cross, a wonderful person and talented writer, thank you for offering a hand in friendship all those years ago. I've never forgotten.

Thank you to Fancy Nancy and the crew and customers at Friday's Crab House, in Friday Harbor, WA. There are no words for the amount of inspiration and fun you have brought into my life. Not to mention fodder for my stories.

And to my Friday Harbor family of friends, thank you for the cheers and support and the wine.

Thank you to Ginny and Fred, and Big Hugh and Mary Lou. I will never forget you, and I will love you forever.

To Bill Chevalier, who would have loved Tsunami Blue's boots, I thank you for your friendship. I'll forever cherish our discussions of movies and books and gossip while sitting at the harbor downing ice-cold beer. I miss you, my friend.

And once again, thank you to Hugh, the amazing man who makes this journey in publishing so much sweeter.

TSUNAMI
BLUE

Chapter One

The San Juan Islands, Washington State
December 26, 2023

"And so, my friends, the moon is full, the sea calm, and the wave?" I dropped my voice to a whisper and clutched the microphone, pressing the cold steel to my forehead. I took a moment, shook my head, and pushed on. "The wave"—I fought hard to keep my voice steady—"the wave, my friends, sleeps tonight. And so can you."

I hung my head and let the mic dangle between my fingers. A few moments passed, maybe minutes even. Then I pulled the mic up to my lips and forced my voice to become much more than just a whisper in the dark. "This is Tsunami Blue, signing off on another waveless night, somewhere in paradise." I paused, took a breath, and then added a tag: "Hang on out there, guys. Just . . . hang on."

My shortwave equipment went to dead air as I snapped the dial off and let the mic slip all the way through my fingertips to fall with a soft thud on the floor.

"Shit." I scrubbed my hands across my face. "What the hell was that about, Blue? When did you become a fucking cheerleader?" But I knew what it was all about. It was about the day, the date, and the ghosts that lived on in my memories.

My dog, Max, jumped up and thumped his tail on the cedar floor. "I know, Max, I know. Language."

I walked over to a small, beat-up cupboard and pulled

a crisp twenty from a thick stack of bills and waved it in front of him. Max, excited almost to the point of frenzy, barked, and started to chase his tail.

"You know what's coming, don't ya, boy. Oh yeah, you *love* this part." I walked over to his bowl where an old Costco pickle jar sat stuffed with twenty-dollar bills. It was near to overflowing. I shoved the bill in. Max went crazy. He knew the drill.

I swear. I pay. He gets a treat.

I was trying to reform, trying to get a grip on my language before it bled into the airwaves. It wasn't easy. I had been surrounded by these words and the familiar smacks and punches that followed them since I was five. But I was older now, wiser. Independent. The bruises had long healed. But learned behavior? Well, old habits and all; they die hard.

However, I knew there was a handful of children out there who could hear me. I had hoped—prayed even—that there were more than a few. In my dreams there were thousands. I would never become anything like the long-defunct Disney Channel or Nick at Nite, but I could be a voice of hope, a voice that could save their young lives.

But, of course, it wasn't working well.

I mean, when you have only a dog to answer to, albeit a *big* dog, well, you get the idea. It's not like he can ground me or send me to time-out. Besides, the money didn't mean a thing, hadn't for at least twelve years. Or was it fifteen? I shrugged. Who cares? When the infrastructure went down, so did our currency. Now all that money is good for is kindling, paper airplanes, and swear jars.

So now we deal in trade. And theft. And murder.

But in the meantime, Max and I had our little game. I liked it. He loved it. I grabbed an extra-large strip of dried smoked salmon and tossed it in the air. Max went airborne, catching it halfway from the ground. I smiled. Someday that dog was gonna take flight.

Moonlight streamed through the window of the tiny one-room cabin, my "beach bungalow." Yeah. Right. But the moon was full, and it beckoned me to the beach and to the inky waters beyond.

It didn't matter that it was past midnight. It didn't matter what the calendar said. It didn't matter what demons I fought in my head. I walk on the beach when the moon is full. I never miss.

And it sure as hell didn't matter that tonight was the anniversary of the end of my life as I had once known it. The life I could barely remember. But what's an anniversary with no one to share it with? After all, this was the anniversary when everyone who had ever mattered to me had died, swept away in the arms of a rogue killer wave. A wave I watched for. Waited for. Daring it to return, claim me, and just finish the damn job.

"Come on, Max," I said as he danced around my legs, "let's see what the water brings us tonight. Let's see if it has anything to say."

I slipped on a too-small Gore-Tex waterproof jacket. Warm and well used, the coat had a ragged hole the size of a small island on the sleeve. But I treasured it. I had only one other spare now. And I just couldn't think about what it would take to get another one. It's not like I could go to the mall.

I pulled on black rubber boots over wool socks; it was December, after all, and everything in my world was soggy. Wet, damp, soggy. Welcome to the Pacific Northwest, or at least what's left of it.

Max ran over, dropped to the floor, and, with his massive head between his front paws, he started to bark at my boots.

"Cut the crap, Max. You've seen these boots for what?

Two years? They're skulls, Max. Painted *skulls.* And you know what I went through to get them. You were there, remember? The wet suit? The dive? The near drowning? Besides"—I stood and patted his golden head—"I like them. They're old-school Goth, they're cool, and they're badass. So as much as I love ya, shut up about the boots, okay?" He shut up.

We pushed through the door together, jockeying for position. Taking turns or bringing up the rear were foreign concepts to both of us, so we did it the hard way every time. Max, through sheer bulk, won, and as always he ran out in front, scouting, smelling, protecting. I smiled. A girl and her dog. Oh yeah, that's what I'm talkin' about. Who says you need a man?

I walked the half mile to the beach, letting my head clear in the cold winter night. Moonlight lit my passage better than any flashlight, which was good, because on one hand, who had batteries anymore? And yet on the other hand, the moonlight lit the beach like Broadway, which left us exposed, vulnerable, an easy target. Danger was everywhere.

But a full moon did enhance my broadcast to levels I couldn't otherwise achieve. They called it moon bounce, a concept that sounds sci-fi, but has actually been around since the 1940s. For one night each month, during the full-moon phase, I could bounce a signal off the moon's surface. My voice echoed in countries and cities and homes that I prayed were still alive with people to hear me.

Mist from the sea floated inland, wrapping around me, leaving the taste of salt upon my lips. I heard the sea in the distance, a pounding rhythm that I'd learned to pay close attention to. Pausing, I wondered if tonight the sea and I would have a conversation.

Max barked in the distance, and I quickened my step.

Even though wild dogs populated these islands, it was still unwise to let him bark too long.

The black sky, like a jeweled blanket, shone with thousands of stars, stars that were familiar, comforting. I smiled up into the breathtaking night as if I were greeting an old friend, and I guess in a way I was. Our landscape may have changed forever, but not the sky. I paused and reached up to trace the Big Dipper with my finger.

Max pierced the night with barking that escalated into a chorus of growls and yelps and howls.

"Max?" I shouted. I cupped my hands around my mouth and yelled again. "Max!" I started to run. What had he found? Or worse, what had found him?

I ran full-out. My cardio was great—I had Max to thank for that, lots of midnight runs. But the boots? Well, not made for speed. I broke through the cedars, tripped on a madrona root, and crashed headfirst into scrub brush that tangled and tore at my cargo pants. I checked for my knife. Yep, still there, lodged safely at the small of my back. I jumped up, and with only my pride stinging, I continued to sprint onto the sand. Yeah, I know, like it's even possible to sprint in rubber boots. But damned if I didn't try.

I could see Max about a hundred feet ahead, his golden coat glowing white in the stark moonlight. He barked and growled and tugged on something long and lifeless. What the hell?

On nights like this the sea often gave us gifts. A flopping sockeye with delicate pink flesh, dinner for the next night. Or Japanese floats, beautiful, handblown glass in green and amber. The hardy glass balls, some ancient and rare, had started to reappear after the last wave, and the sea, as if knowing how much I loved them, made sure I had my share. And sometimes it was a wire trap full of Dungeness crab, lines snapped in the surf or more likely cut by Runners. The traps, brimming with fresh crab, would wash up on the beach, sometimes right at my feet.

But sometimes, just sometimes, the sea would give me the greatest gift of all. It would tell me when to grab Max and run for high ground. Sometimes it even gave me time to broadcast it.

Yes, the sea would tell me when the next wave would come, and in nineteen years, I'd never once heard it wrong.

The problem, in the early years, was getting someone, anyone, to believe me. But Tsunami Blue? Well, people believed her: that solitary voice that floated on the airwaves, the voice that warned and begged and pleaded to please, please believe. Most did. And those who didn't died.

As I ran, I strained to see the telltale glow of a Runner pirate ship on the horizon. I needed to know that Max and I were alone out here with only the sea and surf for company. This island was remote, uninhabited, and wild. We should be alone. But still. They had come once. The bastards would come again.

I needed to know that tonight was not the night we would lose our lives to the light of a full moon.

The horizon was dark, black bleeding into black. No torches glowed, no sirens sounded, no arrows flew. We were very much alone. *Thank you, God.*

Lungs burning and legs screaming, I slid to a stop beside Max. I grabbed his thick rope collar and pulled him away from the form on the beach. Max didn't want any part of giving up his discovery and he tugged back. This was a problem when you had a dog that outweighed you by more than twenty pounds.

"Back, Max, back." I tugged hard. The dog tugged harder still, the hackles on his back raised, his teeth bared. The target of his interest didn't move. I could now see long matted hair, outstretched arms, a trench coat of sorts, legs, boots . . . a *man.*

Max had found a man.

He looked at least six feet tall. Max had found a very large man.

His left fist gripped a long blade, a wicked-looking fillet knife. I had gutted a lot of fish in my time, and I knew a fillet knife when I saw one. I knew what it could do to a dog, or a woman. Moonbeams danced off the metal, taunting and gleaming.

Scared, I grabbed Max's collar with both hands and yanked. "Down, boy, *stand down*." Max whined, but did as he was told. He didn't get "stand down" often. And if nothing else, Max was well trained. After all, my life depended on it.

I kicked the knife from the man's unmoving hand, and it landed far enough away for some comfort. Funny, I didn't feel any safer.

I couldn't see that he was breathing. I couldn't see that he wasn't. I'd have to get closer. Great.

I pulled Max to my side. "If he makes a move, boy, tear his throat out. I didn't name you Mad Max for nothing." Max whined. I knelt in the sand next to . . . what? A Runner? A murderer? A thief? A body?

And the sea gives up its dead.

The words rang in my head. Where had that come from?

I looked to the water and I *knew*, just as I had always known. The words came from the sea. So he really was dead. I wasn't sure how I felt about that. Safer, certainly. But who was he? Where had he come from? Had he been a good man? A bad one? Did he deserve a decent burial? Or did he deserve to be fed, like a bucket of chum, to the sharks?

During these dark years, wave after deadly wave had blurred the lines of human behavior just as certainly as they had blurred the lines of our coast. Good versus evil?

No longer black or white. I had once thought I was good. That was before I took a human life.

I sighed and willed the churning in my stomach to calm down.

I would turn the body over and check for ID, although it was highly unlikely there would be any. Most of us lived in the shadows now, obscure, invisible. ID? Who in this new, wet world would have the balls to check it? And for what purpose? Still, some carried a long-expired driver's license or a tattered and torn passport. Some still clung to the remnants of the old life. Hell, I'd read every single book or magazine I could get my hands on from the old days. My education was steeped in pop culture images that I would never see in person. But most of us knew the truth of it. There was nothing left of the old life. Right now we were all in survival-of-the-fittest mode. And it wasn't pretty.

"Max, come." He'd moved around the body, sniffing and probing like dogs do. But I needed him beside me now. I was going to move the body. And even though I knew the body wouldn't sit up and bite me—death is death, after all—I just felt better with Max, the monster dog, close.

"On three, Max." I frowned at him and he cocked his head as if to say, *What the fu—heck?* Max did not swear; he was good, at least in my mind. "Ready?"

He looked confused.

"Okay, so don't help. Supervise." I took a deep breath. "One." I braced myself in the sand. "Two." I slid my hands and forearms underneath the body. "And three."

I tensed my muscles, shoulders hunched, and did a lift-and-push sort of action. I had a lot of upper-body strength—that I knew—but I still lacked bulk. At five-three and one hundred eight pounds dripping wet (which I was most of the time), I knew some things were just too much for me.

My mother had called me petite. Seamus, the uncle I'd been sent to live with, had called me scrawny. Or scrawny bitch. Whatever. My response: "You have no idea what comes in this small package, asshole."

My feet started to skid backward in the sand. I braced myself with one knee, jamming my shoulder into his. My long ponytail fell forward and caught between us. I yanked at it and flipped my hair over my shoulder in frustration. I tried again, shoulder-to-shoulder, giving it all my strength.

The body rolled.

Hair as black as mine fell back, revealing his face. He looked still, ashen, dead. My breath caught, and a sudden unexpected sadness washed over me.

He was the most beautiful man I had ever seen.

Chapter Two

I knew he was dead.

He had to be dead.

The water had told me. Right?

Max whined, looked at me, then back to the body, then back to me again. He cocked that massive head of his at me and barked. I leaned in, pressing my cold fingers to an equally cold neck to feel for a pulse. Nothing.

"Max." I spread my arms wide as I sat back on my heels. "What do you want me to do? I can't raise the dead, buddy."

I looked at the man's exquisite features, all hard angles and shadows; he looked like a fallen dark angel, silent and tragic in death. I reached over to give Max a pat. Max licked my cheek, then dropped down on the sand, looking at the still figure. The dog went silent. He, too, had given up.

Loneliness and yearning slammed into me.

I wanted this man to be an angel, damn it. I wanted him to be *my* angel. I wanted him to be alive and good and noble. I wanted him to take me away from the waves and the cold and the damp. I wanted him to take away the ghosts. The memories. I don't know why, but looking at this man, so still, so lost, just made me want to cry.

A fine rain started, adding more chill to an already cold night. I hated the way the drops fell and pooled on his closed eyes. The rain looked like tears.

I couldn't stand it.

I pounded the sand with my fist. Max and I were out of here. There was always morning. My head would be clear, no more ghosts, just another body to deal with come first light. I'd done it before, and I would do it again.

I started to push up from the sand. "I wish we could have saved him, Max," I whispered. And then, just as I prepared to stand, I saw . . . what? His coat had draped open, revealing a black thermal shirt stretched taut across a broad chest. Movement. A breath? Not possible. Was it?

Suddenly everything Uncle Seamus had drilled into me came back in a rush of adrenaline. My uncle had been a mean, cold bastard, true, but he did teach me how to survive. My heart slammed against my chest and I felt hot, frantic, confused. I had to think. *Think!* The voice of my long-dead uncle played in my mind.

Pale skin. Appears dead. Body in hibernation. May be alive. May be alive. May. Be. Alive.

Hypothermia.

Of course. The number one outdoor killer. The two top contributing factors? Cold and wet.

My hands shook as I reached for him. I touched his chest, laid my head down to listen for a heartbeat. I couldn't hear. I couldn't hear. I couldn't— Pupils dilated.

Of course. Yes. Of course! I knelt closer and for once I thanked the moon for the light. I gently opened an eyelid and I could see the pupil clearly. Dilated.

I listened once more for a heartbeat. Max knew something was up. He jumped to his feet, barking.

"Quiet, Max, quiet. I can't hear. I can't hear." Max did as he was told and reduced the barking to his signature whine.

Suddenly I knew.

I *knew* he was alive. And I knew I could save him. Maybe. Wait. Not a maybe. I just would.

I turned to the sea and gave it the finger. "Damn you. Just damn you. He is *not* dead." Max started to chase his tail. "Not now, Max," I yelled. The sea, wicked and black, laughed. Laughed! *Fuck it.*

I turned back to the body. No. Not a body. A man. A living, *almost* breathing man. I ignored the sea and let my uncle's instructions fill my head.

Okay, I wasn't able to detect a pulse, so yeah, severely hypothermic. I leaned over, opened his mouth, placed mine over his, and exhaled. I knew that I could increase the rate and strength of his heartbeat enough so that I could detect it. He'd be too fragile for full-on CPR. The pounding alone could cause cardiac arrest. So could moving him. But I couldn't leave him out here, but . . . wait. I was getting ahead of myself.

Get the heart going, Blue, my uncle's voice whispered through my mind. *Then you get your butt going. Don't be a damn sucker. Don't get attached. That's weakness, stupid girl. Whoever or whatever your bleeding heart is tryin' to save most likely won't make it.*

I applied myself with a single-minded goal: *Get a heartbeat. Just get a heartbeat, Blue,* I told myself, *and the rest will follow.*

The next few minutes were silent as only the surf and my breathing filled the still air. The rain had stopped, and Max now watched intently, not making a sound. I could hear the rhythm of my breath moving into his lungs, promising life. I laid my head on the stranger's chest, fingers to the neck, and held my own breath as if not wanting to waste it.

And then, what had it been? Two minutes? Ten? There it was.

A miracle.

Faint. Slow. But steady. Oh, so steady. *A heartbeat.*

"You're a fighter, aren't ya, big guy?" I whispered against his cheek. And then, *Get your butt going, Blue.*

I jumped up fast, startling Max. He bounded up with a sharp bark. I stripped off my jacket and threw it on the sand, followed by my own thermal shirt. I shivered in the cold with only my bra and cargos on as I tucked my jacket around his torso. It was ridiculously small, but still, so much better than nothing. I quickly wrapped the thermal shirt around his head. Dropping to the sand, I tugged off my boots, pulled my socks off, and covered his hands. I called for Max.

"Lie down, boy. Lie down." I pushed him close and snug beside the man. "Stay." Max looked at me like I was crazy. "Stay," I said again, firmly. "I'll be back, boy. Stay. Protect."

I pulled on the boots, hopped up, turned, and ran.

The trick with Max was to not look back. If I said to stay, he would. At least for a while. If I looked back, he would consider that an invite and bolt to chase me down. And that was the last thing I wanted. Max's body heat could have meant life or death for that man.

I swore all the way back, mad at myself for wearing boots that hindered my speed. Time was the enemy. I burst through my door and started to multitask almost to the point of frenzy.

Boots flew off. A log was thrown into the fire; my favorite beach rocks were tossed on a hot stove. I pulled on a T-shirt and a sweatshirt, shoved into old Puma sneakers—my go-fast shoes—slung a thick rope over my head and onto one shoulder, and then ran out the door and back to the beach.

For the second time that night I slid into the sand next to the stranger with my lungs near bursting. His heart still beat, faint but steady. Within minutes, I had the rope slipped under his arms and knotted into a sling that draped across his chest. I twisted my thermal shirt around the rope, padding it against his body. The end of the rope looped around Max, who had a massive chest of his own. A Bernese mountain dog, Max was not only the biggest canine I'd ever seen but also the strongest.

"Let's go home, Max, slow and steady." I led for a few yards, and when Max got the pace, I followed behind with a cedar bough and swept away our tracks. I didn't know where this man had come from or who might be looking for him. And I didn't know how many others he might have brought along for the ride. But I'd get my answers when he woke up. If he woke up.

I bit my lower lip as I watched from behind. An irregular heartbeat caused from rough handling would kill him at this stage. But my Max was doing a great job, and we were almost there. I could see the glow of my lanterns, twinkling, welcoming.

This was one time I didn't mind if Max went first through the door. The three of us piled into my tiny room with me tripping on Max and the rope and a large man who filled my space, bringing me to the brink of claustrophobia.

From that point on everything was on autopilot.

I pulled my futon in front of the fire, a crude but effective cast-iron stove, then checked the beach rocks on the top to see if they were warm. I tossed down my huge sleeping bag, and I started with the basics.

First, strip off clothes.

His trench coat was weatherproof—oilskin, expensive in its day. However, in our current reality? The coat was priceless. I'd known men who would kill for the duster and think nothing of it. Talk about holding value. "Fool," I said as though he could hear me, "a coat like this will get you killed. Haven't you ever heard of a low profile?" But then I saw my skull boots heaped by the door. "Okay," I said, "you got me there."

I hung the coat to dry. I'd check the pockets later. I didn't have time to be a detective. I yanked off his boots: Docs, thick and steel-toed. If he'd worn these in the sea, it was a wonder they hadn't weighed him down and killed him. Shoes like these would drown you. Fast.

Next, the black thermal top. Again, high-grade, military-issue, and didn't that just raise a red flag. I paused, but no, I'd keep going. I'd get my answers later; after all, Max could be pretty persuasive.

I gently pulled on the shirt, untucking it from black jeans. I took as much time as I dared. No rough treatment. I had to protect the heart that I'd worked so hard to get going. I toweled off his shoulder-length hair the best I could and was surprised to see that it really was as black as mine. I brushed it aside as I finished pulling the shirt up and off.

And once again, my breath caught.

His skin was golden, as if kissed by the sun—which, let's face it, in the Pacific Northwest in December was highly unlikely. So, not from around here. My curiosity shot through the roof. So did my anxiety.

His arms were solid, thick, corded with muscle. "Guess I'm not the only one who works out," I said to Max, who looked at me like he couldn't care less.

I ran my hand over his chest. He had a full six-pack of abs, a tapering waist, and well . . . wow, just wow. He was perfect. I rested my hand over his heart and I could feel the beat, soft and sure. I blushed, thinking for a moment that he looked like one of those models from an old Las Vegas calendar I'd found floating in Seattle. A chorus line of gorgeous men from Australia, "the Thunder Down Under," they'd called it. Wait, not models—male strippers.

My cheeks burned. "I can't believe I'm blushing," I said to Max. And then, "Not a word to anyone, buddy. I mean it." Max, who was so used to me talking to him morning, noon, and night, just yawned and rolled over.

I stripped off the leather belt. Black and lethal, it had tiny rows of silver spikes that seemed way too sharp for a fashion statement. The sticky fingers of paranoia crept along my spine.

My hands trembled as I reached for his fly. This was it, and I had to be quick about it. There was no time to lose. No time to be shy. Embarrassed. I had a life to save. And yeah, I hadn't had much experience with men, but yes, I'd seen some naked. Two, actually. As I fumbled with the button and zipper of his jeans, I shuddered at the ugly memories.

One had been dead, murdered and stripped of all his earthly belongings. The thief had gotten away with some ratty clothes, a pair of Nikes, and some photographs. It was the Nikes that had cost the man his life. Maybe our new world wasn't so unlike the old: a life for a pair of designer shoes. It had happened before. I'd found the clothes down the road, thrown away like garbage. The photos of three little kids were stomped and crushed in the sand.

The second naked male, a Runner, had tracked and hunted me for months. One night, hidden in the dark and fog, he'd followed my radio signal and caught up. After stripping off his clothes he came at me. I still remember the haunting, *You won't be so pretty when I'm done, bitch*, in my nightmares. Runners are like that. They like their women beaten, bruised, bloody. He'd come at me and he'd died. By my hand. Uncle Seamus had taught me well. I'd been thirteen. And already lethal.

I unbuttoned the jeans, pulled at the zipper, and peeled the pants down past slender hips and muscular thighs.

Every bit of clothing was soaked, and it was imperative I get him dry and warm. And there was only one way to do it. The jeans came off, leaving only snug black underwear, shorts really, and they had to come off too.

But not before the rocks. I placed my smooth beach rocks, now warmed by the stove, in assorted wool socks. I carefully put the makeshift heating pads on each side of his neck, in his armpits, in his palms, on his soles. Last would be the groin. But first . . .

I stoked the fire for the last time and hung his clothes all around the tiny room to dry. I blew out all the lanterns, so the only light was from the moon, a pale gold streaming through my one small window. I knelt beside him and once more felt for a pulse in his neck. It was there, faint yet stronger. Good. All good.

I had to prevent afterdrop at all cost. He couldn't afford any continuing loss of core cooling, something that could happen during the rewarming process.

And now there was nothing to do but the obvious. I stood up, stripped naked, and caught the reflection of my tattooed left arm, a full sleeve that stopped at the wrist, in the tiny window. The cobalt, aqua, and teal blended to form a magnificent Japanese wave, a tsunami, rising up on my arm and cresting over my shoulder. The name Finnegan was scrolled in the waters, riding the wave upward toward my heart.

As I dropped down to my knees and pulled the last garment from my mysterious guest, I tried not to focus on how magnificent this man, this raw picture of perfection and beauty, really was. I placed the last two stones timidly on his groin, handling his penis gingerly, gently, moving him to a position I hoped would be comfortable.

I climbed in beside him and pulled the oversize sleeping bag closed. The zipper, long broken, dangled in places, so I tucked the fabric around us as best I could. Pressing against him, I gave him my warmth, my life force, and my prayers. *Please, God, let him live.*

My body ached from the long day and the even longer night. My heart ached from the memories of a long-past event wrapped up in a painful anniversary.

Fatigue washed over me, and as I wrapped my arms around him, pulling him closer, every nerve ending tingled with an awareness that was foreign to me. Sweat formed on my brow, and beads of moisture pooled between my breasts. There was dampness high between my thighs and a low pull in my belly. Strange yet tempting. But tempting how?

I closed my eyes, exhausted, and pictured his face, my fantasy angel, my savior for just one night, and I realized that this was sexual. It was pure want, pure need. Pure raw desire. And in all my twenty-four years, I'd never experienced this before. Had never experienced a man before. I wasn't ashamed. My life had been all about waves and survival, and just getting from one day to the next alive. There was never any time for this. There was never anyone for this.

I sighed and let the fantasy of a dark angel with golden skin and jet-black hair take me away to dream. I rested my head on his chest and listened to the steady beat of his heart and thought, Why couldn't I afford to dream for one night? After all, things would be too real in the morning. I'd be back to one day at a time, one wave at a time.

Just before my eyelids closed I saw the glint of silver on his wrist.

The handcuff.

If he survived the night, my guest wouldn't be happy with me. I'd handcuffed him to the cast-iron leg on my stove. He still had one free arm—I couldn't risk both arms exposed, too much heat loss—and yet I would sleep well knowing his fillet knife was somewhere lost on the beach while mine was safely tucked behind me less than an arm's length away.

I couldn't help it. I had to do it.

After all, I was the famed Tsunami Blue, and it seemed that if everyone left in this entire rotten, ruined world wanted a piece of me, then perhaps this strange and beautiful man did too.

To some I was a freak; to others, a fantasy. I was Satan or savior; a witch or a goddess. I was legend; I was lies. And tonight it really was just all too much.

My last thought before blessed sleep took over?

It would be such a shame if he turned out to be a Runner. I would have saved his life tonight, only to have to take it in the morning.

Chapter Three

The dull gray of oppressive morning light seeped into my tiny cabin like the hand of a ghost. I had been dreaming of sunshine and aqua blue water, and a sea breeze laced with Thai flowers that smelled sweet and fragrant. They were the same flowers that my mother had worn in her hair the day she died.

I woke with a jolt. For a split second, I was confused, disoriented. My entire body felt sore, stiff, felt—

I was being watched.

Dark eyes, the color of coal, met mine.

The events of the previous night flew into my brain, and every survival instinct I'd ever know slammed into me.

I sat up, pushed to my feet, and grabbed an old threadbare camping blanket I'd stashed beside me the night before. While holding the blanket to my chest, I reached down with one fluid movement and swept up the bowie knife I'd put under the blanket. I took two steps back, out of danger's reach, pointing the blade at the man who had yet to take his intense gaze off me.

A neat stack of socks with my rocks inside was alongside the stove. Nice to see he hadn't bashed my head in with one. Believe me, I'd thought of it. But I had gambled that dying of starvation while chained to a stove might be a deterrent. Looked like I'd gambled right. Maybe I had a talent for gambling; God only knew I did it often enough. Huh, I might have a new career. Too bad Vegas was underwater.

Sometime in the night he'd kicked the sleeping bag down. It now draped low over his hips, a bent leg exposing a muscular thigh. So, if he was this visible, I figured I must have been too, but for how long? Heat flared, and I didn't need a mirror to tell me that I was blushing. Again. Great.

He held my stare, unblinking, intense, confident, and . . . what was that look? Amused? Arrogant bastard. I might be naked, but, hey, I held the knife.

I wrapped the blanket around me the best I could with one hand and glared. Where the hell was Max? As if we had some ESP connection, I heard Max whine on cue.

"Max?" I called, annoyed that my voice sounded breathy, girly, soft. What the hell was the matter with me? I did not have a breathy, girly, soft voice. I had a soft voice, true, but it was an all-business, kick-ass woman's voice. "Max," I called much more firmly. There, that was more like it, kind of.

The sleeping bag moved, and to my amazement Max wiggled up from the bottom, pawing his way to the top. He stuck his huge head out and licked my . . . my what? My bunk buddy? On the cheek, no less.

"Max," I squeaked. I actually squeaked. *Oh God, Blue, get a grip.*

What happened to the dog that could tear a man's throat out in under a second? The dog that would intimidate, terrify, chomp, maim, chew, and—I swear I was on the verge of hysteria—what happened to Mad Max, the killer?

Max yawned, licked the man's cheek again, and was rewarded with a lazy scratch to the head.

I was so surprised that I lost my concentration. The thin blanket slipped from my fingers and pooled on the floor.

"Shit." I dived forward to grab the fabric, only to have it slip between my fingers again. Max, hearing the cuss-word, tore out of the bag and danced around my legs, tangling the blanket in the process. "Max, move," I yelled while still holding my knife. I tugged at the blanket that was now anchored by a hundred-something-pound dog. It wouldn't give. Heat burned in my cheeks. My long, thick hair was out of my traditional ponytail, but it wasn't long enough or thick enough to cover . . . well, to cover *everything*.

"Fuck, Max," I said out of sheer exasperation, "move!" I realized my mistake the second it left my mouth.

That was all it took.

Max flew off the blanket and started to chase his tail. Any hope that he would turn into Max, killer dog of the north, disappeared with the dreaded F-bomb.

I snatched the blanket up, wrapped it around me, stomped over to the cupboard, grabbed a twenty, stuffed it in the pickle jar, threw Max a tiny—and I mean *tiny*—strip of salmon, stomped back, knelt, and held the knife under the man's chin.

"Who are you?" I asked, and not politely.

He had propped himself up with his free arm using *my* pillow. He looked stern, as if trying to be scary. But his eyes gave it away. He was trying not to laugh.

"Good morning," he said.

His voice, raspy from the previous night's ordeal, surprised me. There was a quiet, silken quality to it. Gentle yet . . . what? *Dangerous* came to mind. I wondered, *Is this what the devil would sound like?*

"There's nothing good about it," I snapped.

His gaze traveled down the length of my body and back again, lingering at my breasts for a brief moment before he met my eyes.

"I'd beg to differ." His mouth quirked into a smile,

sexy and inviting. "It's been a very good morning." He winked.

My heart rate increased, and my palms started to sweat. Being naked and holding a blanket while balancing a knife will do that to you. Plus, I didn't think it was possible for this man to be any better-looking, but the smile . . . Oh Lord.

Even white teeth, twin dimples, dark eyes rimmed in long, inky lashes . . . Oh, man, I was in trouble here. I should just kill him now and put us both out of our misery. But I kinda had a rule against cold-blooded murder. And besides, *he* didn't look anywhere near miserable.

He seemed as though he was enjoying himself.

Still, he looked predatory and dangerous and hot. Hot? Where had that come from? That was it. I was breaking my rule. I was just going to flat-out kill him.

I pointed the blade tip upward into his chin.

Let your guard down, Blue, give away your life.

My uncle's words hung in the air between us. "Yeah, Seamus," I whispered, "it's time to get serious."

He raised a brow. "Seamus?"

Well, now he thought I was crazy. Just as well, because this might hurt.

I pressed the blade, drawing a single drop of crimson blood. My uncle's words had jolted me back into the stark reality of my life. A life filled with waves, survival, death. And after all, I had no idea who I was dealing with. He'd survived the night and, yeah, that was all well and good—what I had prayed for, actually. But if he were a Runner, it would be up to me to survive the day.

"Who are you?" I asked again.

Silence.

"If I have to ask a third time, it won't be a charm."

His demeanor changed; he clearly didn't like the threat.

He lowered his chin into my blade tip, slowly, deliberately, until a fine line of blood trickled along the long blade, tracing down the hilt. The blood dripped over my fingers and along the back of my hand. The entire time his gaze never left mine.

He didn't flinch. He didn't blink.

I didn't flinch. I didn't blink.

Blood didn't bother me. I'd seen too much of it. This show of his wouldn't work on me.

"You're a tough guy," I said, lowering my voice and the knife. "I get that."

I stood, backing well out of his reach, and wiped the blood off my hand onto the blanket. Using the fabric, I cleaned the blade, taking my time. He kept his intense gaze on me as he wiped at the blood under his chin with the back of his hand. I hated that he stared at me with those black eyes, eyes I couldn't read.

Fed up, I flipped the knife, throwing it hard into the cedar floor just beyond his reach. The blade sank deep into the wood in front of his face, and I hoped the message was clear. But just in case, I delivered it personally.

"But I'm a tougher girl, big guy, just in case you thought otherwise. And"—I walked over, yanked the blade up by the hilt, tossing it high in the air, only to catch it right in front of his nose—"I have the knife." He said nothing, just raised that dark brow.

Okay, now I was pissed. I wasn't sure what I was going to do, but I did know one thing: I wasn't going to do it naked.

I turned to collect my clothes, jeans, a tee, socks; where was my bra? I only owned two, one held together by a knot. Man, it was time to go shopping. I needed lots of things: coats, bras, ammo. But considering it was sixty nautical miles to Seattle, where most of the city was underwater and shopping at the mall entailed a wet suit, scuba gear, and a lookout, well, let's just say two bras were good for a while longer. But I had to go soon. Salt water is hard on, well, everything.

"Looking for this?"

I sighed and my shoulders slumped. I knew what was coming. I'd thrown my clothes off last night and in my hurry I didn't know or care where they might have landed. That is, until now. I turned around. Well, so much for the tough-girl image.

He held out my bright pink bra with his long, tan fingers. Good grief, even the guy's hands were sexy. I shook my head, walked over still gripping the blanket, and held out my hand. He tossed the bra my way and neither one of us smiled.

The weak morning light and the absence of warmth in the cabin made for a downright depressing atmosphere. We both knew only too well that this situation could—that is, most likely would—end badly for one of us. And I desperately didn't want it to be me.

I called for Max, who had been sleeping soundly in the corner. Guess all those doggy kisses had worn him out. Traitor. I gathered my clothes and headed for the door.

"Gabriel."

My hand paused at the doorknob. "Excuse me?" I turned slowly and met his dark gaze.

"Gabriel. My name."

I paused, hearing but unbelieving. *Gabriel.* The dark angel, the fallen angel. My fantasy angel from the night before. But this man before me, stretched out naked in my old sleeping bag, handcuffed to an ancient stove, this man was no fantasy. He was flesh; he was blood; he was real. Hell, I'd seen him bleed.

"Gabriel?" I crossed my arms, still holding the knife, and bunched the clothes to my chest.

"Gabriel Black."

Oh, come on. Gabriel and Black? Dark angel? What were the chances? Had I been talking in my sleep? Not possible. Was it? Then again, I could talk to the sea. I could predict the waves. Why not guess a name, or at the very least come close? But Gabriel? A name almost as beautiful as the man himself? I didn't believe it.

"I don't believe you."

He shrugged.

"Fine," I said, bitterness lacing through my voice. "What's a name in today's world anyway? Come on, Max." I turned to go.

"Not much," he said softly behind me, "unless, of course, it's Tsunami Blue."

My hand froze on the doorknob. So he knew who I was. I turned to face him. "You're a genius, aren't you, tough guy? What gave it away? The shortwave equipment?" I motioned to my radio in the corner and was amazed to see it covered with a blue tarp. I guess in my frenzy last night I had thought to try to conceal my identity. So how had he known? As if he'd read my mind, he pointed to the old cupboard, where, pinned on peeling paint, was a yellowed and frail newspaper clipping. The headline could still be clearly read: *Angel of the Beach Saves One Hundred Lives.*

"You're her. You're the angel." He said it without emotion, as if asking, *Please pass the salt.* He shrugged at my glare. "The tat helped, of course."

"I'm not," I said, as I subconsciously rubbed my arm where the elaborate tattoo was exposed. But of course I was. I was that little girl—Kathryn "Blue" O'Malley—on that Thailand beach nineteen years ago who had screamed, "Tsunami!" over and over, alerting, warning, prompting people to run for their lives. On that fateful day, the sea had whispered the word *Tsunami* over and over and over to me. *Scream it, Blue*, the sea had said. *And run, run for high ground while you're doing it.*

Oh, yes, I had saved lives that day—many, I was told. But I wasn't able to save the three most important to me—my mother, my father, and my older brother—if only by four minutes—Finn. Finnegan Patrick O'Malley had been my heart, my life, my twin.

Disgusted, I tossed so-called Gabriel his jeans, which he caught easily in midair. I lifted his shorts with my big toe and kicked them within his reach. If I decided to kill him, it'd be easier if he was dressed.

He reached for his shorts, and the sleeping bag slid dangerously low. I didn't want to think about that magnificent body, the hard lines and muscled thighs. It might distract me from the kill shot.

Gabriel picked up the underwear and held them up. "What's the matter, Blue?" He enunciated my name slowly, softly. "Afraid you might catch something? I think it's a bit late for that, considering"—he raised a knee, and the sleeping bag slid lower still—"that we spent the night together nude."

I narrowed my eyes as I felt the telltale tingle of embarrassment creep into my cheeks. I would not give him the satisfaction of seeing me blush. Again. I had to leave. My pale skin was easier to read than a neon sign. Not that I'd seen neon in more than a decade.

"Just get dressed. I'll be back." I twirled the knife into a blur, which was a habit. I realized it probably looked hokey, but what the hell; I didn't get many chances to show off my knife skills, and he was a captive audience. Literally. "Depending on what I hear," I continued, "if I like your answers, I'll decide if you live"—twirl—"or die." Twirl. Man, I'd just impressed myself with this knife act, set a new speed record, even. I was such a badass. "Max, come."

Max trotted toward the door, but not before stopping to give this Gabriel a lick on the hand. He was rewarded with a lazy scratch behind the ears by those long, slender fingers. Max clearly did not understand the difference between *friend* and *foe*. Or *loyal subject* and *traitor*. And Gabriel Black, if that was truly his name, didn't seem the least bit worried that I was twirling a twelve-inch blade. You would have thought I held a baton, like those bandleaders I had seen once in a parade, and not a weapon that could disembowel him in less than five seconds.

I shook my head. Max was going to make me call him again, wasn't he? Like being naked in front of this guy wasn't humiliating enough, I now had my dog, my monster killer dog, in love with him. What had I done to make my Max turn on me so viciously?

I grabbed the doorknob once more, took a breath to steady my nerves, and yanked the door open. Any second Max would rush in, push against me, and crowd his way out first. I let two heartbeats go by before I peeked over my shoulder. Max was lying on his back now while Gabriel rubbed his belly.

"Max!" *Oh, no.* That was almost a squeak again. I cleared my throat. "Max," I said in a commanding voice. There, that got his attention. That or the strip of salmon that hung drying by the door that I'd nabbed. "Come." Max saw the food, dashed to my side, grabbed the fish, and, just like old times, he pushed and jostled me out of the way. He sprang out the door, snagging my blanket in his rear paw. I held on to the material for dear life. I mean really, I'd had enough nudity in the last twelve hours to start my own camp.

With fish in mouth, Max paused just long enough to see me lose my balance and fall smack on my butt. The knife clattered on cedar planks and my clothes went flying. The blanket, however, stayed anchored. Sort of. A small victory, but a victory no less.

I scrambled, picking up the knife first, clothes second, and my boots, the only shoes closest to the door, third. All the while I refused to look at Gabriel. I was out of the cabin almost as fast as Max. When the door slammed shut, creating a barrier between me and my bunk buddy from hell, I slumped against it, catching my breath. I willed my heartbeat to slow, my adrenaline to quit pumping, and then I heard it through the door.

Laughter. Deep male laughter. And didn't that just piss me off.

I sat on a grassy dune above the gray-blue waters of Haro Strait. A mean north wind tossed and twisted my long hair, obscuring my view. I smelled sea salt and dried kelp and rotting fish. The gulls, loud and boisterous, cried foul. Foul to the weather, foul to the wind, and foul to my dark mood.

The ocean, as if sensing the darkness, was restless today, tossing waves angrily on the beach as if to say, *He should be dead, he should be dead, he should be dead.*

As I brushed long, thick strands of hair out of my eyes, I had to agree. He damn well should be.

But Gabriel Black had not only survived the night, he seemed to have no outward residual effects. It was uncanny. I should be spoon-feeding him warm sugar water, helping him walk, nursing him back to full strength. I picked up a rock and threw it. Yeah, right. Like I could ever be a nurse. I could barely take care of myself. And Max.

With knees drawn up, I watched Max play in the surf. We had kissed and made up. You know, it was that girl-and-her-dog thing.

I had drawn a sketch of Gabriel in the sand, a very bad sketch. I mean, really, how great could it be with a stick of driftwood and no talent? Still, I had tried to show Max who the bad man was. I didn't care how great Gabriel Black scratched or rubbed or petted. I had a sudden vision of him lounging in my sleeping bag naked. Okay, maybe I did care how great he scratched and rubbed and petted. In another lifetime. But right now, I told Max, Gabriel was the enemy, and until we knew more about him, Max was to resume the raised-hackles-and-bared-teeth act. Fake a case of rabies, even. Whatever it took, I told him. He was to remember he was on my side and my side alone.

"Right, Blue," I said out loud before resting my head on my knees, letting my hair whip around me like an angry dark storm. "Now you think you can communicate with dogs. Gabriel Black is making you nuts."

Max's bark jolted me out of self-pity mode. I lifted my head and squinted, out of habit, at the horizon. My eyes expected to see nothing, but my mind said differently. And it was a full twenty seconds before I put it all together to register the sight in my overloaded brain.

Runners.

On my feet, I yelled for Max, studying the horizon, trying to estimate how long. How long before they beached, tracked, hunted, and found us? Thirty minutes? No, I only wished. Twenty? Maybe. Fifteen? *Please, God, no.* The sea was rough today, so beaching would be difficult. Still, not impossible. Not impossible.

Max barreled up the sand dune, dropping a stick at my feet. He stood next to me, growling and snapping at the gray and black sails dotting the horizon. The lead boat unfurled a spinnaker, and the Runners' emblem painted on the sail glared harsh against a bleak sky. The 666 with a dagger running through the numbers did just what it was supposed to: It struck terror in my heart and twisted fear in my gut.

My heartbeat slammed against my chest and my blood pressure mounted. For a moment I could hardly breathe. I doubled over, putting my head between my knees, trying to catch a breath. That was when I saw it. Not a stick. Max had not dropped a stick at all. He'd dropped Gabriel Black's knife, lost from the night before. Scrimshawed in the bone handle was a design: 666, with a dagger running through it.

He was one of them.

I felt angry. Betrayed. But betrayed how? Let's face it: I'd betrayed myself and everything Seamus had taught me. "We should have let him die, Max," I whispered. My mind flashed on the memory of his amazing smile, dimples . . . the wink. Hot tears pricked at my eyes. I willed them away. This was no time for sentiment, for weakness. I didn't know him. He didn't know me. Gabriel Black was a Runner. And that was that.

Runners, the scourge of the sea, the pirates of our new uncharted world, were true devils on and off the water. Psychopaths with no regard for life, human or any other, who robbed and murdered at will. In a few short years their reputation had grown legendary. Almost surpassing mine.

Some said they worshiped the devil. Others said they *were* the devil. Urban legends spoke of human sacrifices and cannibalism. But I knew the legends weren't true. For one thing we didn't have "urban" anymore. We had Uplanders, survivors who were uninformed and isolated, and started rumors out of fear. And we didn't have YouTube, or DIRECTV, or the six-o'clock news. We had me, Tsunami Blue. And thanks to Uncle Seamus, I knew what the Runners were all about. The Runners were motivated by reasons as old as time: wealth, greed, power, sex. And in a world where everything was up for grabs, they had quickly established themselves at the top of the food chain. I should know. Seamus, my coldhearted bastard of an uncle, had been one. And I'd lived among his crew for more years than I cared to think about.

But why come here? Why come to a remote, seemingly uninhabited island with nothing to offer? Nothing to gain? But I knew. They'd come for me.

I chewed my bottom lip, straining to see how many. Ten? Twenty? It didn't matter; even one was too many. But only if they caught me.

The ocean roared in my ears, a frantic, tattooed rhythm all too familiar: *Danger, Blue. Death. Run, run,* run. In the end, in spite of the tricks the ocean played on me, the death and destruction it brought with the waves, it always warned me. And the ocean was always right.

"Run, Max, just run." I turned and raced from the dune toward home.

The last Runner ship had come five years ago. And now they were here, en masse. Whose fault? Gabriel Black's. My life and Max's hung in the balance. Whose fault? Gabriel Black's. Gabriel. It had to be.

Ain't no such thing as coincidence, Blue. If ya think so, you're just like your father, a damned fool.

"Shut up, Seamus. Just shut the hell up," I yelled into the wind. I couldn't afford to think about him, couldn't spare the time. I focused every second on survival: mine, Max's, but what of Gabriel Black? My lungs screamed in protest as I slammed up to my door. I stood with my back to the wood, sliding down into a crouching position. I hung my head. I knew what I would do. And I could do it. After all, Seamus O'Malley's blood ran through my veins, and I could feel the icy coldness of it as it approached my heart, hardening and numbing along the way.

I stood and slowly pulled the knife from the small of my back. What to do about Gabriel? It would be a logical, easy decision for Uncle Seamus. Guess for once in my miserable life I'd make him proud. Too bad he wasn't around to see it. But it didn't matter. I'd made my decision.

I was going to kill Gabriel Black.

Chapter Four

I wanted to kick in the door, enter screaming like a madwoman. I'd plunge the knife into his heart, throw the sleeping bag over his bleeding, dead body, grab my backpack, start the fire, and run.

I would run with Max into the cedars and fog.

Run from the death, run from the terror, run from my guilt. I'd become a monster; of that much I was sure. But I had to start the fire. I had time for the fire. I'd destroy it all—my equipment, my clothes, my bra with the knot, my pretty glass floats hanging from a pseudo Christmas tree—anything to confuse my would-be captors. So why did the vision of the tiny tree lapped in yellow flames bring me near to tears? *Stupid, Blue. Stupid, stupid, stupid.*

Why had I stayed here so long this time? I knew better—I *knew* better. But after the fire, they'd find the body. And it would take them a while to figure out it wasn't me. Not forever, but a while. And a while might be all I needed.

I had a backup plan. I always had a backup plan. Still, I'd gotten too comfortable here. I'd gotten sloppy. I had a plan B, but not a great one. Not a great plan at all, considering it involved a tiny boat in an angry sea on a deadly winter's day. *Shit.* Plan B sounded like a folk song. Again, I knew better.

My hand shook as I reached for the knob; so much for entering like a madwoman. I thought he might be asleep. I thought that I could save us both from the horror. I thought . . . Hell, I didn't know what I thought. It wasn't like I did this every day. I opened the door, sick to my stomach, and walked in.

He lay unmoving, the plaid flannel lining of the sleeping bag folded open. He was partially on top of it, partially in. It was as if in a restless sleep he didn't know whether he was hot or cold, as if he didn't know my warm, naked body was gone, or if he did, he was inviting me back. He lay on his stomach, his smooth, strong back with that sun-kissed skin exposed, unmarred and perfect.

Except for the small tattoo on his shoulder blade.

I had missed it last night. I had let him sleep on his back, too frightened to move him, too exhausted to think of it, too taken by . . . by him. *A mistake, Blue*, I chastised myself, *a deadly one*.

The lines were crude, prison quality, so unlike the elegant, graceful lines that adorned my arm. But the mark was unmistakable: 666, with a dagger running through it.

I was prepared for it. I'd seen it before. Up close and personal on the night I'd almost been raped.

Gabriel had managed to dress in his black jeans, and he'd found what he could within reach: his socks, his thermal shirt, which lay beside him waiting for the handcuff to come off.

I gripped my knife. The cuffs would come off—no use giving the Runners a hint that big—but not until I'd killed him.

Max scratched at the door and whined. Gabriel stirred. I had to move fast, before Max gave away the element of surprise. But in truth? I had to move fast, before *I* lost my nerve.

I hadn't dared bring Max in with me. I had no idea

how he would react to the fire. I had no idea how he would react to my harming Gabriel Black.

I steeled myself as I approached, moving silently, deadly. I knew what to do. I knew how to kill. And I wasn't proud of that.

Softly, so very softly, I knelt. I knew where to plunge the blade, where to strike the death blow. Why did I live in a world where I knew crap like this? Why?

I raised the blade, my hand shook, and a lone tear tracked down my cheek. I hated the Runners. I'd seen what they could do. The trail of blood and broken souls they left behind in their wake. This man deserved to die; they were his brethren, his good-old-boy club, his fucking partners from hell. The knife slammed down hard, tearing through thick fabric and futon, impaling the floor. The blade was a mere inch from his tattooed shoulder.

"Sorry, Seamus," I whispered bitterly. "I won't be joining you or any other Runner in hell. At least, not for this sin."

I moved to retrieve my knife, but not fast enough.

Gabriel moved every bit as quickly, twisting and grabbing my ankle, pulling my legs out from under me. I went down hard, but I wasn't worried. Not yet. He was still cuffed. I had too much fury inside and I took it out on his ribs, kicking him violently with my boot. He let go, and I jumped to my feet. "You bastard Runner," I yelled. "I should have let you die."

Fluid, fast, graceful, he did the impossible.

He stood.

I had it wrong on the beach. Not six foot, at least six-two. He had broad, powerful shoulders, muscled arms, and large fists clenched so tight that the knuckles were white. Okay. So this was not good.

"Great, you're Houdini," I said, now realizing the fatal

mistake I'd made. I underestimated his strength. I mean, I'd thought the man was dying. Who knew he'd turn into Hercules after a good night's sleep? He'd lifted the stove, a *cast-iron* stove, that weighed what? Ten tons? And slipped the cuff free.

"You meant to kill me," he said. His voice had a razor edge of rage to it. Guess I wasn't the only one who was pissed.

"Yeah, tough guy, that was the plan. As you can see, I missed." That was a lie. I never miss. And boy, was I ever regretting my decision about now.

He said nothing. He just reached down and pulled the embedded bowie knife out of the fabrics and cedar plank like he was plucking a feather. *Great. This is the part where I get gutted like a king salmon with my own blade.*

Max was going crazy outside. It sounded like he was going to take the door down. And he was big enough to do it.

"Let the dog in."

I looked at the towering man who now held my knife, and glared. "I don't take orders, tough guy, especially from you." I let my disgust show and added, "Runner."

"Well"—he walked toward me—"to use your words"—he held the knife under my chin—"I have the knife." He held the blade just as I had, pushing the tip into my flesh. It didn't puncture, didn't cut. He was either more considerate than I was or he was saving the good part for later. I'd bet all my twenty-dollar bills that he was saving the good part for later.

I raised my head defiantly and glared into those onyx eyes. I showed no fear. I had learned long ago that showing fear was either the quickest way to death or, even worse, the easiest way to prolong it.

"The dog," he said in that smooth, silken voice. A voice laced with warning. He motioned toward the door with my blade.

I had no choice. "Fine." I raised a brow of my own. "It's your funeral. Hurt me, and Max will tear your throat out." Gabriel shrugged. I turned for the door, paused, and glared over my shoulder.

Gabriel gave my knife a few spins. *Damn it.* He was better at it than I was. Well, that was just what I needed: a dose of humiliation to go along with my murder. How nice.

My hand paused at the door. Fear crept up my spine. Its icy fingers gripped my heart and squeezed.

I wasn't afraid for me. It was Max. He had been such a big part of my life for the last five years, a daily companion, nonjudging, accepting, fun. And of all the things that I'd experienced in my life, fun had been in short supply. Until Max. And I'd just put him in harm's way. I'd threatened Gabriel with him.

"Don't hurt my dog," I said without turning around. "Please." I could hear my uncle laughing from the grave. I could hear his taunts and criticism and jeers. *Trading your life for a dog's. That's rich, Blue. Knew you'd amount to nothin'. You and your bleedin' heart. You really are your father's daughter.*

Gabriel said nothing, and I knew my uncle was right. I hadn't amounted to much, just a voice in the night that tried to do the right thing. Well, right now, right this minute, I was going to do the right thing. I was going to save Max. My fate was sealed. Too much time had passed. Either this Runner or another would determine my fate. And it wouldn't be pretty. I didn't have to take Max down that road with me.

I opened the door. My dog tore into the room, jumping and bounding all over me. He almost knocked me down. And before I could grab his rope collar, the one I'd made with a series of nautical knots, he rushed over to Gabriel.

"Max, no!" A near scream came out of my mouth. "Stand down."

For the first time in five years, Max ignored my command. He proceeded to jump all over Gabriel Black. Max wagged his tail and danced around Gabriel's legs, even licking his hands. Gabriel smiled and, with his cuffed hand, now just a bracelet, he tousled Max's head. The second handcuff swung wildly. The two were having a lovefest. If I weren't in a life-and-death situation—*my* life and *my* death—I might have paused long enough to be jealous.

I bolted for the door.

Two things happened at once.

The knife flew past my left ear and slammed deep into the wall, while a large hand grabbed my neck, yanking me up and backward. I flew hard into a solid chest. It felt like I had hit a brick wall. What was it with this guy and his ripped and muscled body? It wasn't like we had gym memberships anymore. Guess water aerobics were working for him now.

He had me, and before I could stomp on his instep and shove an elbow in his gut, he turned me to face him, sliding his hands around my neck. Gabriel applied just enough strength to let me know he could snap my neck in under a blink.

Max whined and stood, moving his head from one of us to the other.

Gabriel moved close, his mouth next to mine. "Let's not upset the dog," he said.

"Oh, let's," I whispered.

But Gabriel knew what I had in mind, and he moved like lightning before I could land a perfectly aimed blow to his groin. What a waste of a knee thrust.

Gabriel moved behind me and held my arms pinned at my back. I gasped at the sudden pain in my shoulder joints. Max growled. His hackles rose, and I could see fangs. *Oh, good boy. Good. Boy.* I had a moment of hope.

"Down," Gabriel's voice thundered, and Max dropped to the floor, whining. My heart sank. What had happened to my dog?

Gabriel released my arms and once again turned me to face him, this time gripping my wrists. "Like I said, Blue. Let's not upset the dog."

We stood there for a moment, glaring at each other. His dark eyes were unreadable. I had no idea what his next move would be. Or mine.

The Runners' siren cut through the fog and distance, filtering through my open door. Carried on the wind, the warning sounded loud, clear, unmistakable. They'd hit the beach, and subtlety was not their style. They liked to make their presence known. They liked their quarry to run and cry and hide. And they loved the blood hunt. They lived for it.

"Your buddies are here, tough guy," I said, my voice dripping with sarcasm. "You had better hurry and kill me, or you'll have to share."

Gabriel stood like a statue, cocking his head, listening. His dark eyes narrowed and he gripped my wrists harder.

He pulled me to him with such force that I stumbled, falling into his arms. He crushed his mouth to mine in a bruising kiss that both surprised and frightened me. It took my breath away. The kiss ended as abruptly as it had started. He dropped me on the futon like a duffel bag, while he reached down and retrieved his shirt. He looked at me as he finished pulling his thermal over his head. "I don't share," he said.

Why, oh, why, did I mouth off about that sharing thing? My heart kicked into high gear. To hell with showing no fear. I was terrified. He would have me first. Then hand me over to those animals to finish the job.

Bile climbed into my throat, and I thought for a moment that I was going to be sick. I panicked, jumped up, and tried to push by him. He caught my wrist and twisted me toward him. What could I do? He was Goliath to my David. And me without a slingshot. Or at the very least a twelve-inch bowie knife. Max stood up, whining.

"I'm leaving, and you're coming with me. Get what you need—not much, we travel light—and we leave now." He released me and reached for his belt.

"We?" I rubbed my wrist where red welts were starting to rise.

He stopped threading his belt through loops and leveled that dark look of his at me. "You have two choices, Blue. One, you come with me and live. Two, you stay here and die."

My fear disappeared, replaced by red-hot anger. "There is no 'we,' Gabriel Black. Just me. Just Max. Choice three? I take my dog and leave. Without you, tough guy. It's that 'three's a crowd' thing, Gabriel. And don't get your feelings hurt, but you're not invited to the party." I leaned in close. "I just don't think you'd be a lot of fun." I started to shove past him for a second time, heading for my knife.

He shook his head, dark eyes hiding . . . what? That had better not be amusement. I wasn't starring in a comedy here.

A second burst of sirens sounded, and Gabriel grabbed my wrist again. He held up his hand where the cuff dangled. To my amazement, the dangled cuff was open, and in a move that defied logic, he snapped the cuff on me. My bunk buddy and I were now officially hooked up. Unbelievable.

I yanked hard at the cuff in frustration, but he held firm, his wrist hardly moving. For a guy who had been a Popsicle the night before, his strength was amazing.

"Why?"

"Like I said, we're out of here. You. Me. We."

I fought the urge to cry. I just couldn't wrap my brain around the fact that I'd been caught by Runners. But I wouldn't cry. Crying was out of the question. I glared into the darkness of his eyes. "Why the road trip, Gabriel? Why not just get on with it and do what you Runners do best?"

"What is it we do, Blue?" he asked softly.

"Rape. Plunder. Kill." My voice dropped to a whisper. "Torture." Visions of my uncle's mutilated body flashed into my head. I felt sick all over again. "You know," I continued, pushing through the nausea and finding false bravado, "the usual pirate shit. I only remind you that I saved your life, so . . ." I paused and hung my head, not wanting to say it. Not wanting to beg.

"So?" he said.

I raised my head and looked into his eyes. "So maybe you can just skip to the kill part. I mean, come on, tough guy. Give a girl a break. I'm not the party girl you think I am."

The fear must have shown on my face, because his features softened. He looked thoughtful, almost sad. And that scared me. What did he have to be sad about? He was the Runner. He had me cuffed. He had the advantage.

I tried to keep my voice steady as I pleaded in my own proud way. "I'm really not into the whole gang scene, ya know? And I'm not gonna lie, I'm shy that way." There. That was as close to begging as I'd ever get. And I was sure it wasn't nearly enough. I bit my lower lip to keep it from trembling.

I couldn't be sure what emotion passed over his face, but I hoped it wasn't pity. I didn't want his or anyone else's. I just wanted to die with a little fucking dignity. Not like Seamus. Never like Seamus.

He wrapped his free arm around me and pulled me to him. He rested his chin on the top of my head for a moment. And then with a featherlight brush to my lips with his, he whispered, "Like I said, Blue, I don't share. Not ever. You're mine now. And you and I—that is, 'we'—are out of here."

Chapter Five

I paused on the obscure, narrow footpath that wound up through the terrain of Caddy Mountain and looked at the trail of smoke that snaked into a gray, dripping sky.

Remnants of my cabin.

Gone now, along with whatever dreams I had of a stable home. I'd so wanted a tiny dot in this universe that I could call mine. And I almost had it. Almost.

Gabriel gave me a moment before the now familiar tug at my wrist broke my thoughts. And as if sensing my need for validation of the destruction of everything I ever owned, he handed me the binoculars. I held the dual lenses to my eyes, and the excellent optics captured what I'd feared most over the last eleven years.

Runners.

An army of Runners swarmed around the charred remains of my cabin. From my vantage point they looked like nothing more than ants, but I knew up close and personal that they were men of huge stature, with ice for blood and no souls to guide them. I lowered the lenses and took a deep breath before I held the binoculars up once again. I now knew one more thing for certain.

They were coming after us.

"We go off the trail."

Gabriel's voice cut through the silence, and I realized

that I had been holding my breath, as if fearing that the Runners would somehow hear me if I breathed.

He reached for my uncle's glasses and tucked them away in his pocket. Over the years I had wondered where Seamus had gotten such an expensive piece of equipment. Binoculars had all but disappeared over the last decade, along with REI, G.I. Joe's, and Cabela's. Salt water was hell on optics, and to my knowledge, a pair of this quality was rare indeed. Well worth killing for. At least to the right person. A person like a Runner. And Gabriel Black was a Runner. He had already taken them from me. I could only hope he wouldn't feel the need to kill me to make the transfer of ownership final. I glared up at him. "Thief," I said under my breath.

He whistled low for Max, who like always had run ahead, scouting, sniffing, protecting. And with a tug on my wrist we stepped off the deer trail into the dense greenery. Heavy cedar boughs hung over a carpet of moss, and my world darkened a notch as what little sun disappeared.

Max took the lead, crashing through ferns and grass and leaves. On another day, it might have been just Max and me out on a winter's walk.

"Why hide, Gabriel?" I asked, trying to keep up with his long strides. "These are your people. Your 'tribe,' as you Runners like to say."

He pressed ahead, setting a grueling pace, and if I didn't want my arm ripped from the socket, I had no choice but to keep up.

"Bastard," I muttered.

"Like I said, Blue, I don't share."

"Oh, yeah, that so explains it. I guess this is your idea of a date." No reply. I kicked a rock at his back. It bounced off his shoulder; he didn't seem to feel it, thus, no bruise.

Damn it. I sighed and said, "And me without anything to wear."

He stopped so abruptly I smashed into his broad back. He turned and looked at me with those black eyes, narrowing his gaze like a wolf to a lamb.

"I don't think you need anything to wear, Blue. In fact, given what I've seen, I'd prefer it that way."

Heat flooded my cheeks and I was speechless. I mean, really, what could I say? That I preferred him naked too? Laid out and filleted, gutted like a fish? The thought cheered me up.

He turned again, stomping through the growth, tugging me along like a pull toy. "And quit with the rocks," he said over his shoulder. I gave him the finger. Guess it was official: We were just not getting along.

A siren cut through the trees and I quickened my pace, now walking almost side by side with my captor. I was worried that the devils below would catch up. And they would, because besides the sirens, I could hear dogs barking.

A lot of dogs.

Runners bred and trained their own special breed. Think pit bull meets rottweiler meets wolf hybrid. The dogs were famous throughout the islands. They were trained to track, hunt, and kill. That was all. The dogs weren't dogs at all, but monsters, lethal weapons, bred to be as sadistic as their owners. At this point I had to admit that, given the choice—me versus a platoon of Runners and their pets, or a one-on-one with Gabriel Black—I liked my second option better. Seamus had taught me to play poker when I was seven, and by nine, I was beating him soundly. Calculating odds was my talent, and as near as I could tell, Gabriel might be holding the overcards right now, meaning the cuffs and the knife, but he should never underestimate my own hole cards. After all,

I could slit a throat in three seconds, slice a tendon in under two. And trust me, Gabriel Black or any other Runner scum didn't want to see my "all in" move.

We broke through the wooded darkness into a small clearing at the top of Caddy Mountain. Below I could see the crescent shape of Griffin Bay and the angry white-caps stirring more trouble into an already ruined day.

Somewhere down there, hidden among rocks and brush, was my kayak, handmade of deer hide and cedar. The little boat was sleek and fast, but only on seas made of glass. Today, with swells and wind, the boat would trudge and plow like molasses in winter. Capsizing was also a distinct possibility. And that was plan B. *Great, Blue. Just great.*

I brought my hand up to shield my eyes, forgetting for a moment that my wrist was cuffed to Gabriel's. His large hand blocked my view, and in frustration I socked him hard with my free fist in the shoulder. Gabriel raised a brow in question.

"Don't give me that look, tough guy. I'm cuffed to you, for fuck's sake. Cuffed!"

"That mouth, Blue." Gabriel frowned as he looked over my head, listening to a series of barks and howls. I had the distinct impression that he'd just dismissed me, bad language and all. And I hated being ignored.

"So what about my mouth, Gabriel? It's gonna what, get me in trouble? Like being cuffed to a Runner and being hunted by an army of them and their hounds from hell isn't trouble enough? What are you gonna do, tough guy? Wash my mouth out with soap?" My voice rose as a trace of hysteria joined my normal pissed-off tone. It wasn't my fault. I was finding out that Gabriel Black just brought out the best in me.

My world turned upside down.

No, really. Upside down.

Gabriel had swung me up and over his head like a proverbial sack of potatoes in a move that I wouldn't have thought possible with cuffs on. *Great.* He was a contortionist too. I hung over his shoulder and he charged down the slope of the mountain with a speed and agility I'd not thought possible for a man his size. I had no choice but to hold on. It was a long drop from his six-foot-two frame, and I sure didn't want him to go all caveman on me and drag me behind him.

"I can run on my own," I shouted at him. "Just do the right thing and take the cuffs off." He ignored me, of course, and I guess I had to agree: It was damn hard to hold a conversation at this angle, much less make demands.

The ground blurred and twisted beneath me, a blend of ferns and sand and rocks. I felt like an idiot, and Max obviously agreed, racing back and forth to check on me as if seeing me hanging upside down were a novelty of some kind.

A siren blared. Closer. Longer. Max paused as the baying of dogs sliced through the air. Max might try to defend us, but he'd be way outnumbered, and the thought of those mutant mutts ripping and tearing into my dog scared me. I started to encourage Gabriel.

"Run faster, you moron," I yelled, beating my free fist on his back to get his attention. "They're gaining on us." Okay. So I wasn't so good at encouragement. Call it tough love. Still, maybe it was my imagination, but he did seem to pick up the pace.

Gabriel stumbled down the last stretch into pebbles and sand. The beach.

He swung me down beside him, and we both turned to stare at the stream of men and dogs breaking through the clearing above us. Who knew evil could be so fast?

"This way," Gabriel said as he pulled me toward the

water, where now I could see our destination clearly. A sleek black-hulled sailboat bobbed in the waves. With two masts, it was a ketch rig, narrow in the beam, about thirty-two feet long. The boat was as sexy and sleek as its owner.

Sexy? Who thinks of sexy at a time like this? When had this man turned me into a pervert? Sexy, my ass. I kicked his shin.

"Damn it, Blue." He reached down and rubbed his leg. "Stop with the theatrics already. I'm trying to save your life."

"Don't be a wuss. I just wanted to get your attention."

"Try asking."

"Next time, tough guy. Now, what's the plan? How do we get to your little boat out there?"

"Little?"

What was it with guys? Call their toys little and all of a sudden you had an injured male ego. Like I was talking about his personal equipment or something. Which, by the way, I'd seen so up close and personal that the thought made me blush. I mean, come on, there was nothing little about it. The man was amazing.

Heat flared in my cheeks as the visual hit my brain, and I quickly found something fascinating to look at on my boots.

"You doing okay? You look flushed."

Okay. The jury was in: Gabriel Black had turned me into a pervert for real. Great. Just great.

Gabriel motioned to the shoreline, and, not having any choice in the matter, I followed his lead. As we approached I saw my kayak. It had been moved and now sat ready to launch in the unwelcoming sea.

I had built the boat when I was a kid; Seamus hadn't helped, but instead stood watching and criticizing each and every phase along the way. But I was stubborn and I built the boat my way. Strong, durable, fast. I built it with one thing in mind: to escape him. Little did I know that the time would never come. It was Seamus who had left first—left me alone to find him gutted and bleeding and dying on this very beach.

The boat held two, and Max made three. It wouldn't be easy, but maybe if Max was still for once, we could balance him just so, and maybe I could slip the cuff and shove Gabriel overboard. I mean, he did look good wet, and maybe—

"Good work, Black."

We both jerked around to the raspy, low voice. A voice that sounded like its owner had been gargling with nails and rinsing with sand. A voice that sounded mean and scary and so unlike Gabriel's silken whispers.

"If I didn't know better, I'd think you were trying to keep the bitch for yourself. Of course, Indigo wouldn't be happy about that."

Indigo? I looked questioningly at Gabriel. He stood silent and unreadable, as always.

My heart automatically kicked into high gear and thudded against my chest. I hadn't been this close to a Runner since the night I'd been attacked. And now I was looking at three of them, not more than an arm's length away.

The men were huge, all three taller than Gabriel. Raspy Voice had long, tangled black dreads that he'd knotted and woven with seashells and shards of beach glass. He had a massive, serrated shark's-tooth necklace, and long vertical scars ran down the left side of his face. He wore a coat similar to Gabriel's but much worse for the wear. The bloodstains were hard to miss. So were the twin blades he held in each hand.

Gabriel shrugged and reached into his inner pocket and produced a key. I shook my head. My arrogance from the night before had gotten the better of me. I hadn't even taken the time to hide the key. I'd just left it on the counter, so sure was I he'd never reach it. *Stupid, Blue,* whispered the voice of Seamus in my head. *Stupid.* Gabriel proceeded to open the cuff on his hand. So this was it. He was just going to hand me over to these three monsters. So much for not sharing.

"Coward," I whispered.

He looked at me and raised that questioning dark brow of his, and with one more tug, I was sitting on the stern of my little boat, handcuffed to an exposed beam that had rotted through the leather.

"Not that I'd blame you, Black." The man pushed past Gabriel and ran a blade lightly down my cheek. "She's a looker, all right. Look at them blue eyes." He pointed the tip of his knife at my pupil and I refused to blink. He lowered the blade and added, "Scrawny, though. Still . . ." He reached out and squeezed my breast through my Gore-Tex jacket. "She's got enough meat on her for one good ride. Isn't that right, sweetheart?" He pushed his scarred and ruined face near mine and he smiled, showing brown and decaying teeth. His breath smelled rank and rotting, like death.

I'd had enough.

Maybe it was the "scrawny" comment. Or most likely the uninvited hand on my breast might have done it. Not that I'd invited many hands to touch my breasts. Okay. None that I could think of.

Whatever.

I kneed him hard in the groin. I gave it my all, and he went down with a thud like a sack of cement mix. I stood, my cuffed hand lifting my tiny boat off the sand, and kicked him hard in the ribs, wishing like hell I were wearing a pair of those steel-toed boots instead of the rubber skull ones. I wanted to do some real damage. I stomped on a bent knee with my heel and heard a sickening crunch. The man howled in pain.

Max flew past me and launched at a second Runner, sending all one hundred and twenty pounds at him. The man went down, but not before slicing Max's shoulder. Max yelped but continued with the attack, tearing and ripping at the Runner's throat just like I knew he could. But knowing it and seeing it were two distinctly different things. And if I lived, I'd never look at my Max the same way again.

Gabriel had the third Runner, a huge, heavily tattooed bald man, in a death grip. He'd put my bowie knife to good use: It was embedded in the man's heart.

Blood was everywhere, and my mind flashed on Seamus on this same beach, surrounded by so much blood. My legs went weak and I sank into the sand on my knees and tried not to be sick. My vision blurred as the nightmare of eleven years ago pushed to the forefront, taking over my mind. I felt faint. *Not now, Blue. Please, God, help me—not now.* I squeezed my eyes shut.

I was being jerked up by the arm as Gabriel unlocked the cuffs.

"Hang on, Blue. I'll get you out of this."

I wanted to tell him I didn't need saving. I wanted to tell him I wasn't a damsel in distress. But I did, and I was. And right now there was nothing to be done for it.

He pushed me into the front of my kayak, handed me a paddle, and pushed the boat off with his foot. I hooked the surf and, with an expertise honed by years of repetition, I turned the boat out to sea. I looked over my shoulder just in time to see Gabriel kneel and snap Raspy Voice's neck. My stomach lurched, and I saw Max wading into the surf.

I had no intention of leaving my dog behind. Never

had. I whistled and paddled the boat parallel along the shore. I paddled in, rubbing the bottom of the boat against underwater pebbles. I glanced at the approaching army of men and dogs, now way too close. The blare of sirens and shouts and barks was deafening, and I frantically grabbed for Max.

But I'd been concentrating on the wrong threat. So consumed with injured Max, I'd forgotten about Gabriel Black, the biggest threat of all.

Gabriel jumped into the back of my tiny boat, settling into the second seat like it was made for him. He whistled for Max, who went willingly. I couldn't help feeling Max was a lamb being led to slaughter. This boat was made for two. Only two. Three would be nearly impossible. In seas like this, it was suicide to attempt it. Gabriel Black had to go.

Gabriel reached for Max, grabbing him by his collar. The frayed series of old knots stretched and Max slipped out of his collar darting toward me. I reached out for my dog, only to hear Gabriel command him back. I watched as Gabriel bent his head to the dog as if communicating. Somehow, Max calmed.

"Now go." Gabriel boomed the order, and Max turned and ran to the shore, ran into the waiting danger, not away from it.

"Max, no!" I cried out. "Come." Max paused, looked at me, and whined that signature whine of his, and my heart broke.

"Go." Gabriel had the last word as Max, with a final look toward me, ran from the shore straight into the oncoming danger. A dozen or more Runner dogs broke rank and raced to meet him.

Gabriel pushed off with his foot, and with a forceful thrust he sent us into the surf and swells, gliding into the sea.

Hot tears streamed down my cheeks as I lost sight of Max when we dipped into a swell.

"You bastard, that was *my* dog," I turned and screamed at Gabriel. I raised my paddle in anger and he caught it easily, twisting it from my wrist like it was a toothpick.

He pushed the paddle into the angry gray waters and we forged ahead toward the ketch rig and safety. Safety for us, but not for Max.

I struggled to see the shore, but the waves and swells blocked my view. I glared at Gabriel. If I didn't hate him before, I sure hated him now.

"My dog!" I yelled, not ashamed of my tears. "You've just killed my dog, you Runner scum."

Gabriel Black dug the paddle toward the port side of the boat, hitting the waters with force and purpose. He looked at me with sadness in his eyes.

"Not your dog, Blue. *My* dog. I left him behind five years ago when I first found you."

Chapter Six

I hung on while Gabriel used his strength to paddle and fight our way through an unwilling sea. Waves washed over the bow of my little boat, soaking both of us, weighing us down, making our journey hard and dangerous, almost impossible.

Almost.

At last, we smashed into the black hull of Gabriel's boat, and okay, I had to admit, it did look bigger close up. Maybe he didn't deserve the "little" comment, but now, after Max? Hell. He deserved a lot more.

Gabriel grabbed a line he'd stowed in the shell of my kayak and knelt on the deck, reaching up to loop it on a cleat. The water was too choppy to tie it off, and I heard the sea laugh as it tossed and bounced us like a cork. Gabriel managed to grab the stanchions and hoist himself up and over, landing safely on his teak deck. And now it was my turn.

Pulling the boat alongside, he straddled the stanchions and reached down for the front of my coat collar, plucking me out of my boat like I was no more than an errant feather. I went airborne, flying over the steel stanchions and into Gabriel's arms. He lost his balance and almost dropped me. I saw a glint of silver as the handcuffs flew overboard when his coat pocket caught on a stanchion and ripped away. He crashed hard on the deck, flat on his back. I landed on top of him.

My forehead slammed into his for what had to be a record-breaking head butt. Pain shot through my skull when I tried to raise my head, and I saw white spots and blue stars. I laid my head down on his broad chest and had a déjà vu moment.

The thundering of his heartbeat became overwhelmed by the thundering of his voice. "Damn it, Blue. Why is everything with you so hard?"

I moaned. "Why is everything with you so painful?"

I raised my head, glaring into those black eyes. "Look, tough guy, it's not like I asked for this little getaway cruise. And I can't help it that your sea legs aren't working. You pretty much suck as a pirate, you know it? If I were you, I'd stick to being a cabin boy."

"Cabin boy?"

The look on his face was worth the insult. He rubbed his forehead, where a red welt was rising, and I saw the line that held my kayak slip through his fingers and slide from the cleat. We both realized it too late. The sea offered up a swell and the line disappeared over the rail, releasing my little boat into the raging waters. It would no doubt crash against the craggy rocks that lined the shore.

Pushing off Gabriel, I risked the light-headedness and jumped up, grabbing the stanchions to steady my spinning vision and slipping feet. I was just in time to see the tiny kayak swallowed up in angry waters. For a moment, I forgot where I was, forgot Gabriel Black, forgot the Runners on the beach; I just forgot it all.

I looked into the waves and saw my blistered fingers filled with splinters at age twelve when I built my kayak. I saw Japanese floats on a little cedar tree, standing in the corner of my cozy one-room cabin. I saw Max, pushing and shoving to get out the front door. I saw Uncle Seamus on the beach, lying dead in crimson sand. And I saw my mother, laughing in the Thai sunlight, with flowers in her hair.

Hot tears traced down my cheeks.

Gabriel closed in from behind, balancing a foot on the rail. He put his arms around me. We both watched the retreating Runners, no doubt heading to their boats moored on the other side of the island. We were safe for the moment, but pursuit would come soon.

My head swam and I sank back into that strong, broad chest, hating that I needed someone, hating that I needed him.

He nuzzled my neck and whispered in my ear, "I'm sorry about your boat, Blue. I'll build you another one."

That made no sense. Gabriel was a Runner with his own agenda. I was his prisoner. Build me a boat? Still, my mind was mush and I shivered, numb with cold. I thought of Max, and had a vision of him running through the surf trying to get to me.

"Build one Max will fit in?" I whispered, not trusting the strength of my voice, knowing I sounded crazy.

"Sure, Blue. A boat big enough for Max too."

"Max . . . was he really yours?"

Gabriel hugged me to him and whispered in my ear, "In the end, Blue, he was yours. He loved you. You gave him a better life than I ever could." He pulled back from the rails and said, "Come on, little one. I'm getting us out of here. The Runners will be sailing soon."

No one had called me *little one* since my parents died. It jolted me out of the funk and back into survivor mode. I elbowed him out of the way, not hard, not threatening; I needed to see how this boat worked before I threw him overboard. But first, I needed answers.

"Why leave Max five years ago?" I demanded. "What

the hell were you doing watching me? Funny, I didn't peg you as the peeping-Tom type. You're more like the cuff-and-kidnap type." I folded my arms across my chest to try to stem the shivering.

Gabriel nodded, accepting my rejection of our warm and fuzzy moment, and stepped out of the way to let me pass. The sea was rough, and I grabbed for the stanchions as Gabriel pushed the hatch open and motioned me down.

"Not now, Blue. You're freezing. And we have to move fast. Question-and-answer period is over."

He gave me that dark look of his which told me any more probing would be useless. Great.

"Grab a blanket downstairs and try to stay warm while I get us out of here. If all goes well, I'll have us stowed, stashed, and hidden by nightfall."

Gabriel was right: I was freezing. Still . . . "I'll stay on deck," I said. As much as a dry blanket sounded tempting, I needed to see where we were going, where he was taking me. I wouldn't be blinded by hiding in the hull. I needed to plan for the future. I needed a plan for escape. As if reading my mind, Gabriel paused in his preparation and gave me a steady look.

"There is no escape. The ocean will simply eat you up. And if not the ocean, the sharks will."

"And wait, don't tell me. The bogeyman will get me too."

Gabriel came over and looked me in the eyes. "Don't be so sure I'm not the bogeyman, Blue."

Okay. That shut me up.

"I'm hoisting the sails," he said. "Watch the boom. I don't want to have to fish you out of the ocean, strip you naked, and save you from hypothermia."

I rolled my eyes and sat down in the cockpit, shivering. Wrapping my arms around my chest, hugging myself for warmth, I settled in to watch Gabriel work. I hated to admit it, but just watching him move and stretch and bend over to grab a line here and there . . . well, hell, the man *was* gorgeous. And I knew what was under those wet clothes. And even though I hated him—right?—I couldn't help it. I started to warm up.

He'd stripped off his coat and I could see his muscles working under that fitted thermal shirt he wore. Gabriel and his boat moved as one. He anticipated the boat's every move with uncanny ability. His movements were fluid, graceful, efficient. His black hair whipped in the wind, and when Gabriel took the wheel, he looked every inch the pirate. Or at the least, a very dangerous, sexy cabin boy. He had us under way in minutes.

The wind picked up and the sleek boat with the slender hull cut through the water, making its own path in rugged, unforgiving waves. I found the speed exhilarating; I'd never been on a boat like this before. But I'd seen them on the horizon, dreamed about where they were heading, fantasized about stowing away on one, sailing away from the waves and the cold and the loneliness.

"Grab the wheel, Blue. Stay north. I'm going below."

Before I could protest, Gabriel stepped over my head and disappeared into the cabin below. Panicked, I stood, grabbed the helm, and kept the boat on its northern heading. True north. Gabriel had a compass mounted, but I didn't need it. When you grow up predicting waves, tsunami waves, you get pretty damn good at directions.

Wind whipped through my hair, salt spray stung my cheeks, and I was frozen to the bone.

I *loved* every minute of it.

I tasted freedom for the first time in so many years. I saw the possibilities written on the waves. A boat like this could take me away from my islands, could take me to another part of the world entirely. I could search for a better place in this world, a place without waves and

Runners and death all around. I could broadcast along the way, reading waves, saving lives, searching for more survivors, for kids. I could go back for Max. And of course there was . . . Finn. *Finnegan.* I could search for him. It was a search my heart would never let me stop.

The damn tears sprang into my eyes once more. Yeah, I'd had a rough day, but the tears had to stop. *A sure sign of weakness, Blue,* my uncle would have said. *The cat will have a heyday with you actin' like a mouse.* Still, I hadn't let myself think of my brother in those terms for years. "Those terms" meaning that he could be . . . that is, maybe, or perhaps . . . still alive. Logically I knew it wasn't possible. Logically I knew I was kidding myself. I'd seen the wave sweep under his feet, raise him up and up, then swallow him, snatching him from my sight. But if the wave saved me . . . ?

"Stop it, Blue, just stop," I admonished myself as I pounded the wheel. I knew better. Unlike my parents', his body was never found. Just like thousands and thousands of others. Still, something was happening to me as I gripped the wheel of this sleek, fast, and so very cool sailboat.

For the first time in years, I felt hope.

And Gabriel Black, the Runner, my captor, my bunk buddy, my sometime savior, my tough guy, and the father of Max, was going to help me keep it.

I'd just formulated a new plan. I was going to steal this boat.

Chapter Seven

Darkness had fallen and I leaned over the stern of the boat, watching the phosphorus play and dance in our wake. Beautiful colors swirled and flashed in the now black sea. I'd seen the phenomenon before, but never on this level, and I was like a little kid, complete with uttered *oohs* and *ahs*. I knew Gabriel got a kick out of my reaction because I could hear him chuckling behind me.

But I didn't care. I'd been laughed at all my life. It rolled off my shoulders as easily as rain.

I clutched the blanket firmly around me; Gabriel had brought it up from below hours ago, along with a steaming mug of hot herbal tea and salmon jerky. I wasn't too proud to eat or drink. I needed strength. After all, I was slight in stature and I lost body heat easily. Sure, I'd take what he was offering. Up to a point.

The Runners had been lost in our dust—or wake, as it was. Gabriel's boat was beyond fast, and with the winds at peak performance, and a hull designed for speed, we'd buried the rail and the Runners didn't stand a chance. I'd caught sight of them only once, and then they were a mere dot on the horizon.

We were safe. For now.

But really, how safe was I with Gabriel and his hidden agenda? Who was Indigo? And why did he want me? And how in the hell had a sailor as capable as Gabriel Black ended up near death on my beach? I needed answers. And somewhere on this boat, I'd find them.

I had yet to go below. I focused on where we were going and how this boat worked. Thanks to Uncle Seamus, I could navigate by the stars, and I knew we were heading north, into the New Canadian Gulf Islands. Since the age of five, I'd never been anywhere other than my own small string of islands, what was left of the "old" San Juans in what was once Washington State. Now there were no states, just islands. Thousands and thousands and thousands of islands.

"Watch your head, Blue. We're coming about."

Coming about? As in changing direction? Heading back toward the Runners? My heart started to pound. Why? What game were we playing now?

I ducked as the boom swung to the opposite side of the boat and watched as Gabriel trimmed the sails.

"What's happening? Why are we heading back?"

"Not back. Over."

He pointed into darkness and I squinted into the night, trying to see what he could.

Gabriel, seeing my confusion and sensing my fear, explained. "Tonight we drop anchor in what I call the 'new' False Bay. It's similar to the bay off the west side of your island. That is, the False Bay that used to be there."

I nodded, remembering well the hidden beach I played on as a kid. The bay and the beach were long gone, swallowed up by a killer wave.

"We're close to New Vancouver," he continued. "It's about a twenty-four-hour sail from here. I'm entering this bay on a high tide. By morning a minus tide will set in, and the bay will look like nothing but miles and miles of wet beach. That's why I call it False Bay. No one can approach. Plus we'll be hidden in a tiny cove, with deeper moorage." He sighed and pushed a dark lock from his face. "Safe haven, Blue. Not for long, but at least for the night."

Beach? My mind raced. I could do beach. I could walk on beach, run on beach, fight on beach. The beach worked for me on so many levels. I could lure Gabriel off the boat, get him to chase me—

Again, Gabriel read my mind.

"Don't even think about it, Blue."

"Think about what, Kreskin?"

Gabriel shook his head. "About escaping onto the sand. It's linked with tide pools, some deep, some shallow, and all filled with box jellies."

I had nothing to say to that. But the jellies? I could do jellies. Box jellyfish were laced with a poison so powerful their tiny tentacles could cause paralysis in minutes, death in under an hour. Years ago their presence in these waters was unheard-of. But that was before the waves. Now our Northwest waters were home to all kinds of monsters, including—and I gave an involuntary shudder—great whites.

But tonight I dealt with just jellyfish, albeit box jellyfish. I had my badass rubber boots on. Jellies couldn't begin to penetrate them. That alone boosted my confidence. My ego kicked in. I was raised around the water. Tide pools? I wasn't afraid of no stinkin' tide pools. Bring it.

"The tide pools . . ." Gabriel continued.

Oh, boy, I thought, *here it comes.*

"Well, the sand has changed. In this bay, it's quicksand. Once you're stuck, trust me, babe, you're stuck."

Babe? What the . . . ? I wouldn't think about that now. I knitted my brows and thought about the pools. Quicksand, huh? Well, that just didn't sound good. That is, if I believed him. I'd wait and see what daybreak revealed.

"Believe it, Blue. Wait and see for yourself, in the morning."

Damn. Maybe he was a mind reader.

A few minutes later Gabriel maneuvered the sailboat into a tiny cove. I could see the shadows on the water of crooked madrona trunks from the shore as they twisted into the moonlit sky. The wind had died down to just a whisper, and a soft rain started to fall. Time to go below. And didn't that just bring a whole new set of circumstances to worry about.

"Time to get below, Blue."

Damn it. I wished he'd stop doing that. It was beginning to freak me out.

I huddled in the blanket, watching him stow and stash, as he'd promised. With the boat and sails secure he approached, and I trembled with anticipation. *What now, Blue? What now?*

Gabriel pushed the hatch back and went below. Moments later a soft glow filtered up to the deck, and he stuck his head out, offering a hand. "Come on, I know you're hungry. You're freezing. You're"—he lowered his voice—"you're scared." I glared at him. "And for that," he continued, "I'm sorry."

I thought about my tiny home, my little boat, about Max and the Runners. I thought about the voice of Tsunami Blue, now silenced, maybe forever. I rose, not feeling I had any choice in the matter. What good would it do to freeze and starve? I needed my strength. I needed time for my plan. I reached for his hand. "Not sorry enough, tough guy."

I stepped down into a teak wonderland.

Gabriel's boat may not have been the biggest on the water, but it had to be the cleanest, the coziest. The lanterns cast a warm hue over the highly polished wood, and the small stove radiated blessed heat. I smelled cinnamon and herbs and a pleasant musk that was pure Gabriel Black.

I looked around, astounded by the order and neatness. Who knew a Runner lived any other way than like a barbarian? Where were the gnawed chicken bones, the tobacco butts, the severed arms and legs?

Instead, there were shelves of books, lots of books, and carefully labeled jars of herbs and maps and—

"You need to get out of those wet clothes, Blue. You've been in them for hours." I didn't move. He looked at me and shook his head. "Stubborn to the core, that's what you are."

"Well, forgive me if I take offense, but I haven't been down here for more than, what, two minutes? And already you're talking me out of my clothes." I wrapped the blanket tighter.

"Look—"

"Don't 'look' me, Gabriel. Damn you. Take off my clothes, huh? Whatever happened to dinner and a movie?"

He laughed. It was warm, rich, unassuming, and I swear, it must have been contagious, because I laughed too, in spite of myself. We both knew there hadn't been movies for well over a decade, and dinner? Pretty much grilled salmon, barbecued salmon, smoked salmon, salmon jerky, and on it went. Reservations and candlelight? No way. Chance of us "dating"? Double no way.

He took two strides and approached, reaching for me. I flinched and backed away from his touch. Old habits again. He withdrew his hand and I bit my lower lip, trying to stop the trembling. He was too close. I felt crowded, scared, confused. And I hated it.

"What do you want with me?" I whispered. "I have a right to know."

"In time," he replied softly. "I mean you no harm—"

"No harm?" My temper flared, and I let the blanket drop to the wooden floor.

I shoved my bruised and battered wrist in his face to

show him where the cuff had made its mark. "No harm?" I pulled the neck of my thermal top down and showed him the fingerprints he left on my neck. "No harm?" I didn't stop there. In blind anger I pulled the shirt up, revealing my pink bra and the ugly purple-and-blue patch over my ribs, where they had taken a beating bouncing over his shoulder. The bruise looked neon against my pale skin. "No harm?"

He looked at my midriff and closed the space between us, catching my wrist with one hand and circling my waist, pulling me into him with the other. My hand flattened against his chest, and he was so close I couldn't breathe.

In the warm cabin light, with shadows that fell on his beautiful features, I thought again of dark angels and flesh pressed against flesh. Our flesh. Anger melted, and that strange sensation I'd felt the night I slept next to him returned low in my belly, and I felt my pulse race and my breath become shallow.

He pressed my wrist to his lips, and with a soft kiss, he dropped my hand and gently touched my exposed skin with both his hands. I gasped as he ran his fingertips over the damaged area, skimming the bottom of my breasts with his thumbs as he pushed up under my bra.

"Blue"—he looked into my eyes with that dark gaze of his—"please believe me when I tell you how sorry I am." I read raw hunger in his eyes. His thumbs rubbed back and forth, pushing farther under my bra. For a moment, for a heartbeat or two, time stopped.

And then the fear kicked in.

He was a Runner. Runners raped. Runners killed. Runners were not gentle, they were not sorry, and they did not care. Not ever.

I used all my strength to push him back. And just like that he let me. My shirt fell back in place, and I trembled from cold and nerves and something else I didn't want to think about. Gabriel ran his hand through his long black hair in frustration. It was a moment before either one of us spoke.

"Go change, Blue." He pointed to the bow of the boat, where I could see a bunk and not much else. "Please. I've laid some clothes out for you on the V-berth. The door slides shut. It won't lock, but you have my word I won't come in. Just please get warm. I hate seeing you this way. I hate"—he paused and took a breath—"I hate what I've done to you."

I read the sadness in his eyes, the conflict. As if he were in a struggle within himself. How could I fight when I didn't know what I was fighting? Why was I here? It was a mystery, one I had to solve, but for now he was also right: I had to get out of these clothes. I felt sick with the cold and the damp.

Walking past him to the bow of the boat, I reached the V-berth, the bunk, stepped in, and slid the teak door closed behind me. I breathed in the familiar scent of the sea and leaned against the smooth, warm wood and tried like hell to calm my nerves.

There on the bed were clothes carefully laid out like I was an expected guest. I looked closely at them, touching and caressing each piece in wonder.

There were black jeans, like his, stonewashed and soft. There were cargo pants and two long-sleeved thermals, pretty in cream and cornflower blue. The underwear, black panties and bras, were my size exactly. A fisherman's sweater of soft wool hung on a hook, a women's size with a large cable-knit pattern. And there were pajamas, cloud-soft flannel. The matching tank top and short bottoms were decorated with tiny dragonflies and Asian coins for a pattern. I'd never owned anything as extravagant as pajamas before; at least, not since I was five years old.

Lying on this little bunk were more new clothes than I ever remembered owning all at one time. Where? And how? New Seattle? Not possible. The malls were underwater; nothing this nice could have survived. Then where? I thought of Gabriel's sun-kissed skin, and I remembered my first impression: *Not from around here.*

I stripped off my clothes, slipped on the silky underwear, and climbed into the black jeans. They fit perfectly, hugging my body like an old friend.

I marveled that I actually had a choice of clothing. I chose the cream thermal and fisherman's sweater. Oversize, it hung to my knees, and the sleeves covered my hands to the knuckles. It felt warm and cozy and welcoming. I loved it. But what I really wanted to wear were the pajamas. I couldn't help handling them, rubbing them against my cheek, smelling the newness of them. But when, if ever, I'd wear them with Gabriel so close . . . well, for now it wasn't possible. It just wasn't.

I smelled a heavenly aroma coming from the cabin and my mouth watered with hunger. Time to face Gabriel. And then what? Thank him for the clothes? Thank him for planning ahead, for knowing my size? That was creepy on so many levels. I had so many questions. But would he answer them? And if he did, would there be any truth in his words?

I turned to leave when I saw a small mirror hanging flush on the door. Standing on tiptoe I peeked at my reflection. I looked at the dark circles under my eyes, the paleness of my skin, and the tangled mess of my hair. I looked at the lump on my forehead that matched Gabriel's goose egg perfectly. A shadow of a smile passed over my face as I touched the painful spot. Guess both of us were pretty hardheaded. As bone-weary fatigue crept into every part of my body, I knew no amount of new clothes would help sort out the mess I was in. Sighing, I put my hands on the door and got ready to slide it open.

Taking a deep breath I prayed. *Please, God, just get me through this night. Let Gabriel Black be different from all the rest of the Runners out there. Let me rest. Let me sleep. Let me regain my strength. And please, please, let me live through this night.*

Chapter Eight

The aroma of something wonderful hit me the moment I slid the door open. My stomach growled and my nose told me I wasn't in Salmon Land anymore. I smelled fresh bread and roasting vegetables and some kind of simmering meat and . . . wait, was it even possible?

Coffee?

Did I smell coffee?

I closed my eyes and inhaled deeply through my nose, almost tripping as I made my way toward the aroma. Seamus had introduced me to coffee when I was seven, and by the time I was eight, I was the one making it. I was on the top of New San Juan, waiting on high ground, the day one of the worst waves took a giant swallow out of New Seattle. The sea took away the last vestiges of coffee, canned, freeze-dried, whole beans, or any other. My New Seattle coffee runs came to a halt.

It was the beginning of a two-month-long caffeine headache for me. Which was my own personal hell. Even Max hardly recognized my normal pissed-off personality. I'd gone from marginally pissed off, to off-the-friggin'-Richter-scale pissed off. Looking back on it, I was surprised Max stuck around at all. At the thought of Max, my eyes stung and I quickly blinked back the threatening tears.

Stopping coffee runs was just one more door closing on my interaction with people. Which was probably for the best. My blue eyes and tattoo had been drawing too much attention anyway.

As things in our world got worse, the hatred for me grew. And who could blame them for hating me? Every time they heard my voice, death and destruction followed. No matter how much I read from the books and magazines piled in the Runner kindling dump, I never could find any explanation for my abilities. People didn't like what they couldn't explain. Some thought I wasn't human, that I was something evil. Their superstition, desperation, and fear overrode hope.

Gabriel had set up a tiny fold-down table for us; he'd even lit a candle. He sat with his back to me, sipping a cup of Joe, as Seamus called it, reading a chart. His long black hair had been brushed out and hung loosely around his shoulders. It looked shiny and thick and glowed blue-black in the candlelight. It was beautiful.

I had the urge to walk up and yank it. Hard. But I really, really, *really* wanted a cup of coffee, so for now I'd try to play nice. Try.

"Have a seat," he said without turning around. "Make yourself at home."

I slipped onto the bench across from him, folding my hands in my lap, and waited expectantly. He would feed me, that much I was sure of, but I just didn't know how to go about "making myself at home." This wasn't my home. This was my prison.

My stomach growled and he looked up and smiled. Twin dimples appeared and white teeth flashed. I must have been starving, because Gabriel Black looked good enough to eat. He had to quit smiling. It was unsettling and interfered with my thoughts of escape and stealing his boat and throwing him overboard.

He put the chart aside and leaned across the table. "Hungry?"

I nodded.

He looked at me appraisingly in the sweater, tilted his head, and whispered, "I know I am."

Why did I think he wasn't talking about food?

I felt the familiar heat climb into my cheeks.

"Your eyes look even bluer when you do that, as if that's even possible."

"Do what?"

"Blush."

"Oh. I mean, I wasn't."

His black eyes sparkled with humor. "Oh," he said. "The sweater looks terrific on you. I knew it would."

I hardly knew what to say. *Thanks for being my secret shopper*? *Thanks for stalking me for five years and getting my underwear size right*? I decided to say nothing.

He continued to stare.

"Um, Gabriel?"

"Yeah?"

"Food?"

Now it was his turn to look embarrassed. He blinked. "Of course."

Gabriel brought two heaping bowls of stew and placed one in front of me. I bent my head, breathing in the enticing aromas.

"It smells amazing. This is so not the fish chowder I'm used to." I looked at him. "Venison?"

"Sirloin."

I almost dropped my fork. Sirloin? Who had sirloin anymore? Sirloin was from cows. Cows had disappeared years ago. Hadn't they?

There was warm wheat bread and tiny salt and pepper shakers, which blew me away, and then the magic words: "Do you want some coffee?"

It was all I could do to hide my excitement. "Um, yeah, sure." I could do casual. I wasn't a heathen.

"Cream?"

"Cream?" My voice squeaked and I dropped my spoon, sloshing the stew on the table. Okay. So maybe I was a heathen. Still, I was so surprised I could have fallen off a chair. Good thing my chair was a bench.

"Something wrong?"

I couldn't stand it another second. I lost it. I picked up my spoon, pointing it at him like it was my knife. In my anger I might have even spun it, which was really embarrassing. I raised my voice anyway.

"Wrong? Wrong? Why would anything be wrong? Sirloin? Cream? Salt *and* pepper? And coffee? Who the hell has coffee these days?"

He looked confused. "What? You don't like coffee?"

"I love coffee. *Love. It.* But that's not my point."

"What is the point?"

God, the man was dense. Who knew? But I guessed this was our first real conversation. We hadn't had time to talk. We'd been too busy trying to kill each other.

"Okay, Gabriel. I'll speak slowly."

He frowned.

"Once upon a time there was a series of giant killer waves." He sat back with arms folded, clearly not amused. "And they pretty much wiped out just about everything we humans had taken for granted. Things like cows and cream and pepper and *coffee*." He gave me a blank look. I sighed, rubbing my temples. "The next thing you'll tell me is that it's Starbucks."

"Christmas Blend."

"What?"

"The coffee. It's Starbucks' Christmas Blend."

"Un-fucking-believable."

He raised a brow. "I like to eat well."

"That's my point. You eat well." I spread my arms out in exasperation. "How?"

"Uplanders."

His answer blew me away.

"Uplanders?" I hated that my voice sounded weak, uncertain. Scared.

"In part. The coffee is mine, though. It's like gold. It makes a good trade."

I put the spoon down and shook my head, amazed at this information. "How is this possible?" I demanded. "Uncle Seamus said Uplanders were no better off than the Runners—worse, even. He said the few of them who remained lived like animals. He said they weren't worth saving. He said they'd kill me just as sure as—" I stopped. The look on Gabriel's face said it all.

Seamus had lied.

How could that surprise me? Seamus had always lied. It wasn't until now that I realized the true extent of it. The extreme measures he went to just to keep me isolated and alone. To be his personal Weather Channel. I saw the look of pity in Gabriel's eyes and I hated it. With fists clamped against the anger and hurt, I hardly trusted my own voice. I held his gaze and then asked coolly, "May I have that cup of coffee now?"

"Of course."

As Gabriel brought the steaming mug of coffee and set it in front of me, I kept my gaze down, intent on staring at the stew. It probably tasted wonderful, but I'd lost my appetite. I'd lost my fire, my will, my focus. Even the aroma of Starbucks Christmas Blend couldn't rouse me.

Today I'd lost everything. My home, which now seemed like a lie. A lie because there were more people out there in more communities than I could have imagined. People who raised cows and had cream. I didn't have to live alone, isolated on a remote island because Seamus O'Malley had put me there. And then I thought again of Max and realized that I hadn't been truly alone for the past five years. But even my dog had been a lie. Max hadn't been mine at all. And now he was gone.

Sitting in this stranger's boat, held captive, my future in question, I felt as alone as the day they told me my family was dead.

I realized I was over-the-top feeling sorry for myself. Drowning in self-pity. But when most everything you thought was real wasn't, well, it was a lot to process.

"Blue, you have to eat."

Gabriel's silken voice cut into my thoughts. I looked up into his intense gaze now filled with worry and I thought, *Why does he care?*

I wrapped my hands around the mug, letting the warmth seep through. I felt completely and totally lost. Where was my place in this world? Where would a freak who could read waves and talk to the water fit in? Would Gabriel, a Runner, even give me that chance? Or was I once again a pawn for someone else's agenda? Someone like this mysterious Indigo.

Gabriel reached out and wrapped his hands around mine for a moment. His hands covered my own completely. I couldn't help but flash on how easily those same hands had snapped Raspy Voice's neck. I started to tremble, in spite of my efforts not to.

"There's so much you don't understand," he said in a soft, low voice.

Releasing my hands, he reached for the cream, held it above my mug with a questioning look. I nodded, unable to find my voice, and watched as the white liquid dropped into a dark landscape, turning it into lighter shades of brown.

"Please, Blue. Take something hot. You need it."

I stared into the coffee, watching the light swirl with

dark. I listened to the rain beating a soft rhythm on the deck above. But most of all I listened to the waters of the bay, tapping out a faint tattoo message against the hull.

A message I'd heard before.

My heart rate increased tenfold, and blood roared in my ears as my blood pressure skyrocketed.

Gabriel and the lantern lights faded away. The swirls in my coffee moved faster and faster, forming peaks and foam. Sometimes it worked like that, like a message in a bottle. The sea talked to me in many forms: a tide pool, rain puddles, once even in Max's water bowl. Why not a cup of coffee?

It was a summons. A summons to listen.

Gabriel's voice seemed distant now. All I could hear was the voice against the hull, tapping out a warning.

A wave, Blue. A wave. A wave. A wave. A big wave. Huge. A monster.

A tsunami.

I gasped and the message continued.

Unmatched. Unstoppable. Unbeatable.

I gripped the mug tighter and the hot liquid sloshed out, streaming over my hands. Gabriel was on his knees now, kneeling before me, gripping my shoulders, calling my name.

I was Tsunami Blue, all right. And I was living up to my name. A wave was coming, unlike one I'd ever seen before. None of us had. And just before my world turned to gray and then to black and I passed out in Gabriel's arms, one thing and one thing only resonated in my mind.

The wave was coming.

And very few of us would live to see another.

Chapter Nine

I woke up in Gabriel Black's arms.

He was asleep, I was awake, and all I could think of was that we were in bed together. Again.

We were in the tiny stateroom, snuggled up on the V-berth under a cozy down comforter. And even though the comforter covered us completely, I knew immediately that I had on my new pajamas. The baby-soft flannel felt as good against my skin as I knew it would. Still, that left the million-dollar question. Not that a million dollars was worth anything, right? Or was it? I didn't know anymore. Still, I hadn't put on the pj's. So?

So once again Gabriel had seen me naked. Or gotten me naked. Shit, I guess both were technically right. *Well, that's great, Blue. Just great.*

I tried not to panic as thoughts of what might have happened raced through my mind. But no, my body would tell me; I would know. And I sure as hell would have woken up. A wave vision might lay me out for the count. But render me unconscious while I had wild, raw sex with a Runner? Not a chance in hell. I was an extremely light sleeper. And I was pretty damn sure sex with Gabriel Black would wake me up.

And as for Gabriel? I looked at him sleeping, one arm over my stomach, the other under my head. Inky lashes lay against bronzed skin, and his black hair mingled with my own, hard to tell where his started and mine left off. He looked amazing as always, but somehow in his sleep he looked . . . what? Not harmless, no, never not harmless. Honorable?

Okay. Get a grip, Blue.

I'd just visited the planet Delusional. Had to be lack of food. Or more likely the cup of coffee I missed out on last night. Something that traumatic would mess with anyone's mind. I mean, come on. It was Starbucks Christmas Blend. With cream.

I held my breath and peeked under the comforter, lifting it slowly. Gabriel was completely dressed, except for the nasty spiked belt he favored. Thank God. I mean, really, that belt could have snagged the hell out of my new pj's.

The daylight from the tiny hatch above filtered gray light into the cabin, and I concentrated on the sounds that surrounded me: Gabriel's even breathing, an eagle's cry, the breeze slapping a line against the mast, and the sound I listened for the most: the water. And there it was, lapping at the hull, steady, constant, and nothing more. No warnings, no words, no rise in my blood pressure, except for when I looked at Gabriel sleeping next to me—nothing.

A wave bigger than any other.

I fought panic. I had time to figure this out. I always had time. Not much. Two weeks, tops. The ocean would tease me with clues, give me facts mixed with fiction. It would lie, promise, renege, and then promise all over again. It was a dangerous game that had led to false alarms at times, which only further enflamed those who believed I was evil—that I somehow caused the waves.

I closed my eyes and tried to relax, tried to think. Whatever the sea was selling, I would buy. And I'd keep buying until I got it right. Eventually I would. I was Tsunami Blue, after all, and it was the one thing I could be proud of: In the end, I never, ever got it wrong. And when I figured it out, I'd take to the airwaves. But just like the boy who cried wolf too many times, there were people who refused to believe. And they paid for that with their lives. Our new world was filled with so much fear. It was easy to blame me. Still, I saved lives, so I'd keep on the air and— Wait. My equipment. My now burned and destroyed equipment.

I had more; I wasn't a complete moron. I'd stashed shortwave radios all over the San Juans. Each had been jury-rigged to my own specifications. I'd been collecting the hand-cranked units since I was kid, back in the days when no one would listen. But we were headed north. Away from everything I needed. I had to tell Gabriel. We had to turn around. Now.

I shot up, so caught up in my thoughts I didn't realize that Gabriel's arm no longer lay across me, and once again, I collided with his forehead, a complete repeat of the day before.

"Damn it, Blue." He flopped down on the bed.

"Oh, damn," I said, crashing back on the bed in a heap next to him. Both of us put our hands on our foreheads, groaning.

He spoke first.

"You're a painful woman," he said with a grimace and a moan.

I rolled over on my side and glared at him. The movement more than gave me a headache; the white spots and stars threatened again. His eyes were still closed and his fingertips rubbed his forehead.

"Serves you right for sneaking up on a girl. And"—I punched him hard in the arm—"that's for seeing me naked. Again."

The punch didn't faze him, of course, but he did open one eye and look at me.

"If you want to get physical, Blue, I'm game."

He moved so fast, I was totally unprepared. He'd straddled me in under two seconds. Pinning my arms over my head, he pressed his weight onto my stomach and lowered his face close to mine. I felt my pulse jump and caught my breath. Was this it? Was this when Gabriel Black, the Runner, showed his true colors, turning into an animal? I could taste the fear in my mouth, and I tried like hell not to show it in my eyes.

He narrowed his own dark eyes and his intense gaze said it all. He was pissed. But not murderous. I was raised around Runners. I knew the difference. I started to breathe again.

"Blue, you will listen to me. From your reaction last night, I have to believe another wave is coming. And I have to know when. And where."

I said nothing, just glared. I knew he wasn't through yet.

"You will get up, you will eat, you will fight to keep your strength up, and you and I will talk. Or rather, I will talk and you will listen. Understood?"

Oh, I understood.

I'd understood my whole life. I'd been pushed and punched and ordered around my entire childhood and then some. But when Seamus was murdered and I was left alone at thirteen, I'd been the boss of me ever since. And I liked it that way. But I also knew enough to know that I wasn't holding the right cards. If I'd been playing poker, I would've folded this hand. Besides, Gabriel had something I desperately wanted: a way back to my radios. *And let's not forget the boat.*

Still, old habits and all. I glared defiantly at him. "And if I don't, tough guy?"

"Then you don't get any Starbucks."

Okay. He had me.

"Christmas Blend?" I asked, mad at myself for being so cheap and easy and, well, easy.

"Christmas Blend."

"Cream?"

"Will you listen, Blue? Will you eat? Will you"—he released my arms and reached up and touched his forehead—"will you give my head a break?"

I nodded, my mouth already salivating for the brew.

"Deal." My thoughts of the rich, dark coffee were interrupted by a loud, "Wow."

Wow? Where did that—

"Hey, Nick, look. Gabe's got a babe down there."

Babe? Did I hear that right? Babe? And from who? I looked over Gabriel's shoulder to the skylight hatch and saw a boy's face was pressed against the thick panel. It distorted his features, but not enough. I could tell it was a kid.

"Damn it," Gabriel swore. "I never even heard those two board."

Two? I looked harder over his shoulder.

He looked at me, exasperated. "You're such a distraction, Blue."

"Me?" I asked, incredulous. "Me? You're the one who's distracted me. From my entire life."

Dark, shaggy heads, almond eyes, perfect noses—it might have been the distorting glass, because both kids looked exactly the same. From what I could tell, they were going to be heartbreakers when they grew up. They were brothers, of course, most likely twins. And, being a twin myself, I was fascinated. I waved.

The boys laughed and knocked on the hatch. "Hey, Just Gabe. Who's your girlfriend?"

"Yeah, for a while there, we thought you might be gay," the other chimed in.

Gabriel raised both dark brows and I couldn't hide my amusement. He sighed and leaned in closer. "We have to give them a show."

"We do?" I couldn't read his eyes, but I'd have sworn they'd gotten darker.

He leaned in and kissed my neck, now holding my arms to my sides. "Play along," he whispered.

"Because they think you're gay?" I whispered back. "There's nothing wrong with being gay." I was pretty damn sure he wasn't, but the look on his face was . . . How did that old commercial go? Ah, I got it. *Priceless.*

He scrubbed a hand over his face. "Because they can't know who you are."

"They can't? Why?" I whispered back. *Damn.* Now he was getting serious. I trembled in spite of myself, having Gabriel so close, so intimate. So *not* gay.

He bit my earlobe gently and I gasped, as more whispers from Gabriel came and went.

"They can't know." A kiss to the neck. "It's too dangerous." A caress up my bare arm. "Try to understand. They're just kids."

"And?"

"And kids talk."

"They do?" He kissed me on my neck. I gasped. "I mean they do. Of course they do." What the hell was wrong with me? I couldn't think straight.

"These two do. A lot. And if they think they have met Tsunami Blue, they'll want to tell the world."

"Follow my lead." He traced my collarbone, and my nipples tightened. It was a raw sensation for me, and I was now noticeably trembling. "You're beautiful, Blue, beautiful." Then, just before the kiss, I saw it in his eyes. The desire. And the fear. Then a few more whispers. "They can't know right now. Your life depends on it. Please let me protect you." He looked into my eyes and I couldn't look away. "I can't lose you."

Then he kissed me.

And I'd never been kissed like this before.

I'd had only one attempt in my teens, when the tattoo artist who had worked on my arm had become close with me. My full sleeve had taken a number of days, almost a week, and I so enjoyed Jake's company that when it was over and our time together was drawing to a close, I let him kiss me. I hadn't known what to do. It felt awkward and wrong.

It hadn't felt like this.

Jake, with his red hair and freckles, was a sweet, talented kid. Nothing like my tall and dangerous Gabriel, my dark angel, my tough guy. Only faintly was I aware I called Gabriel *mine*. I couldn't think, couldn't process. I didn't know what I was doing, but at this moment, knowing his fear and tasting his desire, I didn't want it to stop.

And when Gabriel's lips explored mine, soft yet demanding, I did as I was told and followed his lead. He opened my mouth to his, and when his tongue touched mine I couldn't help it: I moaned softly, circling his back with my arms, leaning into his solid chest. My breasts, so sensitive now, pressed against him. He slid off and pulled me up from the bunk into his embrace; I went willingly into his arms that felt so safe, so amazingly strong and secure.

Tears pressed behind my eyes as I thought of Jake, his twisted and bloody body lying among spilled ink and smashed tools. He'd died because of me.

Runners, knowing Seamus had once made his home in the islands of the Pacific Northwest, had come looking for their prize, Tsunami Blue. After all, to own Tsunami Blue would be to own the power of the sea. To know when and where the next wave would strike would give them control over who lived and who died. The bastards could play God. Who wouldn't pay dearly for information like that? Who in this changed, damp world didn't want to fight for survival? To live? Who didn't want to hope and pray for a better tomorrow? For most of us, that possibility, that shred of hope, was all that kept us going.

They'd somehow heard I'd been with Jake, and he'd paid the price.

Before Jake's death, I had ventured out, paddling to outer islands, mingling a bit with fringe folks who lived like me; low profile, antisocial, scared. But as word grew about my talent, about the color of my eyes and my unusual tattoo, I knew it was time to keep my head down and stay hidden.

What if Gabriel Black was headed toward the same destiny? Would he deserve it? Would I care? For the first time in longer than I could remember I was afraid of something other than a wave or Runners. I was afraid for someone else. Someone I shouldn't care about, much less trust.

A tear escaped. Gabriel felt it, pulled from the kiss, and whispered into my hair, "I'd never hurt you. You must believe that." He wiped the tear with his thumb and kissed me again. This time he held back, aware of our underage audience of two. He broke off the kiss reluctantly.

"Ready?"

I nodded. "Do I still get coffee?"

He smiled that killer smile of his. "To quote someone I've been hanging with lately, abso-fucking-lutely."

I shook my head, embarrassed. "Max and I were working on it, you know. The language thing."

"I know." He smoothed my hair. "That's what I love about you. You have a unique way of doing things"—he winked—"and wording things. I find it quite adorable."

Adorable? I'd been called a lot of things in my life, but I was pretty sure that *adorable* had never been one of them. What was happening to my tough-girl image? When I got my knife back, I'd have to kick his ass again. But out of respect for my Max, I was really gonna work on the language thing. One way or another, I'd be talking on the airwaves soon. And if I understood Gabriel correctly, there were more children out there than I could have dreamed of. Hell—that is, heck—two of them were on this boat.

I glanced at our little audience above and I knew they'd seen just a good-morning kiss, albeit a really, really good one. Gabriel was fully dressed and I was well covered; still, I felt raw and vulnerable and exposed. All because of one kiss. Okay. I admit it: one amazing kiss.

"Cool tattoo," one of the kids said. "Looks like a wave."

"I wonder if she has big boobs," the other one said, louder than he meant to.

I burst out laughing. "The boys are going to be disappointed."

Gabriel jumped up and flattened his palm on the glass, scaring the boys into flight. He could sure play the tough guy. But I thought I'd seen a glimpse of the real Gabriel Black, and maybe, just maybe it was time I listened to what he had to say. If I didn't like it, I could still throw him overboard.

The boys thudded across the top deck.

Gabriel bent down and brushed his lips on mine. "They won't be disappointed, Blue. They'll fall in love."

As he left the tiny stateroom and slid the door closed behind him I heard him yell, "Get your butts down here for pancakes, ya little gangsters."

Chapter Ten

I sat across from the twin boys on my little bench and ate pancakes while drinking Starbucks Christmas Blend. With cream. I was on my fifth cup.

The boys hadn't been able to take their gaze off me and I could see that their curiosity was killing them.

"Better slow down on that coffee, Bambi," Gabriel said. "Might make you edgy."

I gave Gabriel the look. The exact same one I'd given him forty-five minutes ago when he first introduced me to the boys. As Bambi. I mean, really. I remembered a small ad on the back of that Thunder Down Under calendar from Las Vegas, the one where Gabriel Black looked like Mr. December. *Come see Bambi and her amazing pole*, it read. Somehow, I didn't think they were referring to the Disney deer.

"So, um, Bambi. How'd you and Just Gabe hook up?"

The boys, ten-year-old twins named Nick and Alec, had shortened Gabriel to "Just Gabe." It seemed to be an inside joke between them. According to the boys, Gabriel was quite the mother hen, always giving advice, hovering, worrying, lecturing. The boys had taken to exasperated sighs, eye rolling, and saying in unison their favorite expression, "Don't worry, that's Just Gabe."

I glanced at Gabriel and tried to picture him as Just Gabe. Or maybe Just Good Old Gabe. Nope. It wasn't workin' for me. Just Gabe was still just good old pain-in-my-ass Gabriel Black. Kidnapper. Runner. Pirate.

Still, as I watched Gabriel around the boys, dishing up pancakes, making them drink their milk, smoothing their wild hair, I saw something else. I saw the way he looked at them. I saw pride in the way he would pat their shoulders, I saw worry when he examined Alec's skinned elbow, but mostly I saw love in those dark eyes. These boys were special to him. And honestly? I didn't know how to process the boy's version of Just Gabe with my version of Gabriel the Runner.

"Hello? Bambi? How'd you hook up?" Nick asked again impatiently.

Hook up? I tilted my head toward Twin One and thought of the cuffs. *Let's see, how to answer?* "Well, Nick, I guess you could call it more like a 'linkup.'"

"A linkup?"

"Yeah. You might say he *captured* my attention."

"How?" Now it was Alec's turn to ask questions.

"Well . . ." I looked at both boys. "It all started with a *bracelet.*"

Gabriel almost dropped his mug and I smiled smugly at him.

"A bracelet?" Nick asked Gabriel. "Where'd you get a girl's bracelet, Just Gabe?"

"Unisex," I said.

"Huh?" the boys said in unison.

"What I mean, guys, is that the bracelet is good for a male or a female. Although, I must say, I think it looked way better on his wrist than mine."

Gabriel gave me a warning shake of his head.

"Can we see it?" Alec chimed in.

Gabriel set his mug on the teak table hard, and I jumped in my seat.

"Sorry, boys," he said. "It's gone."

"Yep," I joined in, not able to help myself. "Lost overboard. It was all I could do to keep Gabriel from jumping in after it. I mean, he was so attached to it."

The boys looked genuinely disappointed, and I started to feel guilty for the tall tale. Damn Gabriel and his girlfriend, Bambi. Even if she was me.

We were interrupted by barking.

Barking that sounded just like Max. I couldn't help myself. I started to jump up, nearly spilling my precious coffee, and yelled, "Max!"

Gabriel placed a hand on my shoulder as the boys hurried to climb the steps leading to the cockpit.

"Bacon, knock it off. We told you to wait!" Nick shouted.

"No barking, Bacon," Alec yelled after him.

I pushed Gabriel's hand aside and followed the boys up the ladder and out into the morning sun. Shielding my eyes from the brightness of the winter morning I was met with more than one surprise.

First there was Max, as big as life, sitting in a steel drift boat that had been modified with skids and poles. Second, as far as my eyes could see, the bay, now only mud and sand, was pockmarked with tide pools.

My breath caught.

The tide pools were teeming with box jellyfish, some sporting tentacles as long as fifteen feet. So Gabriel hadn't been lying. Interesting.

I leaned over the stanchions, looked around, and shuddered at the sight, knowing full well the danger the jellies presented. Even a feather touch of those stinging tentacles would cause paralysis. Then my organs would shut down one by one and, within an hour, death. I was nine when my uncle put a knife through a fellow Runner's heart after tangling with a jelly left him begging for a quick death. I secretly suspected that Seamus had enjoyed the kill a little too much. Turned out I was right. All the dead man's belongings ended up in our cabin.

The dog looked ready to jump onto the sailboat to greet me. But if Max missed his mark, there were jellies between us, surrounding the boat, everywhere.

"Max, no!" But I was too late. The giant dog flew into the air. My voice was joined by a chorus of others.

"Dang it, Bacon."

"Not again, Bacon."

"How many times have I told you guys? No dogs on board."

And then, "Duck, Bambi, duck."

And just like that I was on my back, covered in fur and slobber and dog breath. Tears sprang to my eyes as I hugged Max to me, so glad he had made it on board, so glad he was alive, so glad— But wait. Through my tears and as the boys yelled and tugged I could see the top of Max's head. Not at all like Max. To much brown, not enough white, the black markings off. Like a patchwork of soft fur and colors, this dog was beautiful. And the weight, while suffocating, not as suffocating as Max's. Not as big as Max. Not my Max. An almost an exact copy but not. Not.

I felt my heart break all over again.

Alec was beside me helping me up. "Sorry, Bambi. Bacon just gets excited when she meets someone new. She didn't mean any harm. Sorry if she hurt you." He looked down, embarrassed. "We—that is, Nick and me, and Bacon, of course—didn't mean to make you cry."

Gabriel was next to me, his arm securely tucking me in next to him.

"She's okay, boys," he said before I could find my voice. "Bacon just caught her off guard."

I nodded, still not trusting my voice. I looked at Bacon, held back in Nick's arms. This dog was certainly not Max. Could never be Max.

"She's beautiful, boys," I said at last, hoping my voice didn't sound as shaky as I felt.

"Did you have a dog like her, Bambi?" Nick asked as he let Bacon go and she trotted over to my side. " 'Cause you called her Max. Just Gabe had one too. Bacon's brother."

I knelt and held the dog's massive head in my arms. "Once," was all I could get out.

"Hey, Just Gabe," Alec said. "Maybe Bambi's dog was related to Bacon and Beans."

"Beans?" I looked up at Gabriel. "Please don't tell me you named your dog Beans." I had a hard time keeping the ice out of my voice. Max was magnificent, not a joke. Not deserving of a name like Beans.

"It wasn't Just Gabe," said Nick. "The breeder named them."

"The breeder?"

"Yeah. They were the second litter, the B litter. Bacon and Beans. Just Gabe took Beans and gave us Bacon."

"Yeah," said Alec. "Right after our parents died. Bacon's been our family ever since."

"Bacon and Just Gabe," Nick said, shrugging. "When he's around."

"I'm around, boys," Gabriel said, "even when you don't realize it."

I stopped petting Bacon and looked at Gabriel, surprised at the raw honesty in his voice and the intensity of his words. Sadness creased the corners of his eyes and I realized the investment he had in these boys. He loved them. Pure and simple. It was evident in his voice. In the way he looked at them with pride, the way he patted their shoulders, the way he tossed their shaggy hair.

What was it like to be loved like that? My family, now a faint memory, had loved me like that. Hadn't they? Loneliness and pain filled my heart, and as I gazed upon the boys an awkward silence filled the air around us. A sorry little band of misfits, that was us: a rogue Runner, a freakish captive, orphaned twins, and one huge dog. Sounded like characters in a classic work of fiction. If only we could all have a happy ending. But with a monster wave coming, I knew it wasn't possible.

I stood and walked to the bow, inching out on the narrow wooden sprit. The tide was closing in and the pools were melting into one another, releasing the jellies to travel on the current, final destination unknown. The air smelled of sulfur and salt, and the winter sun felt warming yet waning, as the sky filled with clouds promising another overcast day.

One of the boys padded up behind me and I turned and looked into the hazel eyes of Nick. I thought of him and his brother, alone after their parents' deaths, and I couldn't help myself. I had to ask.

"How did they die, your parents?"

"Wave."

"Oh," I said, my voice a whisper. Didn't I just know how that felt. I turned and faced the boy, so close to being a man, and yet closer still to a child. My heart hurt for them both.

"Tsunami Blue saved us, though."

Shocked into silence, I didn't know what to say.

"We heard the warning on the radio. Alec and me, we got to higher ground and got ourselves up a tree. That's where Just Gabe found us. He's been looking after us ever since."

Nick settled on the deck and crossed his legs. "Have you ever heard her, Bambi? Tsunami Blue?"

They can't know who you are. They can't know. Gabriel's message played in my head. "Can't say that I have," I replied, hating the lie and hating Gabriel for making me tell it.

"She saved us. Wish we could meet her someday. That's what Alec and I want more than anything."

Anything? "How come?" I found myself asking.

" 'Cause when we hear her voice she makes us feel safe. Kinda like Just Gabe does. We don't think she's a witch or anything."

Well, that was a relief. "You don't?"

"Naw. She's probably old. Like a grandma. That's what we think."

Great. "Yeah," I agreed. "Old like Just Gabe."

"Yeah."

The little joke cheered me up.

"Time to go, Nick. Tide's in." Gabriel stood at the rail and lowered a large package of supplies to Alec, who was in the skiff with Bacon. I walked along the railing, and Alec scrambled from his steel craft and climbed under the stanchions, flying into my arms for a hug. Surprised, I hugged him back. He bounded back with a, "Nice to meet you, Bambi," only to be replaced by Nick giving an identical hug.

"Hope to see you soon," Nick said as he released me and hopped over the rail to join his brother.

I watched the boys deftly push off with poles and the tiny craft floated and gained momentum on the tides. They started to drift away and something squeezed at my heart. What would become of them? How could Tsunami Blue keep them safe this time?

A wave like you have never seen, the sea whispered at me.

I clutched my stomach in fear.

"Gabriel. We can't just leave them. A wave is coming. I don't know when, but they are out here alone and—"

Gabriel put his arms around me and held me to him. "I need to know everything you know about this wave."

"I only know that it's coming, soon—"

"And you don't know where?" His voice was soft, steady, but I could hear the stress in it, the carefully masked fear.

"Not yet." I wish I did. But this was the sea's game, and as always it had a head start.

"Look." He released me and pointed toward the boys as they drifted away. "Look at them, Blue. They are the innocent in all this. Do you want them to die?"

"That's not fair." I turned to face him. My anger flared. I carried enough guilt on my shoulders. Guilt for knowing I could always save myself. Guilt for knowing there were people who would never listen to me and die because of it. Guilt for not being able to stop the waves. I would not add the twins to that burden. I would not. But as I looked into Gabriel's dark eyes and read the worry written there, I knew I was kidding myself. I was fond of those kids. I already felt partly responsible for them.

"You're the one leaving them alone. Not me." I couldn't hide the defensiveness from my voice and I tried to step away form him. He stopped me.

"Not alone, Blue. Never alone. Look." He turned me around. He pointed to the horizon, where the sand spit reached out for miles. A light flickered, a signal in the distance.

Gabriel released my shoulders and, cupping his hands to his mouth, he shouted, "Follow the signal, guys. Stay on course and stay out of trouble."

"Yeah, we're on it," one of them yelled back. "Take care of Bambi. It's not like you have a choice of girl-friends, ya know."

"Yeah," came the second voice, "and you'll never find a prettier one, that's for sure."

I felt myself blush at the backhanded compliment. I shrugged at Gabriel. “Kids,” I said. “What are you gonna do?”

Gabriel looked at me with that dark, intense gaze of his. “I agree,” he said. “I’d never find a prettier one.”

“Bye, Bambi,” I heard the boys yell one last time. “Be careful and have fun.”

Fun? Well, that was new. When had anyone told me to have fun? And with Gabriel, the kidnapper? Yeah, like that was gonna happen. I yelled back, “Bye, guys, and don’t worry about me.” I glared at Gabriel. “Me and Just Gabe? Well, we’re livin’ the dream.”

And with that I pushed past Gabriel and headed down below for cup number six of Christmas Blend. But not before I landed a kick to Gabriel’s shin as I passed.

Chapter Eleven

Through the porthole, I watched the last trace of the boys and their tiny silver boat disappear into the horizon. I heard the last echo of Bacon's bark and thought of Max. My heart squeezed and I blinked back the tears as I saw the signal flash once more from a distance impossible to judge. Runners?

Were the boys being raised by Runners? Just as I had been. And if they were, didn't I just want to hate Gabriel Black for that. What kind of life was that for them? What kind of future? That is, if any of us had a future. Still. I finished my coffee and climbed topside once again. If I had a chance to save the boys and anyone else, I had to learn how to sail this boat. With or without Gabriel Black.

We were under sail and I stood at the end of the tiny bowsprit once again, watching the jellies float and scatter and disappear in our wake. Overwhelmed, I felt my shoulders slump in relief. I stared down at my rubber boots and had to admit that even with skulls, the badass feeling I got when I wore them had left me. Let's face it: The jellies had unnerved me. I'd never seen so many in one place. And my rubber boots and I weren't about to go wading at New False Bay anytime soon.

I watched an exceptionally large one disappear under the hull. Make that anytime ever.

I had watched every move Gabriel made as he readied the boat for sail. If I wanted something badly enough, I could be a quick study. And I wanted this boat more than badly enough.

The winter breeze turned into a stiff wind, and the boat picked up speed. I knew without turning around that Gabriel was watching me. I ignored him. As much as I could ignore a Runner who looked like a pirate who looked like Mr. December, who looked like . . . like what? Like sin and danger and sex, and like someone I had recently kissed in a way I had never kissed anyone before. Like someone I wanted to kiss again. *Damn it.*

I couldn't help it. I turned and looked.

Sure enough, his dark gaze was on me. Not on the sails or sky or scenery. On me.

"Just stop," I shouted at him.

"Stop what?"

"You know damn well, Gabriel. Stop with the staring."

"I'm not."

"You are."

"You're in my line of vision."

"Well, not anymore, tough guy." I couldn't exactly stomp off to the other side of the boat. My sea legs weren't working. Okay, I didn't have sea legs yet. But I would. I worked my way to the port side of the boat, hanging on to the stanchions as I went. Gabriel continued to watch, ready to pounce if I slipped or got tangled up in the lines or tumbled overboard. I scowled at him. He scowled back.

I sat down on the deck and let my legs hang over the edge of the boat, well above the waterline. Slipping under the stanchion was a distinct possibility. Not that I would let that happen. Still, it made Gabriel anxious, I could tell. And that made me feel like I had control again. I stretched and let go of my safety rails, watching for his reaction. He paled. So I really could make him nervous. Fearful even. He needed me for something. Or someone. I thought of Indigo. Wow. It was so nice to feel wanted.

We neared the mouth of the bay, and my heart pounded as we headed out to open water. The sky was an endless gray, the sea an endless blue. No land lay before us. Where were we going? And why? And how could I escape?

Before I could muster the nerve to work my way to the cockpit where Gabriel manned the helm, I saw the last remnants of a dead buck being swallowed by a pool of sea and sand. The vacant, lifeless eyes stared into mine before the water rushed over the carcass, sucking the deer from sight in moments. My fist tightened on the railing until my knuckles turned white. The quicksand warning resonated. Gabriel had not lied. False Bay was a death trap lying in wait. And if it weren't for the boys and Bacon, I'd be glad if I never came again.

"Not pleasant, is it?"

I jumped, not realizing that Gabriel was behind me until he spoke. Damn, but the man moved like a cat on this vessel; a large cat. A jaguar came to mind. I turned and looked up at him. He towered above me, casting a shadow as dark and ominous as the man himself.

He extended his hand. "Come away from the railing, Blue."

It was a request of sorts. Underscored with a demand. His tone let me know once again who was running this ship, and who was not. I, of course, was the "not."

I shrugged and grabbed his hand and let him hoist me to my feet. What was I gonna do? Jump? Besides, maybe if I played nice, I'd get some answers. It was worth a try.

As he steered me toward the helm, I jerked from the grip he had on my arm. Clearly a mistake. A sail shifted and I lost what little balance I had. I fell back into Gabriel's arms, but he too was caught off guard. His arms circled me, cupping my breasts in the process. I struggled to stand, to regain my balance; he struggled to help, tightening his grip. My nipples peaked under his hands. My stomach knotted and thoughts of Gabriel naked on my old futon jumped into my head. Heat climbed into my cheeks as I felt the now too familiar burn of embarrassment once again.

And I felt something else.

Leaning back into Gabriel, I felt the hard, muscular line of his body. And I felt something else decidedly male. An erection.

He wanted me. And my traitorous body wanted him.

The boat lurched into a building swell and the sea laughed, rolling over the bow, covering both of us in salt spray. The cold water caught us by surprise, dousing desire and passion and spontaneity. Replaced with guilt—his. I sensed it in his, "Sorry, Blue." For me it was embarrassment. Like that was new. And then we both heard it.

The siren.

It shattered the morning silence, the gulls screeched in warning, and my heartbeat jumped; while all along the sea continued to laugh. There could be no mistake: The siren signaled Runners.

"Shit." Gabriel released me and, just as quickly turned me toward him and swept me up in that damn over-the-shoulder sack-of-potatoes position. My bruised ribs screamed in protest and I yelled, "Hey, tough guy, I've been at this rodeo before. I didn't like it then and I sure as hell don't like it now."

Gabriel didn't answer, just moved.

Once again the man ran on a moving boat with me over his shoulder like he did it every day. Hell. Maybe he did. We sped along the deck, into the cockpit, and down the ladder into the cabin. I was plopped on the hard bench, and now it was my rear end that screamed in protest. I opened my mouth to complain, only to be met with a kneeling Gabriel with a finger to my lips. His eyes had never looked darker; he'd never looked so dangerous.

"Listen, Tsunami Blue, and listen well." His voice was low, intense, frightening. I wasn't an idiot: The man had something to say. And as furious as I was, not to mention sore, I was in no position not to listen. The sirens sounded louder. They were almost upon us. And who was I fooling? My heart was now beating out of my chest. Terror didn't begin to cover the emotions I was feeling.

"You will die at their hands, you know this?"

I nodded.

"I can't say what will happen or how long it will take to be rid of our company, but if my guess is right, they will be with us all the way through the Canadian Gulf Islands and on to New Vancouver. And there is nothing, and I mean nothing, I can do about that. I have to lead them away from the bay. Away from"—he became deadly serious—"away from Nick and Alec."

I felt myself pale at the thought of the boys at the hands of the kind of Runners that we left dead on my beach. I hadn't grasped exactly what kind of Runner Gabriel Black might be, but I'd bet my life he was not one who would toss a kid into a pit of wild dogs and take bets on how long he'd last before he became puppy chow. How I wished that kind of evil didn't exist. But it did. I had seen it.

"But I can hide you," Gabriel continued as he grabbed my shoulder and gripped so hard I winced. "Sorry." Gabriel softened his grip and began to gently rub my arms where bruises were sure to form. "I can save you."

He put his forehead to mine and whispered, "I'm so sorry, Blue. I forget my strength, my passion to keep you safe, to . . . keep you alive."

He pulled back and looked at me with desperation in his eyes, something I hadn't seen before. And that scared me almost as much as the impending Runners.

"Trust me," he whispered.

"I can't," I whispered back.

"Then try. If only for twenty-four hours. Just until we reach land. Try."

Heavy footsteps echoed above me, thundering through the deck and resonating in the teak floors. They rattled not only the small walls that enclosed me but my nerves as well. Loud voices mingled with Gabriel's and I knew the boat had been boarded. By how many men was a mystery. By what men was only too evident. If the swearing hadn't given them away, the sirens certainly had.

Gabriel had hidden me under the floorboards where a now-defunct engine sat. Gas and diesel were nearly impossible to find in today's world. A boat hauling an engine used it only for ballast or trade for scrap and parts. But leave it to Gabriel Black to make use of his engine for something else entirely.

Camouflage for a shortwave radio.

And not just any shortwave radio. But an elaborate one with more bells and whistles, as they used to say, than I'd ever seen. It made my little hand-cranked jury-rigged units look like children's toys. It made the midnight deejay in me salivate.

So he'd been listening in. A lot, it would seem. I could tell by the "reading material" he'd inadvertently left me. The walls were plastered with newspaper clippings; old, wrinkled, and yellowed with age, they mapped out the time line leading up to the death and destruction of our world.

My head began to ache with the headlines that surrounded me in my new cramped quarters.

First, the clipping about the tsunami in the Indian Ocean, where it all started. Photos showed the decimated beaches of Phuket. Second, a photo of my family pinned on the teak wall stared back at me. I fought tears as I reached up to touch the faces of my mother and father and, finally, Finn.

My beautiful mother had laughed at the photographer that day and he had captured her radiance—no, her spirit—in the snapshot. Finn and I sat on my father's lap, two dark-headed kids who looked so much alike. My father was looking at my mother with such love and pride that I choked back the sob that threatened to betray my hiding place. I hadn't seen the photo since I was nine. It had been lost to me forever when Uncle Seamus, in a fit of drunken temper, burned it in front of me.

A clipping from Thailand reported elephants as far away as Sri Lanka moving away from the ocean before a sound or warning was heard. Another reported waves rising to one hundred feet as they swept ashore and traveled miles inland.

Aftershocks.

Thousands dead.

Billions donated.

Ghosts sighted in Phuket. And so it went. On and on, and on and on.

There were newspaper clippings tracing the origins of the waves. The "how" of it all.

None of us who had survived had been able to answer the "why" of it all.

Why test nuclear weapons? Why the underwater

explosions that wiped out reefs and ecosystems and life as we all once knew it? Why global warming and the subsequent earthquakes and landslides and raging infernos of fire? Why did the meteorites fall and the tides turn?

Why is God punishing us? read the last clipping, dated around the time that printing presses stopped and the infrastructure crashed. *Why?*

I heard loud footsteps pounding on the small ladder leading down to the galley and living quarters. I heard thunderous voices laughing and swearing. And I heard the sea outside my small prison of hand-polished teak, whispering the headlines that surrounded me.

Freak wave. Rogue wave. Monster wave. Killer wave. And then . . . *A wave like no other.* I tried to breathe, knowing it was coming. Knowing I couldn't stop it. *Coming,* the sea tapped against the hull, *coming, coming, coming for you, Tsunami Blue.*

The nausea and bile rose in my throat, and my world started to fade to that shade of gray I know to dread.

Not now, I screamed in my head. *Please, God, not now. Not when I need my wits, my skills, my fuc—friggin' A-game. Please don't let me pass out into a helpless heap. If they find me, let me go out fighting. Please,* I prayed. I knew it shouldn't matter—it had to be my ego—but I wanted a little honor in death, a little satisfaction that I might rid the world of at least one bastard Runner. 'Cause if they took me down, I sure as hell would take at least one of them with me. I still had lethal weapons. My hands. My feet. My teeth.

I lay back on the quilt Gabriel had thrown down and closed my eyes against the panic, forcing myself to calm. I focused on each breath. I blocked the sound of the ocean. I shut out the sound of the footsteps above, the sound of voices. I focused on Nick and Alec, and how I needed to stay alive to save them. And Bacon. And I thought of Max.

And then I thought of Gabriel Black.

Why, I don't know. I just did. Maybe it was because I could hear him above trying to explain the neatness and order of the cabin. I half smiled at the, "What the fuck, Black? This boat is *Better Homes and* fucking *Gardens*."

"What's in the hold, Black?" Another gruffer and meaner voice demanded.

Hold? My eyes shot open. This could be the hold. Right?

"Supplies." Gabriel answered, as if it were the most boring conversation in the world.

"Supplies, my ass, Black. I saw something over your shoulder through the binoculars. Who ya stashin' in here?"

"Supplies," Gabriel answered again. This time with ice in his voice. I sat up, wondering what the hell to do.

"Guess I'll just check out your supplies then, Black."

"Suit yourself."

Suit yourself? Suit yourself? The bastard.

I dived under the blanket, rolling up as small as I could and trying to look like a discarded piece of nothing. Shouldn't be a stretch; after all, I'd felt that way most of my life. I tried to take steady, even, quiet breaths, but it was hard. I was pissed. And, okay, big-time scared.

I heard the lock turn, the hatch above me flew open, and a voice that was nothing like Gabriel's shouted, "Explain what the hell this is, Black. Looks like a body to me."

Chapter Twelve

I heard the thunder of boots landing inches from my head. I heard the knife find its mark with a dull, sickening thud.

Thank God it was in something other than me. I knew this because I wasn't howling like a madwoman, I wasn't bleeding, and my cover wasn't blown.

The sack of potatoes, however, didn't fare nearly as well.

"Wow, Snake. You just killed you some mighty mean-lookin' spuds. What are you gonna do next? Fry 'em?" Raucous laughter filled the air.

Snake? Why did Runners have names like Snake? Whatever happened to Bob?

"That's what you saw over my shoulder." Gabriel's voice had that sharpened edge of steel to it. "Now get out of my hold." Snake may not have known it, but he really should get out of Gabriel's hold.

Really.

I held my breath, waiting. No one moved. The blanket was suffocating. And the stench of the Runner scum wasn't helping. I held perfectly still, allowing my breath to seep out in minuscule streams, so as to remain undetected. It was a game I played with myself when I was a child. I'd hide, my uncle's drunken tribe members would seek, and when I lived to see the morning sun, I knew I'd won.

I had every intention of winning this round too.

"Yeah, you moron," said the first monster, "get out before the potatoes jump up and bite you in the ass."

Snake apparently didn't much like his tribesman. Either that, or being called a moron just hit a nerve. A big one.

"Long sleeve or short sleeve?" Snake said under his breath, as he followed the man back up the ladder into the cabin leaving the hatch open behind him.

My stomach turned. I knew what was coming next. The unsuspecting Runner in the cabin never heard the threat, and it wasn't like I could warn him. And if I could? Well, not likely. It was times like this that reminded me of how much of my humanity was lost. My mother's smile from Gabriel's photograph floated in my mind. What would Lilly O'Malley think of her little girl now?

Something dropped through the open hatch and landed next to my head. I pushed the blanket back and peeked out.

A hand.

I fought back the nausea. The Runners had taken a lesson from the history of the Dark Continent. During the days of the Sierra Leone diamond trade, rebels in Africa had randomly chopped off limbs of anyone who got in their way. "Short sleeve or long sleeve?" they'd ask. It didn't matter what the response was. The whole point was to prolong the mind game and heighten the terror. Word had it they did it just for fun. The Runners loved the concept and adopted the practice as their own.

The scream of outrage resonated throughout the tiny engine room; the echo of pain rang in my ears. The sickening copper smell of blood filled my nostrils. I willed myself not to gag. I'd dealt with plenty of blood in my time. It was just that, in some remote area of my very frightened brain, I wasn't a hundred percent sure that limb didn't belong to Gabriel.

I should have known better. It wasn't his voice that was screaming. And screaming still. And it wasn't Gabriel's style to be caught unaware, unprepared. I remembered when he stood up in the living area of my small cabin, confident, strong, in control. Losing a limb to scum like these men? Not possible. No way.

The cries continued and I knew Snake had not stopped at a hand. He'd gone for the gut, moved to the heart, and now he'd take out the throat. Limb, gut, heart, throat. The best Runners could complete the kill ritual in seconds. The bastards took pride in it.

Snake chased the man, thumping up and out of the cabin and onto the deck. The hatch slammed shut. I could breathe again. So why couldn't I catch a breath?

I pushed out from beneath my quilt, my body hot with fear. The sweat pooled between my breasts and trickled down my temple. I tried to push my hair from my eyes; so much of it had come loose from my ponytail when Gabriel did his upside-down trick on me once again.

Blood smeared my cheek, and as soon as I felt the dampness I looked at my hands and realized that blood covered the floor and my quilt had acted like a sponge. It soaked into my new cable-knit sweater. I knelt, frantically pulling the garment off my body. I never wanted a Runner's blood on me. Not ever again.

The events of my thirteenth year slammed into my memory. I remembered wiping the blood of the man I had killed on both my cheeks with my thumbs, smearing my face like a badge of honor. I'd been in shock and took to my victory like an animal. It was as close as I had ever come to crossing the line and becoming one of them. It wasn't until I'd seen my reflection in a tide pool that I realized just how close I'd come to that kind of insanity.

The roar of Gabriel's voice brought me up short. I

crouched at the wooden hatch, straining to catch every word, every nuance. "Get off this boat before I throw you overboard. And take the body with you."

"Sorry to fuck up your pretty little ship, Black. But it's 'bout time you made ready for Indigo. A little blood on your teak floors will make him feel much more at home."

"Go."

"We travel together, Black. And you'll lead us to Tsunami Blue."

My heart stopped.

"I don't have a lead on her."

My heart started again.

"That's not what's in the wind."

In the wind. Another phrase for *on the airwaves.* Even without cell phones and e-mail, word traveled fast throughout the islands. It was only a matter of time before these Runners verified what the San Juan Island raiders knew.

Tsunami Blue was last seen in the company of the Runner Gabriel Black.

Lucky for me the various factions of Runners often warred with one another. Operating much like the now-defunct Crips and Bloods of LA, or the Mexican and Russian Mafias, they happily lied and cheated and murdered one another. So much for brotherhood. And until the word circled a time or two and accounts were verified, I had a little time. But only a little.

Gabriel knew it too. "If you believe what you hear in the wind, Snake, you really are a moron."

Shit! I thought to myself. *What are you doing, Gabriel?* I wanted to scream. *Don't you remember what just happened to the last guy who called Snake a moron?*

An animalistic growl rose from the throat of Snake, and I could hear the rush of bulk and speed tearing a pathway through Gabriel's little teak table. I heard it splinter in what sounded like a thousand pieces. Was it possible that just an hour or so ago I was sitting at that same table eating pancakes with two cute kids and being called Bambi?

What a difference an hour made.

I heard a sickening snap and an accompanying scream.

"And just for the record, Snake," Gabriel said in that low, lethal voice of his, "you're not only a moron"—I heard him drag the moaning man up the ladder and through the cabin hatch onto the deck above—"I think you're an asshole too."

There was a loud splash as Gabriel threw Snake overboard. Moments later another splash followed as Gabriel threw the body off the railing, shouting, "You seem to have left something behind."

I sank to my knees. They were gone. At least off the boat. *For now.* Exhausted, I sat back on my haunches and put my head on my knees, willing my pulse to slow and my breathing to calm. I wondered when I would wake up from this nightmare. And if I'd wake up alive.

I could decipher two things from the yelling going on around the boat. One, Snake was still alive and being fished out by what I had to assume were equally bad men. Or, as Gabriel had so aptly put it, assholes. Damn. Where was a great white when you needed one? And second, Gabriel was right. We would have company on our voyage into the New Canadian Gulf Islands. Lots of company, bearing the same spinnakers as ours: a 666 with a dagger running through it. *Great. Just great.*

After we'd been under sail for hours, I realized I'd have to give over to that trust factor Gabriel had asked of me. I'd just have to have faith that he could keep me safe. I trusted him to distract the other Runner who had been put on board to watch him. And from the booming, raucous laughter filtering down from above, I could only assume it was working. Gabriel had kept me hidden, and I trusted him to continue to do so. Really, what choice did I have?

I'd thrown the quilt over where I believed the most blood was pooled. My bloody sweater covered the severed hand.

I refused to wear clothing drenched in Runner blood. It brought back too many memories and too much pain. I'd rather sleep nude. But what I longed for was a hot shower, my new pajamas, and, most of all, Max.

With the discovery of Gabriel's shortwave equipment, I knew in my heart that there was no need to circle back to New San Juan Island. Once I gained control of the boat, escaped the Runners, and found out when the killer of all waves was coming, I could broadcast at will. So what if my to-do list was a little daunting? I'd just start small. Like with stealing the boat.

But without returning home, there was no chance to find Max. Dead or alive. And didn't that just make me want to cry all over again. And I would have if I could have afforded the energy. *Self-pity's a weakness, Blue. It'll get you killed.* Uncle Seamus. For once his words rang true. They were still echoing through my head as I finally drifted off to sleep.

I awoke to a hand cupped over my mouth and a velvet voice whispering in my ear, "Don't scream. It's me, Gabriel."

Well, of course it was. Who else could have sneaked down here with the silence of a cat? Who else had that amazing voice made for dark nights and the wee hours before dawn? Who else had that unique smell of sea and surf and sun?

Gabriel Black, of course.

So I didn't scream. I bit. Hard.

"Damn it." His hand shot away from my mouth. "What is the matter with you?" he whispered through teeth I knew were clenched with anger. Even in the dark I could easily picture his scowl and dark gaze. And why not? It wasn't like I made the guy smile much. Such a waste of dimples.

I whispered back in anger, "You just don't sneak up on a girl uninvited, tough guy. Especially one who's half-naked."

Silence.

And then . . . "You're half-naked?"

Shit. "No."

He slid his hand down my arm and on across my belly. His touch was feather-soft, and I pictured those long golden fingers against my pale Irish skin. His hand played on my stomach, rubbing gently, slowly.

"So you are," he whispered in my ear. "Why?"

I almost didn't trust my own voice. I let out a deep breath. "Blood," was all I could say.

He folded in next to me, taking me in his arms. His whispers came rapidly, intensely. Sincerely.

"I'm so sorry. I'll make this right, Blue. I'll protect you, keep you safe, die trying; trust me. Trust me, Blue."

I lay in his arms and listened, lulled by his reassurances and yet overwhelmed with physical awareness at the same time. His breath teasing my hair, the moist heat at my ear, his hard muscles at my back. I felt a pull of desire low in my belly. I was glad of the dark, for the burn of the telltale blush had returned as my nipples hardened and ached.

I listened to the sea sweeping against the hull with a message of its own. *Trust him, Blue. Trust him, Blue. Trust him, if you dare.*

And so when his lips met mine with a tenderness I didn't think possible, I gave in and made way for trust.

If only a little.

If only for a moment or two.

His kiss deepened and I pressed into that lean, strong body of his. His hand rose to cup my breast, and I reached up, threading my own hands through his hair.

I had just one wish.

If only I were someone other than Tsunami Blue.

Chapter Thirteen

"Black, get your ass up here. Dude, ya gotta see this killer light show."

Gabriel gripped me tighter, as if he couldn't bear to let me go. I pushed away from him hard as my heart kicked into high gear at hearing the stranger's voice so close.

He released me, albeit reluctantly. He was probably afraid I'd make a scene. You know, the one that would attract too much attention and get us both killed.

"Don't make me come down there and drag your butt up here. I don't give a damn if you are Indigo's favorite boy warrior; you sure as shit aren't mine. Where are you, man?"

My stomach flipped. Indigo's favorite?

The man stumbled and went down hard. The boat rocked to one side. It would take a lot of bulk to do that. He must be huge. I thought of myself at the hands of this beast, being torn, ripped, beaten. I trembled in the dark, a sudden chill invading my core, turning my blood to ice. I sat up and, in spite of the dark, I covered my breasts with my arms. Pushing with my feet, I moved away from Gabriel. From Indigo's favorite. What had I been thinking?

"Gabe, where the hell are you?"

The man slurred his words, and it was only too apparent that he was drunk. Drunk and mean.

"Hey. Boy wonder. I call. You fucking come. Remember? Just like the good dog you are."

Okay. Mean and getting meaner by the minute.

Gabriel stripped his thermal off and put it over my head. And before I could protest, he was up and out of the hold, tossing a knapsack at my feet.

His catlike feet made no sound as he moved about the cabin. I pictured him putting on a tee, but not before I pictured him without one. Not that he wasn't beautiful, but again, what was I thinking? I raised my fingertips to my lips, tracing the feeling of where his had been on mine.

Pathetic. Was I really so lonely that I would risk so much of myself? And to a Runner, no less?

"Back off, Charlie," Gabriel yelled. "I'm bringing up more absinthe."

Absinthe? Was he really giving Charlie absinthe?

The liquor had once been banned in the United States and most European countries. But human nature being what it is, once the ban was lifted, the liquor flowed again, and now, in our new ruined world, it was a highly sought commodity.

I only knew about it because Uncle Seamus and his tribe members had celebrated for a week straight when they found—that is, stole—a month's supply from a traveling merchant mariner. The merchant had died, of course, and my uncle and his friends had nearly gone mad from the stuff. The extreme alcohol made you both suicidal and homicidal. Not to mention completely insane. I'd left the camp, disappearing into the safety of Caddy Mountain, surviving as best as I could until the madness died out. That is, until the liquor ran dry. When I returned, eight Runners lay dead; two had lost a hand, and Uncle Seamus? Unfortunately, he'd lived through it all. And he was all the meaner for it.

So Gabriel was plying the Runner Charlie with absinthe. That was either brilliant or sheer stupidity. The man would either succumb to alcohol poisoning or go completely mad, and with the strength of ten men, tear Gabriel Black into shark chum. I prayed Gabriel knew what he was doing.

Pulling Gabriel's soft shirt over my arms, I took a fraction of a second to relish his lingering scent. Then I pushed the image of him lying naked under my old sleeping bag out of my brain and sat back to listen to the show unfolding on deck.

"There you are you, asshole. What took you so long?"

"Calm down, Charlie. I got it right here."

Gabriel sounded just like one of them. His easy banter with the man ran from friendly to insulting to dangerous, then back to friendly again. Typical Runner.

"So, Black," a very drunk Charlie said, "what do you think of Wave Girl?"

Wave Girl? I strained to listen. Huh, Wave Girl. Well, that was a new one.

"Tsunami Blue?" Gabriel asked, like he couldn't care less.

"Yeah. What do you think she looks like, man? Do ya think all that talk about spooky blue eyes and a wave sleeve tat is true?"

"Does it matter?"

"Does to me." Charlie barked out a mean laugh. "Hell, yeah. I want her to have really big tits. You know, like in them Hooters joints that used to be around before everything turned to soggy shit."

I shook my head in the dark and looked down at my small chest. Men and boobs. What was up with that?

"Why?" Gabriel asked, and I could hear the ice creep into his voice.

"Shit, man. Why do you think? Me and the boys are breaking her in before Indigo gets his hands on her."

"You are, huh?" Charlie was just too wasted to realize the danger in Gabriel's voice.

"Hell, yeah. You know what Indigo will do. Once he figures out the whole wave deal, he'll ruin her, man. I mean, he'll keep her alive and shit so we're the only ones who know where the waves are, but it's not like he won't screw her every chance he gets."

That didn't sound good.

"Nah," Gabriel said clearly trying to soft-pedal the subject, probably for my benefit. "He'll want to make sure his precious forecaster is well cared for."

"Come on, Black. You dense? Shit, you of all people should know. Indio's a sick bastard and you know it."

"Shut up, Charlie, and have a drink. Nothing you said matters. We don't have Tsunami Blue. And even if we did, I heard she's old and deformed and ugly as hell."

Ugly as hell? Thanks, Gabriel. You couldn't have just stopped at old and deformed?

"So if that's the kind of woman you're into," he continued, "be my guest."

"No, you shut up, Black."

Oops. The absinthe was kicking in. I could hear it in Charlie's voice. *Be careful, Gabriel.*

"Relax, Charlie. I'm just saying no one knows for sure. Just have another drink, okay, buddy?"

Gabriel was now using his reassuring voice. The one that didn't work on me either.

"Black, you're a bastard, ya know it? You want her for yourself. And she's not ugly."

Thank you, Charlie.

"And she's mine," he went on to say.

Ah, no thank you, Charlie.

Charlie was up on his feet; I could tell by the listing of the boat as he moved on deck. He stumbled but gained momentum. And that concerned me. But what exactly was I gonna do? Having two men fight over me was something new. Not that I enjoyed it. One was Runner scum who would pass me around like a bottle of absinthe after he was finished, and the other was . . . was what? A Runner, certainly, but what? Why couldn't I just toss Gabriel Black into the category where he belonged? Also Runner scum.

"Charlie, sit down before you fall down," Gabriel said.

I heard the *thump-thump* of footsteps as Charlie charged, and then a crash as both men hit the deck. Not what Gabriel had in mind, I'm sure.

"Damn it, Charlie. Don't make me kill you. I've already had enough blood on my boat today."

I thought of the severed hand still in the corner hidden under my sweater and I couldn't have agreed more.

The noise from up above was deafening as the men fought and rolled. Clearly, Charlie the Incredible Hulk disagreed. Not that Charlie was green. But I was sure his teeth at least were. The boat rocked wildly.

"You're dead, Black."

"Whatever you say, Charlie."

"Not just dead but sliced open and your heart used as bait."

Gabriel groaned.

Was that in pain? Had he been cut? I thought of how hard Max and I had fought to get his heart working again. The idea of Charlie slicing and dicing his way toward it sat wrong with me on so many levels.

Now I was concerned. And pissed. To hell with staying below.

I lifted the heavy teak door above my head and had a new appreciation for the strength of the Runner Snake and Gabriel. Man, was the door heavy. My biceps burned as I lifted the door and swung it back, where it crashed on the floor.

"What the hell was that?"

Damn it. Charlie. But subtlety was never my nature. And besides, I didn't hear anything from Gabriel. So to hell with the element of surprise. I had no knife, no weapon of any kind. But I thought I had figured how to get his attention and get in close for the kill. With my bare hands, if that was what it took.

I picked through debris that looked like pick-up sticks, clambered up the wood ladder, jumped into the cockpit, and made my way to the bow.

I was greeted by a winter chill and soft mist rising from the sea. The air smelled fresh and pure, so different from the mingling odors below of drying blood and Runner stench. I glanced at the midnight sky, glad to see my old friends the stars winking at me.

I only hoped I'd live to see them another night.

Charlie's giant form loomed ahead, highlighted in the night by torches and moonlight. Luckily the other boats were a distance away, too far to see my silhouette. Still, my breath caught and for a few seconds I lost my nerve.

There were hundreds of ships.

Ahead of us. Behind us. To each side. What was it Gabriel had said? We *might* have company? Couldn't he have mentioned it might be an entire Runner armada? If he wasn't already dead, I was gonna kill him.

Charlie grunted and I jolted back to the project at hand. The kill-Charlie one.

He had Gabriel pinned, a knee to the throat and a wicked bowie in hand. His leather pants sagged, unable to cinch around the waist due to a huge belly. His plumber's crack looked like a plumber's Grand Canyon. I wanted to look away. Unfortunately, that was not an option. Some girls just had all the luck.

"Hey," I yelled. "Charlie boy. Over here."

Foggy from the absinthe, he looked my way, then back to Gabriel. The knife threatened.

"Hold your horses, fella. I'll get to you in a minute. I have a face to rearrange." Getting back to business, he bent over Gabriel.

Fella? Had he just called me fella? Did he have no clue who I was? I was his Wave Girl. His— Wait. Did he say rearrange a face? I thought of Gabriel, the flawless golden skin, the perfect cheekbones, the straight nose and even straighter teeth. And how about those twin dimples? Rearrange his face? No.

I stripped off Gabriel's thermal and pulled my long hair out of my ponytail. I stood in the moonlight naked from the waist up with long hair blowing this way and that in the night breeze. The chill surrounded me, and my nipples hardened against the cold. My snug new jeans were low-rise and hugged my hips, leaving no doubt what was under them. I was all girl.

And I might not have the size double-D breasts Charlie-the-horn-dog-Hulk was fantasizing about, but it was my guess they'd be good enough. I mean, come on, how many women could a man like Charlie get? At least willing ones.

"Oh, Charlie, over here, baby."

I willed my voice to be like the girls of the old days who worked the 1-900 phone lines. That kind of quality. I knew what they sounded like only because I had listened in on some of Uncle Seamus's calls. I had just turned six. I had been with Seamus a year and thought it might be my mother. Boy, was I wrong. Seamus had been furious, and that was the first time he'd hit me hard. I still had the scar by my temple to prove it. That was the last 1-900 phone call Seamus had made. Shortly afterwards the waves came and took the phone lines with them. So, yeah, I knew what the girls sounded like, and hey, I was used to being on the airwaves. Fake the voice of Bambi the pole dancer? *Damn right.*

It worked.

Charlie, in his absinthe-induced haze, froze, staring and staring some more. He couldn't lift his gaze from my breasts. So. I guess they were big enough. The thought pleased me. Gave a girl a little more confidence going in for the kill. He rose slowly to his feet.

"Just call me Wave Girl, baby."

"I'll call you any damn thing I want to, bitch."

"Now, see," I said, gathering my hair and tossing it over my shoulder, "just when I thought we could be friends, you've gone and hurt my feelings."

"Oh, I'll hurt something, all right," he said, grinning in the moonlight. I was right: His teeth were foul. At least, the ones he had. "You can count on it, girly."

At least all thoughts of Gabriel Black had left his mind. I could tell, because he dropped his knife, which was good for me. On the other hand, he pulled down his pants. So *not* good for me.

Still, thank you, God, for underwear.

Ratty and torn, Charlie's Hanes were a marketing nightmare. But at least he wore them. So many didn't bother anymore.

He had trouble lifting his legs out of the leathers. His cumbersome boots caught and snagged. The man lost his balance, teetered, and I chose that moment to rush him.

My mistake.

I had misjudged and he freed himself of his pants just before I reached him. Like a lightning strike, he grabbed a fistful of hair, snapping my neck back and slamming me into him. Unlike Gabriel, his body was soft and jelly-like. Impact wasn't so bad. Except for the smell.

I had a jolting flash of pain and hoped the huge clump

of hair in his fist was still attached to my head. I should have been more worried about my neck, but sometimes I was such a girl. I just couldn't see myself walking around half-bald. If I lived to walk around.

I slammed my heel on his instep, and even through the rubber boots the impact connected. I'd be bruised. And Charlie would have some broken bones in his foot.

He howled in pain, but gripped my hair even tighter. I jabbed my elbow deep into his gut, trying like hell to get him to release me. He had to let go. I needed to be facing him when I gouged out his eyes.

It worked.

He freed me, and as I turned, my instincts told me to duck, but I caught a glimpse of Gabriel from the corner of my eye. He too was moving, and I was so relieved to see his beautiful face unmarked and not bleeding, I didn't see the blow coming.

And damn, Charlie boy packed a punch. Catching the full force of it, I flew back on the deck more mad at Gabriel for distracting me than at Charlie for punching me. After all, with Charlie, I was trying to take out an eye. Or two.

My head smacked on the teak deck and once more I saw stars. This was getting really old. I turned my head and was relieved to see that my hair wasn't lying in a clump.

But something else was. I took a deep breath and tried like hell not to go down for the count.

Charlie's severed hand was tangled in my long locks, his crimson blood mingling with my midnight hair.

I gave up, closed my eyes, and let the darkness take over. My last words I whispered before I passed out?

"Long sleeve, Charlie boy, long sleeve."

Chapter Fourteen

I saw Gabriel the moment I opened my eyes. I was confused, and the first words out of my mouth were, "Am I naked again?"

"Only half," he said, smiling, his dimples making his features soft and inviting and—okay, I admit it—amazingly sexy.

"You should do that more often," I said.

"What?"

"Smile."

He frowned and there it was: that familiar scowl of disapproval. *So here we go again.*

"You scared me half out of my mind, Blue."

"Only half?"

"Not funny."

"Where's Charlie?" I asked, trying to see past Gabriel.

"You don't want to know."

"Oh."

I tried to sit up and encountered a wave of nausea. The stars, always friendly and inviting, now spun in vicious circles. I gasped and Gabriel caught me in his arms, holding me up like I was made of handblown Chihuly glass.

"I'm small, not breakable," I said. If I weren't so weary and sore, I might have launched into that whole tirade about being able to take care of myself, about not being his personal damsel in distress, and not needing anyone. But tonight my heart just wasn't in it. I had been captured by a Runner. I was now surrounded by them. I didn't think I'd be convincing with that argument anymore. And how I hated that I was starting to doubt myself.

"You have a concussion," Gabriel said. "I don't think you understand yet what a blow you took to your head. Shit. Why in the hell did you come up here?"

Why? *Why?* Was he kidding?

"To save your sorry ass, that's why. But if you don't want to thank me, fine. I should know better than to think a Runner might have manners."

Holding me with one arm, he rubbed a temple. "I had it under control."

"Charlie had a knee in your throat and a knife in the air. Don't know how to break it to you, but you weren't winning, tough guy."

"Ever hear of playing dead? About the element of surprise?"

That did it. I jerked out of his arms. If I could get up, he wouldn't have to worry about playing dead. He would be dead. The condescending ass. I tried to sit up. My world swam and faded to gray.

He was saying something about my head. But I was so sick from the motion as he picked me up, I couldn't focus.

"I'll be with you, Blue. You have to wake up every hour on the hour. The checkpoints will last all night."

All night. He was saying something about lasting all night. That was good, right? Most women wanted a man who could last all night. I remember that from Uncle Seamus's 1-900 hot-girls line.

He wrapped me in sailcloth to disguise me from prying Runner eyes and took me down the stairs, slowly picking his way through scattered debris and splintered wood. He headed straight back into the V-berth and put me down like a china doll.

My head throbbed, and my cheek and eye, which had taken the brunt of Charlie's punch, were tight with swelling. I didn't need a mirror to know I'd have one hell of a shiner.

Gabriel covered me with a soft flannel camping blanket, which reminded me of the old threadbare blanket I'd used to cover myself the morning I had woken up with him beside me; which reminded me of my little cabin on the beach; which reminded me of Max; which reminded me that I wasn't going to cry anymore. At least, that had been the plan.

I put my arm over my eyes and squeezed them shut, fighting off the pain and loneliness and heartbreak. Still, as hard as I tried, one lone, hot tear streamed down my swollen cheek. A gentle thumb brushed it away.

"I'm sorry, Blue. I put us in the thick of things, but I can get us out of this."

I heard him unwrapping something and I dropped my arm to focus. "My eyes are watering from the dizziness," I lied.

"Of course," he said, clearly not believing me.

I hated seeing the pity in his eyes, so I closed mine once more. Something cold and soft touched my cheek and my eyes opened to see Gabriel trying to adjust a raw steak against the side of my face.

"Please tell me that is not prime rib."

"It's not."

"New York?"

"Underwater, I hear."

"Don't try to be funny. Comedy is so not your thing."

He raised an eyebrow.

"Seriously. Do not waste a steak on me."

"I don't consider it a waste."

"It is if you don't eat it."

"Not hungry."

I thought of all the salmon I had consumed in the last, oh, say, million years, and the thought of a perfectly good steak going to waste . . . "Damn it, Gabriel." I made the mistake of trying to sit up again. The moment I pushed up from the bunk the tiny cabin swirled and the cold steak slipped from my cheek and eye, the throbbing flaring to a new level.

I dropped back on the bunk. I reached for the raw meat and placed it on my face again. The relief was immediate.

"Let's not eat the steak and say we did," I said. "Okay?"

I heard a chuckle and then, "Okay."

I thought of Snake and Charlie. I chewed my bottom lip. "Um, Gabriel?"

"Yeah."

"Not that there's anyone around to tell. Right?"

"Yes, for now. Although I can't be sure they won't send another babysitter around for me."

"They might reconsider. You seem to go through babysitters pretty fast."

Gabriel laughed, and I couldn't help smiling as his face softened and the twin dimples danced to the surface. I reached up and traced the dimples, resting my hand on the side of his face. He looked amazing when he smiled, and yeah, he always looked amazing, but when he opened up like this, so warm, so inviting, I almost believed he was so much more than a Runner. Who was this man, really?

Indigo's favorite.

I jerked my hand away, suddenly afraid.

He grabbed my hand back, pulling it to his lips so he could kiss my palm. He placed my hand on his chest. I felt his heartbeat, a beat I'd worked so hard to bring back to life. I wondered again, and not for the first time, whether, knowing what I did now, if I had to do it over, could I let him die? I didn't want to know. Not really. I didn't want to know that all my humanity may have slipped away that night.

"This belongs to you now," Gabriel whispered.

"What?" I whispered back.

"My heart. You saved it. You saved me."

I looked at him and pulled my hand from his. Not in anger, not in haste. I just couldn't bear to touch him, this dark angel of mine, not knowing if he was my savior in the midst of all this evil or the root of the evil itself.

Below, the shortwave radio crackled to life. Runners had the best equipment around, and Gabriel's was no exception. They went to great lengths to tweak and detail and trick out their equipment. It was such a Runner thing. But they also went to great lengths to hide and camouflage their babies from would-be thieves, and, if truth be told, from each other. Paranoid didn't begin to cover it.

"Gabriel Black, answer or we board. Your decision."

Gabriel sighed and looked intently at me. "I'll buy us some time. For tonight it's the best I can do."

"What if your best isn't good enough?" I whispered.

He didn't answer, just got up, ran his hand through his thick, dark hair, and made his way down to the hold, where his shortwave radio spun static and noise.

I lay unmoving, listening intently, knowing how shortwave broadcasts were prone to serious interference from the atmosphere, from the season, from the time of day even.

Shortwave signals skipped and bounced in the atmosphere, so the sound was variable. Therefore, when the Runner voice faded and cracked, I wasn't surprised; still, desperate to hear my fate, I risked the nausea and spinning and sat up on the bunk, straining to hear.

Holding the steak to my eye, I slid to the floor so I could hear better, fighting the rising bile and closing my eyes to the dizziness. I heard Gabriel first, his voice almost unrecognizable with hatred and malice.

"Send anyone else over and they die tonight."

"Tough words."

"I'm tired of the bullshit, Trace."

Trace? Who was Trace?

"How can I trust you?"

"You have me in your sights. I'm surrounded. Where do you think I can go?"

A new voice: "You've slipped by us before, Black, you slimy bastard. And now you've broken my arm. We aren't letting you go nowhere. And I'm counting the minutes till we meet up again."

I knew that voice. Snake.

"You can count?" Gabriel again. I smiled at the crack. Maybe I misjudged him. Maybe he could do comedy.

"Snake, get the fuck off this channel. Now."

Trace again.

"Tomorrow," Gabriel continued, "I sail for New Vancouver in the Canadian Gulfs."

"Your business?"

"What it always is, Trace. Nothing's changed."

"The wind says differently."

"When do you put stock in anything that comes down the wind?"

Silence.

Then the crackle and pop of interference over the airwaves. Trace's voice moved in and out like a child playing with the volume on a radio.

Then I heard it. My name. There one minute, gone the next. I crawled now, letting the steak drop. I had to hear; I had to. And then, there it was.

"Tsunami Blue." Interference. Then, "Hunt. Find."

Crackle, static, then, "Indigo." Fade out. "Proud." Fade back in. "You'll be a rich man, Gabriel, if you pull this off."

Trace was coming in loud and clear again.

"Yeah. And when I do, I just might remember who my friends are. So how about letting me get a decent night's sleep by not sending me any more losers?"

"Fine. I'm tired of arguing with you. We're done for the night. And, Gabriel?"

"What?"

"Where's Charlie?"

"He's taking swimming lessons from the sharks."

I heard Trace chuckle. And even though I'd tried to encourage Charlie to take a swim myself, I failed to see the humor in it. And then Trace was back with one more question.

"Short or long sleeve?"

"Long."

Trace laughed. "My personal favorite. That's what I like to hear, bro."

I immediately had a vision of Charlie's hand gripping my hair and how the blood from the severed limb had soaked and matted it into impossible knots.

I couldn't contain my nausea any longer. I threw up what little I could and continued retching with dry heaves until my body couldn't take it any longer.

As I laid my bruised and swollen cheek on the cool teak floor, I waited, too weak to move, listening for his familiar catlike footsteps.

He wouldn't be pleased I'd ventured from the bunk.

Well, to hell with him. I wasn't pleased that Trace considered him his "bro."

Gabriel was a monster, albeit a great-looking one, but still a monster. I'd bide my time. Keep my cool. Learn to sail this boat, throw him overboard as I'd originally planned. See how he liked swimming with the sharks.

I wouldn't mention his "bro" relationship with good old Trace. Nope. I'd just stash that little bit of info away for a rainy day.

"Blue, what the *hell* are you doing off the bunk?"

I couldn't move my cheek from the cool floorboards. It felt too good. I felt too weak to lift my head. But I could yell. Or at least die trying.

"Well, hello yourself. Tell me, how's your 'bro,' Trace?"

Me and my temper.

Guess that rainy day was now.

Chapter Fifteen

So apparently we were taking a shower.

With the coast clear for the night of unwanted baby-sitters from hell, Gabriel suggested I—that is, *we*—shower. He said I couldn't do it on my own. Gee, I wondered what gave it away: the puking, the dizziness, or the just plain passing out.

Long overdue, he said.

Not a nice thing to say to a girl, I said.

I said no.

He said yes.

When I still said no, he pointed out that I had blood in my hair and other unknown bits of Charlie yet to be named. I considered all the blood and gore I'd witnessed and worn today, and all of a sudden, I couldn't get in the shower fast enough.

But not before I reminded him that he was to blame for the mess in my hair and the mess in my life and mostly likely the mess in the entire world.

He said that part didn't make sense. How could he be responsible for the waves and the destruction that followed?

Spawn of Satan? I suggested.

And that was when we stopped talking.

Still, if only I were a better communicator. I had always let my knife do all the talking. And it wasn't like

I ever had a boyfriend or a real relationship. I had Seamus, but I'd done everything in my power not to talk to him. Not to have a relationship. I didn't want to feel anything when he died. It hadn't worked.

But then I had Max. I knew how to talk to Max. How to love Max. And the best part? He never, ever in five years, talked back. If only Gabriel Black were that trainable. Then he might make a good boyfriend. Boyfriend? What? Where had that thought come from? *Had* to be head trauma.

"Blue, we're ready."

"You are, maybe. Me? Not so much."

He came into the tiny stateroom where I was lying with the steak over my eyes. Even the tiny candles that had been lit tweaked my vision and made my head swirl.

I opened one eye and saw he had his shirt off and his jeans still on. With his golden skin and the candlelight flickering off him, he looked like Mr. December right off the Vegas stage. And with a stubble of beard that only added to the tall, dark, and dangerous mystique, I had to admit Gabriel was even better.

Better because he was real and standing right in front of me.

I gazed at his lean and muscled torso, the tapering waist and slender hips. I didn't need to see more. I knew every inch of this man.

I'd rubbed and stroked him, massaged him.

I'd brought him back to life.

And I was ashamed to admit it, but I so wanted to put my hands on him again. I wanted to feel his warmth. His shelter. I needed the power that radiated from him, that made me feel somehow protected, even if we were enemies.

There was no denying it: There was a connection.

I had risked my life for him. It was that undeniable

pull that made me charge on deck and take on Charlie, a man a gazillion times my size. And Gabriel had done the same for me on New San Juan, where he was outnumbered and overmatched. And then again with Snake and Charlie.

What was it with us?

"Come on, Blue. You'll feel so much better after a shower."

I let him lift me in his arms, and the steak slipped from my fingers on the stand next to the bunk. What a waste of such a good-looking piece of meat. A *New York*. Guess it was nice to know that in his eyes I was worth the price of a premium cut. And in today's world, I was thinking, that had to be a lot. It wasn't like we had Safeway and shrink-wrap.

Gabriel had rigged a makeshift chair in the head by padding the toilet seat with a towel. The plan? The two of us would squeeze into the tiny room, and I was to sit on his lap while he handled the portable hose and showerhead. From a holding tank, he would pump the water with his foot into the system, which fed through the hose, and like magic we would have a nice, steamy shower.

In theory.

But first we had to negotiate shower rules.

Number one, he could take off his jeans. It was December, and there was no way they would dry easily. So I'd given in on that. But he would wear underwear. I requested the black number from his washed-up-on-the-beach day. He said I'd get what he had on: tighty whities.

Number two, I could wear a tank top with my panties. Which he thought was ridiculous, since I'd spent time with him in the hold topless. Not to mention time with Charlie. I pointed out that I'd been wearing a blanket, and Charlie had the whole absinthe-haze thing going on, so technically he didn't really see me. He saw double-Ds. I won, of course.

And now we were ready.

But the shower wasn't.

I'd taken so long to negotiate that our hot and steamy was barely lukewarm. Gabriel started over, warming kettle after kettle of water.

I sat on the side bunk in the main cabin with the camp blanket wrapped securely around me. My spinning world had stopped, replaced by a headache of all headaches. Gabriel said that was to be expected and insisted again that I needed to be woken up every hour. *Great.* Because my sore and aching body screamed for sleep. Ten straight years should do it.

I looked around the cabin and marveled at the amazing job Gabriel had done cleaning up after Snake and company while I'd slept. I knew without asking that the blood and hand would be gone from below too. Knowing I might have to spend more time in the deep bowels of the boat, Gabriel had made it tolerable for me. That was the kind of guy my kidnapper was.

Gabriel had brought up the knapsack he'd tossed down below to me earlier and it sat beside me. I was unsure what was to be done with it. It was for me; that much I knew. And the curiosity was killing me.

"Blue." He walked over and sat beside me on the small bunk. "Open it."

I placed the small canvas bag in my lap. The blanket slid down, revealing my full tattoo from shoulder to wrist. I knew Gabriel was staring at it. At the name *Finnegan* scrolled through the waves, reaching upward toward my heart. But I ignored him. Some things I never discussed. And Finn was at the top of the list.

I opened the bag and there, gleaming in the candlelight, were three Japanese float balls. I recognized the blown-glass amber and green ones right away, those colors I had seen before. They were like the ones I had lost in the fire. But the third was new.

New, and oh, so amazing.

I fought back a laugh of sheer joy but couldn't contain my smile as I brought out the rare and much-sought-after cobalt blue one.

"Oh, Gabriel," I whispered, truly in awe. "It's beautiful."

"Like you," he whispered back.

Not wanting to ruin the moment, I ignored his comment, but as usual, the tingling in my cheeks warned of impending blushing.

"This float is as sought after as . . ." I trailed off, humiliated at what I was about to say.

"As Tsunami Blue," he finished for me.

I could only nod, knowing the truth of his words. Everyone had wanted a piece of me since I was a little girl. The Southeast Asian press, Seamus, Runners, and now, most likely, Gabriel Black. I had a very big fan club. And not in a good way.

I held the glass up to a nearby candle and let the blue shine through, beautiful and bold. I'd never been given anything so wonderful before. The feeling was simply overwhelming.

"It matches your eyes."

I lowered the ball and tucked it safely back with the others. I'd revisit it later, alone, when I wasn't feeling so raw and exposed. "Thank you."

"There's more."

"There is?" I said, surprised.

My hands shook slightly as I pulled out an envelope. I opened it and saw that it was the clipping of my family. The one he had taped up down in the hold. I guess it was mine now. After nineteen years, my mother's smile matched my memories perfectly. I touched her face, then my dad's, and finally, I lingered on Finn, the only other person in this entire world who truly had known me. Had known my soul, my heart. My goodness.

Silent tears traced down my cheeks and I tasted the salt of them on my lips. For once I didn't wipe them away. I wasn't ashamed of the tears I'd shed for what had once been the best part of me.

"Thanks," I breathed into the dark cabin as two of our three candles went out. "I-I don't know what to say. Just . . ." My eyes were brimming with tears. "Just thanks."

"You're welcome," he said softly.

I was so grateful for the dark, I almost missed the third and last item in the bag.

Max's collar.

The one I had made myself out of a series of intricate nautical knots. I gripped the collar to my chest as the pain of losing him slammed into me all over again. The tears I so desperately tried to control tumbled down my cheeks.

Gabriel was at my side and took me in his arms.

"We'll go back for him, Blue."

I jerked my head up. "Can he still be alive?" I thought of the hounds of hell, their sheer numbers and size. How was it possible?

"I taught Beans—that is, *Max*—to survive. Without you to protect, or me, he may have just done what I'd trained him to do: run for his life. As soon as we left the beach, the Runners were after us. Why stay just to hunt down one dog?"

"But their dogs, those monsters—"

"Would leave with the rest of the scum. Max has a chance. Please understand that on that day, in that boat, in those waters, we would have been killing him—and us too—to take him with us. There was no choice."

I nodded, understanding the logic. Still, my heart pounded in my chest.

"But is it really possible he's still alive?" I reached for Gabriel, dropping the collar and grabbing his shoulders.

Gabriel shrugged. "It's possible, it is. But in reality probably not likely. I hate to get your hopes up."

"We still have to go back."

Gabriel covered my hands with his and pulled my wrists to his lips. He kissed my palms, then looked into my eyes. "We'll try. If we get out of this mess, we'll try. I promise."

I looked back into the darkness of his amazing eyes, searching for answers, for reassurance, for a promise I knew he couldn't keep. Couldn't keep because, as I looked past Gabriel's shoulders at the lights of the Runners' many ships, I didn't really believe we could get out of this mess.

The kettle whistled.

Gabriel kissed my forehead and rose to get the last of the hot water.

Chapter Sixteen

I sat on Gabriel's lap, resting my head against his solid chest, and let the hot water wash over me. Gabriel was right about two things, not that I'd admit it.

First, the shower did make me feel better, and second, the tighty whities were just fine. Okay. More than fine. What that man could do for a pair of underwear. Wow. Let's just say that color does not matter.

Gabriel had started with my hair. I watched the dark, almost black blood circle the drain, until finally the water ran clear. His hands were gentle as he massaged my head, careful where Charlie had done his best to scalp me.

He lathered up the most amazing soap I'd ever experienced. It was even better than the handmade oatmeal soap I'd rescued from an upscale boutique in New Seattle, just before most of the city went under in the last big wave.

Okay. Not rescued. Stole. But the bars were floating, so in my mind, technically, they were used.

Gabriel's bar smelled of vanilla and almond and honey, all mixed as one. It was creamy and foamy, and I couldn't get enough of it. As I breathed in the scent, I relaxed completely for the first time in days.

I let his hands trail over my shoulders and arms. He paused at my tattoo, tracing the intricate wave design.

"It's beautiful," he murmured in my ear. "It's as though the wave comes to life."

I smiled. I knew exactly how he felt. The first time I was caught out in the rain after I had gotten my tattoo, I saw the same thing. The aqua wave seemed to roar to life, dancing, shimmering under the water. My wave was a thing of beauty, just as all waves should be. Just as all waves would be again someday. In my heart I believed it. That was why I had gotten the tat. It was my private symbol of hope. And that was why I had insisted Finnegan's name be added. Seamus had called me stupid and delusional. I had called him asshole and asshole.

My head rocked to one side, and I let Gabriel nuzzle my ear as he smoothed his hands under my tank and along my ribs. His thumbs caressed the underside of my breasts, and he slipped his hands up to cup them gently. My nipples hardened and pressed into his palms.

I opened my eyes and, repositioning myself on his lap, I touched his muscular thighs for balance. He had his hands on my breasts. And I wasn't sure how I felt about that. It was wonderful; it was terrifying; it was— And that was when I felt it. Strong and hard. Demanding.

That low, low pull in my belly.

I felt dampness deep from within, pooling between my legs. I felt the push of Gabriel's erection pressing on my bottom.

And I panicked.

I tried to stand. Too fast. My headache roared, and the dizziness returned. I lost my footing, slipping in the suds, and Gabriel caught me in strong arms.

"Blue. Please." He pressed me onto his lap. "I'm sorry; I'm so sorry. I'd never make you do anything you weren't ready for." His voice caught. "Never."

He lifted me easily so I sat sideways facing the door. Facing escape. He'd done it on purpose, buying back my trust, hoping to build my confidence that I was in control. Still, he held me fast in a possessive embrace.

So much for control.

Sensing my discomfort, Gabriel let go and pushed his hair off his forehead in frustration.

"Look, I'm sorry about the hard-on."

I raised my eyebrows.

"My, um, erection. But damn it, I'm a guy. And you're a beautiful woman. One I've seen naked. A lot."

Well, that was embarrassing.

"And," he added, "I like you. A lot." He narrowed his eyes and lowered his voice. "Maybe more than a lot."

"You're a Runner, Gabriel. That makes you an entirely different kind of guy. You know, the kind you don't take home to Mother. So don't be getting a crush on me."

He looked insulted. "A crush?"

"And for the record," I continued, "I've seen you naked, and you don't see me groping you at every chance. I don't know if I like you, even a little."

He looked at me with that dark expression. The dangerous one. "You like me, Blue O'Malley. And you want me. You just don't recognize it."

O'Malley? I hadn't been called by my last name in a decade or more. I was Tsunami Blue. I didn't know who Kathryn O'Malley was anymore. And Gabriel was right: I did want him. But I did recognize it. I also recognized the danger that went along with it.

Using the last of the hot water, he rinsed us off from head to toe and back again.

He looked stern, bothered, and miserable. I noticed that his erection was gone. Guess he didn't want me anymore. So now I was miserable. And that made absolutely no sense. *Damn it*, I chastised myself, *what do you want?* His words weighed heavy on my heart: *You want me. You just don't recognize it.*

As he picked me up in his arms and carried me to the

bunk in the V-berth, I saw regret flicker in his eyes. He pulled out a clean, well-worn T-shirt and tossed it my way.

"You should get out of the wet clothes." He frowned at my frown. "Please?" he added. "You can't afford to get sick on top of a concussion."

"On top of a black eye, on top of a swollen lip, on top of a bruised—"

"I get it, Blue."

I was taken aback at the anger in his voice. I was trying to lighten the mood. I sighed. Guess I wasn't much of a comedian either.

"I'm sorry I haven't been able to take better care of you." Sadness and regret laced his voice.

"I'm still alive," I said softly.

He punched his teak cabinet hard and the drawer popped open. Turning his back to me, he skimmed off his wet underwear. And even with my messed-up vision, I could clearly see what a magnificent butt he had. Damned if he didn't have magnificent everything. Why did he have to be a Runner? Why couldn't he just be Gabriel, my dark angel, and call it good?

He reached back into his drawer and brought out a clean white tee, then turned to face me, holding the garment just so to cover that part of him that terrified me the most. It was the part that fascinated me the most too.

A single candle burned, and its flickering light danced and played along the hard lines of his body. He looked beautiful. Darkness and danger just rolled off him naturally. What was it about a bad boy?

I never realized until that moment that I could want any man as much as I wanted Gabriel Black.

He leaned across me and blew out the tiny light. But not before he saw me flinch away from him, a reflex as second nature to me as breathing.

"Nice," he said with a sigh. "Like I could ever hurt you. Nice."

I woke with a start to that voice of silk I'd recognize anywhere. Even in my dreams. Dreams that were leaving me damp and wanting and frustrated.

"Wake up. It's time to check your eyes."

I groaned. "You just did."

"That was an hour ago."

"They're still blue. Good enough?"

He ignored me and reached over to light a tiny tea candle next to the bunk—with matches, of all things. Not a flint and stone for a spark. Real matches.

"Matches?" I asked in amazement.

Gabriel reached across me and opened a teak drawer. He grabbed a handful of matchbooks and scattered them on the blanket before me.

There were matchbooks of all sizes and shapes. They were imprinted with things like *Tony and Angela's Wedding*, and I wondered if they were still married. Or still alive after the waves. I hoped they were. Then there was *The Martini and Bikini Bar*, which sounded like fun, but I'd never owned a bikini, so maybe I couldn't have gotten in. And bikinis usually required big boobs, so there was that. And, of course, there was my personal favorite, *We Leave Bite Marks Club.*

That sounded like my kind of place.

Gabriel said it was a vampire-wannabe club in what had once been Vancouver, that it had been all the rage before the waves. Now it was gone, swallowed long ago by a tsunami that came in the dead of night, which I guessed was sort of appropriate. Still, I told him that sucked, no pun intended. I really was disappointed.

He brought the light over and shined it in one eye, then the other. Satisfied, he blew out the candle.

"You go back to sleep now."

"Can't do it."

I heard a long sigh and then, "Why?"

"I need answers."

"Now?"

"Why not now?"

"I thought you wanted to sleep for twenty years."

"Ten," I said.

"Whatever. Just go to sleep. Trust me: You'll need your strength in the morning."

"Yeah. Call me crazy, but hiding from Runners is exhausting that way. Trouble is? I've got a Runner in my bed."

"My bed."

"Small details."

"Still, it's mine."

"Well, you were in my bed. Until you burned it up."

Silence. And then, "Couldn't be helped."

"Sure it could have."

"How's that?"

"You could have not visited my island. You could have not washed up on my beach. You could have—"

He rolled over and kissed me. Hard. It so surprised me that I melted into him for a moment, not sure what had just happened. Was happening. And by then, I wasn't sure I wanted it to stop. But he stopped. *Damn it.*

"You want answers?" He reached under the blanket and rubbed the top of my thigh with lazy fingers. "How about a trade?"

"A trade?" That sounded like something my alter ego Bambi would do. And I kind of liked it. "What type of trade?" I whispered.

"The kind we just did."

"Um, the kind you did."

"You were there too."

I touched my swollen lip, which throbbed some from the pressure of the intimate kiss. Yep, I sure was there too. And I had to admit, I wouldn't have missed it for anything. Not even Christmas Blend.

"Okay, I'll play." *Why not?* I told myself. Bambi needed answers. And let's get real: So did I.

He started to kiss me. "Hey." I pushed him back. "I go first. No freebies."

"Then go. Let's get this game started."

I thought I detected a little excitement in his voice. And that in turn excited me. At last, answers to my questions. Now all I had to do was concentrate.

"How did you end up unconscious on my beach?"

He rolled partially on top of me, his leg straddling one of mine. "I fell in the water," he whispered. Then he kissed me. Careful of my swollen lip, he nuzzled my mouth open, biting softly on my lower lip.

I loved it. My nipples hardened, and the twinge in my belly roared to life. I was scared. I was thrilled. *Shit.* How'd I get so sidetracked? I pushed him away.

" 'I fell in'?" I asked. "What kind of answer is that?"

"Ask better questions."

"How? How did you fall in the water?"

"My Zodiac capsized. The surf was too strong."

He kissed me again, this time more demanding, deeper, with tongue involved. And hands. He caressed my thighs under the blanket with feather-soft strokes as he moved on top of me, careful of his weight. I almost moaned in pleasure. I thought using his hands was cheating. But hey, I wasn't a referee, right? *Right*, said Bambi.

I pulled away from the kiss, gasping at his nearness. Nothing was making sense. He was too good a sailor to try to beach in a midnight winter surf. I tried again.

"Are you a good Runner?"

"There are no good Runners." Gabriel shifted his

body on mine, and I felt his erection hard against my thigh.

The kiss lasted longer this time, and my bearings slipped farther away. My mind was mush, while my body ached for something I'd never had.

"Who's Indigo?" I asked when I could breathe.

"Someone to avoid."

And the kiss started all over again and went on and on and on.

"Why do you want me?" I asked after a ridiculous amount of time of kissing and touching.

"Because you're beautiful." Kiss. "Because I don't share." Kiss. "Because you're mine." A longer kiss.

That wasn't what I meant to ask. What I'd meant to ask was, *What do you want to do with me?* No, that wasn't right. He was showing me what he wanted to do with me. Hell, he was doing it with me. And I was doing it right back. This question-and-answer thing was just not working out.

My breasts ached for his touch, and when he skimmed the T-shirt off my body and put his lips to my nipple, I moaned soft and deep. "Okay," I whispered in his ear as I ran my hands through his silky hair, "that's a bonus question."

"Whatever you say."

My body arched into his, and I closed my eyes to the anger and hurt and pain of the past. Something was happening, or maybe about to happen. I didn't know for sure. I'd never been with a man before. And I was pretty sure that after tonight, I'd never want to be with any man other than Gabriel Black. And didn't that just scare the hell out of me. I mean, I really didn't know who he was. Or what he was. I knew only that for now, for tonight, he was everything.

And I was ready for everything. Wasn't I? Ready for

him. I thought of Gabriel in my bed the night I'd found him. I knew his size, knew every inch of him. It was intimidating and scary and thrilling all at once to think of him and me together in that way. But hell I was a twenty-four-year-old woman. I was ready, right? In surroundings like this I could die at any time, and I wanted this experience. Didn't I?

I did. From start to finish, I wanted all that Gabriel was offering.

"Gabriel," I said. He lifted his head from my breast, and I pulled his shirt off the same way he had mine.

"What did you mean," I said as I ran my hands down his chest, "by not doing anything I'm not ready for?"

Gabriel paused and cocked his head. I could see his expression in the moonlight. Thoughtful.

He rolled off me and pulled me close to his body as if to protect me. He shoved his hand through that black hair of his and sighed.

"Look, I didn't mean for things to move so fast for us."

"You don't want this?" I tried to keep my voice steady, to keep the hurt from seeping through. I'd been rejected before. This wasn't new. But I was lying to myself. Everything about this situation was new.

"Of course I want this. More than you can know. But I want us to be ready." He pulled me into him and whispered, "I want you to be ready."

"Make me ready. Please."

He kissed my lips softly and guided my hand down under the covers and placed my hand on his penis. I gasped at the sheer size of his erection. Maybe I wasn't ready. And for the first time in bed with Gabriel Black, I felt real fear set in.

Sensing my panic, Gabriel turned and faced me. "Tonight, we prepare, Blue. You have nothing to fear. I could never hurt you."

He moved my leg over his, opening me to his touch. I gasped as he touched me there, where the dampness and desire had grown.

Gabriel moved his fingers over my tiny bud in a rhythm that started slowly and built to a pace that had me panting. A strange sensation was building, strong and fierce. And when the feeling rose to the surface, I whispered his name over and over. My voice became louder as the sensation grew, and when the scream broke from my lips, Gabriel was there to meet it with a kiss to end all kisses. And as I collapsed, my strength gone and my body limp, he slipped his fingers into me, probing, teasing, stretching. I was slick with desire, and the sensation felt wonderful. I wanted more.

Gabriel whispered that this was how he would wake me up every hour on the hour. And soon enough, in a few days, he promised, I'd be ready for him.

All of him.

Chapter Seventeen

Gabriel's twenty-four hours turned into forty-eight. The winds were up and the sea seemed angry to have so many ships gathered with a single-minded purpose: finding me.

So the sea delayed the mission, tossing some of the small ships like corks caught in a whirlpool. One tiny vessel capsized. No one stopped to help.

But Gabriel hid me well, and the sea rewarded him by sending him smaller swells, less chop, and mist over the bow instead of freezing waves.

Every moment I listened for a message and watched for a wave. Unfortunately, if I saw it before I sensed it, there'd be no surviving it. No one would.

I was sicker than I'd ever been.

I still hadn't earned my sea legs, and having to hide below from the Runners only enhanced my seasickness. The concussion didn't help. I had to hand up a bucket to Gabriel periodically after emptying my stomach of its contents, which I found humiliating. But Gabriel understood and would ruffle my hair and wink as he took the foul container.

I longed for the fresh open air, my New San Juan Island beach, a run with Max. I looked at the dog collar Gabriel had hung on a hook meant for his Atlantis rain gear. He'd tossed the jackets in a heap to hang the collar where we both could see it. It was a constant reminder that once we were out of this mess, we were going back for him.

Gabriel had promised.

And I believed him. A promise from a Runner. Uncle Seamus would have had a good laugh over that one.

Trace had radioed over from his boat a time or two, and when I asked Gabriel about him, how he got his name, Gabriel said I wouldn't want to know.

But I'm the type who likes answers, and I refused to drop it.

After he told me how people tended to disappear around Trace, like they'd never existed—you know, without a trace—I wished I had listened to Gabriel. I wished I hadn't asked. I could have lived without knowing, especially the part about the human ears he kept as trophies.

But the night had been a different story.

Anchored away from the pack, Gabriel could sneak me above deck to breathe in the fresh sea air and gaze at the stars.

We huddled under a quilt, and as my head and stomach calmed, we "practiced," getting me ready for him with an intimacy that seemed as natural as breathing. With the magic of his fingers and powerful kisses, we practiced and practiced until the sounds of my moans and muffled screams became too loud. Too dangerous. Guess there was a little Bambi in me after all.

I passed the night in Gabriel's arms, sometimes playing our trade game, where he continued to cheat. I mean, come on.

But mostly, we slept. Even a man as strong as Gabriel Black had to sleep sometime. With his arms around me, his leg pinning my body, there was no escape. There was no place to run, to hide. And if I were honest, I didn't know that I wanted to leave him. I knew only that given the chance, I would have to.

Now, forty-eight hours after my concussion and counting, we were at New Vancouver, the only remaining hub of humanity in the New Canadian Gulf Islands.

It had to be a sight from the shore, a hundred or more Runner ships approaching the harbor, sporting spinnakers and flags with the daggered 666. A handful of boats had skulls attached to their bowsprits. Gabriel said I was to avoid those vessels at all costs.

Sirens cut through the afternoon fog, a deafening sound that scattered the people onshore like ants at a picnic. All because someone showed up with Raid.

I watched from my vantage point, my head peeking up through the forward hatch. It was the same hatch the boys had peered at Gabriel and me through when we had shared our first real kiss. Even if it had been for show.

Given how far we'd come and all that had happened? It seemed like decades ago.

Gabriel knew there would be no keeping me down below once we entered the harbor, so he'd outfitted me in a black hooded sweatshirt and shades with skulls on the side. "Cool," I said. "They match my boots."

"They hide your eyes, Blue. You may not realize it, but your blue eyes are legendary."

"I did not know that," I said sarcastically. "As you might recall, I don't get out much."

He'd given me that scowl I knew and loved. "Down, girl."

Gabriel passed me on deck and reached down to push my head below. Again. I felt like one of those groundhogs in a carnival game I'd seen at age six, where when they popped their heads up, they got smashed back down by a toy mallet. I'd been good at it. I'd taken out all my anger and pain on those poor mechanical heads, and when I broke the game, Uncle Seamus and I had been thrown out of the park. I think he had been proud of me. It was one of the few times I'd seen him laugh.

I popped my head up again.

Danger was all around, but my excitement grew with each passing minute as we sailed farther into the harbor. My heart pounded a fast rhythm while adrenaline shot through my veins. I couldn't wait to get to shore.

I wanted to see a cow and see how they made cream. I wanted pepper and salt; Gabriel was almost out. I wanted more matchbooks; I was thinking of collecting them now. I wanted to do my first trade; Gabriel would give me some freeze-dried packets of Christmas Blend, wouldn't he? What were a few packets to Gabriel Black, the Juan Valdez of the West Coast? What might they be worth? A cool mill? Or how about one new pink bra? Or maybe a blue one, turquoise, like the colors in my tattoo. Gabriel could use a little color in his life. I almost laughed out loud, thinking the bras were more for him than me.

Giddy didn't begin to cover what I was feeling. I'd lived a solitary life for so long that this was like a hundred Christmases rolled into one.

But most of all, I wanted to see children. Lots and lots of children. I wanted to tousle their hair and pinch their cheeks. I wanted to make sure they were real. I'd dreamed of broadcasting to a planet still alive and brimming with the hope for a future that only children could bring. And I had dreamed over so many years that one of them might be Finn.

"It's not what you think, Blue."

So lost was I in my thoughts, I didn't hear Gabriel approach from up above. He'd lowered all the sails but one, rolled and packed the spinnaker, and tied off all the lines. I'd been watching along the way, learning what I could, but this time I was so distracted from the excitement, I doubted that much had registered this time.

"What's not?" I asked, not taking my eyes off the shore. I was holding my sunglasses in my hand, clearly against the Gabriel rules, and shielding my eyes, squinting to see. I heard him sigh. He knelt beside me.

"Please, Blue. Keep the glasses on." He touched my chin with his fingertips, turning my head to face him. He ran his thumb over the purple-and-blue flesh surrounding my right eye and pulled the hood lower. I could read fear in his eyes. "This is not a game. There are those who would kill you on sight, out of fear. There are those who would do much worse, out of hate."

So we were back to that. I was the devil; I was a God. I was good; I was evil. I was pissed.

Didn't these people know that I had just sailed in with the devil? Why did I get the bad rap? What had Tsunami Blue done but save lives?

"People fear what they don't understand, Blue." Gabriel was doing the mind-reading thing again, and it wasn't helping. I was angry and I wanted to stay that way. If I stayed mad, I wouldn't be so disappointed later when he told me I couldn't go ashore. Okay, I admit it: devastated.

"Look, Blue."

Oh, boy, here it comes. I turned away.

"Blue," Gabriel said in that smooth, annoying voice he used when he wanted to soft-pedal bad news, "you can't go ashore."

I didn't look at him when I gave him the finger.

Out of respect for Max, I didn't say it, but I had to express it. I had to do everything in my power to stay angry. If I didn't, I might cry. And I was so damn tired of tears.

Gabriel sighed. "Shit," he muttered under his breath as he peered through his expensive binoculars. Shaking his head, he lowered the glasses and knelt once more to talk to me. I didn't want to talk to him. But I did want to know what had prompted the "brown word."

"New Vancouver is a dangerous and ugly place," he said.

"I just want to see a cow." I felt like a little kid, and if I could have, I would have stomped my foot in anger.

"I know you do, Blue." He knocked the hood back and stroked my hair. "But this is not the time or the trip. Look around you. Never have there been so many Runners in one place. Never."

As I glanced around, I felt my blood pressure rise a notch. Make that two. My heart skipped a beat, then settled back into a regular rhythm. But just barely.

I'd been so caught up in the harbor and the activity onshore that I had just dismissed the Runners and all their ships. I now realized Gabriel was right. There was nothing little about this gathering.

Gray and black sails filled the sky, blocking the few winter sun rays struggling to get out. Sirens still blared at will, while the harbor filled as more and more ships entered through the breakwater. The noise grew, and the cursing and shouting floated across the water. A fight broke out on a ship close to us, and two men ended up in the freezing sea.

Only one surfaced.

The other was slowly drowning, and I watched in horror as money, even though completely worthless, changed hands to see how long he lasted.

He didn't last long. Some unknown assailant helped the man along by throwing a knife into his neck. Others joined in, using the man for target practice. His body quickly filled with arrows and knives and even a gaff hook.

And these were the men who sought me. In numbers too vast to count. I felt the color drain from my face. I put the hood up and the glasses on.

The water turned red, but the worst was still to come. The sharks swam in and the feeding frenzy began. With five rows of razor-sharp teeth, jaws that unhinged, and a lust for blood greater than a Runner's, the sharks made quick work of what only minutes ago had been a living, breathing man.

The only consolation as I dropped back into the boat tumbling on the V-berth? At least his screams had stopped.

Gabriel was being invited to a party.

"Guess I'm not welcome."

"Be thankful you're not, Blue."

I didn't have to think about that long. I crossed my booted feet and propped them up on a sail bag. "Will you be late, dear?"

"Funny."

It wasn't supposed to be funny. It was supposed to be a roundabout way of asking if he'd be home before dawn. Or before a day or two. Or maybe a week, for all I knew. It wasn't like I hadn't been at a Runner party before. Seamus had been legendary for them.

The other thing that concerned me were the female voices floating across the harbor from the other boats.

Gabriel looked good enough to eat in black jeans and a black thermal that hugged every hard line of his body. He'd donned that lethal-looking belt he favored, which only added to his dark and dangerous appeal. Gabriel Black was cut, lean, strong, and beautiful.

And he was mine.

I touched the back of my head where I'd hit the deck. It was tender and still had a swollen knot the size of a golf ball. Not that I'd ever played golf. You needed dry land for that. Dry, flat land. But yeah, a bump that hard might have shaken up my brain some. At least enough to get it wrong about Gabriel Black. He was not mine. Would never be mine. I didn't want him to be mine.

I heard the sea outside the boat whispering to me, *Are you sure, Blue? Are you sure, Blue? Are you sure?*

"Yes, I'm sure, damn it."

Gabriel paused midway through putting on his duster and looked at me in surprise. "Sure about what?"

Well, if that wasn't embarrassing. The sea, as usual, laughed. I shook my head. "It's not funny," I whispered.

"Blue?"

I glared at Gabriel, mad that he'd caught me being a freak. Mad that I was a freak. "Just go," I told him.

He shrugged and walked past me. As he started up the ladder, he stopped, came back, and knelt beside me. I stared at my hands. He lifted my chin and kissed me on the nose. "Remember what we talked about. Don't go topside, lie low—"

"Make no noise," I joined in, "and if I have to fight, survive."

"No one will dare board my boat without permission. It's understood in my circle. It's a death sentence."

His circle. The Runners' circle. I couldn't ever forget.

I looked into his eyes, black like the night he was about to venture into. He grinned and twin dimples danced to the surface. I gave him a halfhearted smile. Then he surprised me with a kiss, deep and passionate and wonderful.

"I'll be home in plenty of time to practice."

It was a good thing Gabriel had given me that kiss. Because when a dinghy hit our hull moments later and a female voice, sultry and seductive, called out to him, I just might have tripped him on the way up. Or broken his leg. Or worse. I peeked through the porthole and saw a tall, luscious blonde sitting next to him.

Too damn close.

I wasn't worried about her seeing me. She only had eyes for Gabriel. Great.

Her platinum locks bore a stark contrast to his midnight hair, and I couldn't help wondering how different the strands would look tangled together. How unlike my dark head, where you couldn't tell where his hair started and mine left off. I had a pit deep in my stomach as I saw her reach up and run her hand down his back. I felt sick and I knew damn well it wasn't from my head or the sea or the blood of a stranger.

It came from my heart.

As they rowed away I saw him flash a brilliant smile, complete with twin dimples. *Great. Just great.*

Chapter Eighteen

Gabriel did not come back to the boat all night.

By dawn my body ached for him to the point of physical pain.

It was a new kind of pain for me. Foreign and unfamiliar. It was pain that couldn't be treated with smelly remedies or by slamming whiskey or old medicines. No this pain was lodged deep in my heart. And I didn't know what to do about it.

I really didn't.

I longed for his touch, his kiss, his warmth, for, well, for everything that was Gabriel Black. *I'll be home in plenty of time to practice.*

I had believed him.

And now I didn't. It was that Runner thing.

But it still didn't make me feel any better.

And the sea had been restless too. All night it had whispered and taunted: *Coming. Coming. Coming.*

Finally, just as the colors of daybreak streaked across the sky, I rolled off the bunk and got dressed.

I wore all black, to match my mood. Black jeans, the black sweatshirt, black shades, and my boots.

And when I slid into my skull boots, that badass feeling came roaring back. All I needed was my knife. It was then that I realized I'd stayed at the party too long. I had been captured by a Runner, abandoned by a Runner, and been made love to by a Runner. Almost.

And what had all this drama gotten me? An ache so deep in my soul I didn't know if I could ever regain the numbness I had lived in for so many years. And I desperately wanted to reach numbness again. Because when I did, this pain—this raw, twisting pain—would go away.

I made myself some Starbucks and contemplated my next move. Escape was always an option. But I wanted this boat. I needed this boat. With the impending wave, I needed to broadcast, and Gabriel had the means to do it right here on this little ship.

A ship that was now mine.

It must have been the coffee kicking in, because I had just commandeered this vessel and claimed it as my own. *Now, see?* I told myself. Gabriel should have just come home last night and none of this would have happened. At least, not this soon. After all, if truth be told, taking the boat was always the plan. But I had been reconsidering the throwing-him-overboard part. Until this morning, when I woke to a cold and empty bed.

So I guess it was official. I was one of those woman-scorned types. Who knew?

I hummed an old Taylor Swift song from back in the day, and when I reached the part about saying no and coming home, I threw caution out the hatch and belted out the lyrics as loud as I could.

There. I felt better.

Until I heard the approaching dinghy and the loud, gruff voices that went along with it.

I peeked out the porthole. *Shit.* Runner scum. Two of them. Well, I hoped they liked country and western. If not I was pretty much dead. Oh, who was I kidding? I was pretty much dead anyway.

I watched, crouched in the V-berth, out a tiny porthole. I should be okay. Gabriel said they wouldn't dare board. He said they'd be dead meat, he said— *Shit.* They'd just boarded.

Did they have a death wish? Didn't they know Gabriel would kill them for trespassing on my boat? I meant his boat. That was now my boat. Whatever.

Exasperated, I scrubbed my hands on my face. Of all the mornings for Gabriel to have pulled an all-nighter. He needed to be here to kill these people. What was he thinking, leaving it up to me like this? And I'd had only one cup of coffee. I needed at least seven Christmas Blends—with cream—to kick their Runner asses.

They were talking at the moment, not seeming too interested in coming down here. This, at least, was good.

"Did you hear singing?"

"Thought so. Pretty bad. Hurt my ears when we were rowing over. Sounded like that country crap to me. Probably came from across the water from Horse's boat."

Pretty bad? What? A Runner critic? Are you kidding me?

"You mean Horse's ass, don't ya?"

Both men laughed at their little joke. I shook my head. Now they were comics and critics. Well, they were just annoying. They either needed to come down here and kill me, or I needed to go up there and kill them. Whichever. It just needed to happen soon.

"So who's gettin' Black's boat?"

I raised my hand.

"Trace."

What? The thieving bastard. Well, see, there you go, Blue. If someone was going to steal this boat, I just knew Gabriel would rather it be me than "Mr. Missing Persons" with a fucking ear fetish. I felt bad about thinking the F-word—I was trying hard now that I knew kids were around—but really. Jars of ears stacked around this boat for decor? No.

"That bastard, he always gets the good ones."

"Yeah. Guess that's what happens when you're Runner royalty."

"What makes that bastard royalty anyway?"

"Black has them convinced he's the only one who can bring in Tsunami Blue. Alive. Untouched. In one piece. Now I ask you, where's the fun in that?"

Runner royalty? And they believed this crap? That was it. I was heading up. Gabriel must have a knife hidden nearby. I started searching.

I listened to the men walk around topside and complain about how this went to Trace and that went to Trace, and to tell the truth I'd pretty much tuned out both of them and written them off as whiners, until, ". . . when Gabriel Black dies tonight." Now, that brought me up short.

"Indigo won't be happy when his precious Gabriel doesn't show in Seattle next week."

Precious? That wasn't good.

"He'll be even more unhappy when he finds out Gabriel had Tsunami Blue in his sights and lost her to Trace. Black was supposed to deliver her personally, with a bow around her scrawny little neck."

"He had her? Actually had her?"

"Naw, but Trace thinks he was close. Trace figured she had to be in the area, because that's where Black was headed. With the net Trace is casting, it's only a matter of time."

I really hated the word *scrawny*. But what I really, really hated? Was that Gabriel Black was nothing more than a delivery boy.

"Yeah, and I just bet that bitch gets delivered without any ears."

"Count on it, bro. I want to be there to ask her if she can still *hear* the waves coming."

"Man, that's messed up."

"Not as messed up as when we did those girls, remember? Trace paid pretty damn well for the ear with that pretty little diamond in it."

I heard them high-five each other and laugh like a pair of donkeys. I was frantic for a blade now. I couldn't wait to get up there and feed them to Jaws.

My hand closed around the hilt of a mean-looking hunting knife. Nice. What better to gut two Runners with? Gabriel had hidden it well, but I had been raised by Seamus O'Malley. Nothing eluded me for long.

Except Gabriel, the sea whispered.

"Not now," I said in anger, my voice carrying up and away.

"You hear that?"

The Runner's voice, nasal, nasty, and mean, hurt my ears. I would kill him first. Just because I couldn't stand the sound of his voice.

"Hell, yeah, I did."

Like nails on chalkboard or a screeching wrong note, I hated the second Runner's voice even more. Well, it was his lucky day. I just bumped him to the head of the line.

They met me coming down. I met them going up.

Both were armed with those long, skinny fillet knives Runners favored. And it just didn't matter what I was armed with. I was lethal with any blade. And so much better than they could ever hope to be.

"Which of you wants a go at me first?" I purred with my knife behind my back.

"Who the hell are you, girly?"

"Baby," I said in a sultry voice, "it's just little old me, scrawny Tsunami Blue." And then I added, "Your worst nightmare, asshole."

He came at me. Just like they always do.

I met him halfway, cutting his Achilles' tendon in one swipe and slicing into the femoral artery on two. He'd bleed out in minutes, but I hadn't the patience or time to watch him die. I delivered a kill shot to the heart, the same one I had planned for Gabriel on that first morning. The next time I saw him—and there would be a next time—I just might use it.

The second Runner screamed, jumping me from behind. Just like I knew he'd do. I turned with such speed that he couldn't see the blade until I had sunk it into his stomach. He came down on me hard, and on my blade harder. A belly stab is the worst; it can take the longest time for the victim to die. But I needed him alive for a few minutes. I had a few questions. Like where in the hell was Gabriel Black?

It took a full ten minutes to get the info I needed. The Runner was . . . how should I put it? Not willing to share? Shy? Yeah, that about covers it. But in the end, I got what I needed. Gabriel was scheduled to fight in the cage at midnight tonight.

And all bets said he wouldn't come out alive.

Chapter Nineteen

As dusk seeped into twilight I maneuvered Gabriel's sleek, black-hulled sailboat out of the harbor, past the breakwater, and steered her out to open water. I thanked God for the absinthe and parties and the violence that engulfed Runner mentality when darkness fell. No one cared about an unmanned boat they figured would be fine until morning. What I would have given to see the look on their faces when they woke to find Gabriel's boat gone. Now that would have been a Kodak moment.

The winter winds were up and I was under way in no time. I trimmed the sails the way I'd seen Gabriel do it. He had made it look easy; there was nothing easy about it.

But then, he knew what he was doing.

Still, with twice as much work, blistered hands, and a rope burn, I persevered.

It was official: I was stealing Gabriel Black's boat. And it served him right. He had stolen my heart. And it wasn't even a fair trade. He could easily get another boat. I couldn't get another heart. But I would try to find him tonight, confront him, and I would do my best to make myself hate him. Only then did I have a prayer of reclaiming the pieces of what was left of my heart.

I could admit it out here, alone on the sea with only the wind and clouds across the moon for company. I could admit that I had fallen in love with him, crazy as it sounded.

Probably on that very first night. But it was over for me. I'd been used again, just as I'd been used all my life. Nothing new there. It just hurt more this time. A lot more.

Tonight, under the cover of darkness, I would find him.

I didn't know what "the cage" was, and it didn't sound good, but I needed answers too much to be intimidated.

I was going to find out once and for all who Indigo was and what he wanted with me. I needed to know what I was up against. Then I'd leave Gabriel Black and never see him again. He found me once, but it wouldn't happen twice. Tears came to my eyes, and for one self-indulgent moment, I let them tumble and fall.

After a minute, maybe two, I wiped them away with the sleeve of the black fleece Gabriel had given me. I vowed those were the last tears for Gabriel Black, my dark angel, my delivery boy, I would ever shed.

Blood still marred the teak where the two thieving Runners had met with their little accident. The "little accident," of course, being me. I had waited to throw the bodies of the two men overboard until just past the breakwater. Not that anyone would have noticed. Around Runners, bodies went into the water all the time. No one noticed anything out of the usual. The *unusual* would have been if someone didn't try to steal Gabriel's beauty of a boat at morning light. I was so happy to beat them to it.

I suppose I should have spent more time contemplating the undeniable fact that I had just taken two more human lives. I should have felt bad, prayed for forgiveness, something. But I felt nothing for the men I had killed. In fact, out here on the water, with only the wind and waves for company, I was damn glad. Glad I had ended their miserable lives. I felt relived. Relived that they would never rape and murder a young girl again. Or cut off her ear. The left one, with the tiny diamond in it she had gotten for her birthday one week before.

"In the wind" works both ways. People listen to me. And I in turn listen to them. I'd heard about the little Uplander girl. And Max and I had vowed revenge if the killers ever crossed our path. At least, I was sure Max would have if he could people-speak. Who knew that would be today, on a beautiful little sailboat that I was stealing from the man I loved? Crazy.

Leaving the harbor behind, and with the guidance of the moonlight, I hugged the craggy shoreline of New Vancouver Island, looking for a small point of land. It looked like an arrow pointing inland. Inland to a small, hidden bay. A bay Seamus had told me about when I was young: close access to shore, a back way into New Vancouver, and loaded with sea piranha. *Don't dip your toes, Blue*, he had said. *They'll eat 'em and come back for more. Eat right up your leg, they will.*

I saw it. It seemed so obvious, but that was the beauty of it. Unless you knew what to look for, you'd see nothing. Nothing but a craggy, unwelcoming shoreline that screamed, *Go away.*

The bay was perfect: sheltered and hidden, and, man, did I need to take precautions. A boat like this would be missed in the harbor by the right men—men like Trace. Or, as I preferred to call them, monsters like Trace. I had no doubt that he would be looking for this boat, maybe within hours. I didn't even know what he looked like. He was only a voice on the airwaves to me. I guess we had that in common. I shuddered. Just thinking about him made my ears burn.

Still, if I could steal this boat, someone else could too.

Dropping anchor was easy. Securing the sails, coiling lines, stowing the gear . . . well, that was flat-out exhausting. I hated to admit it, but it took me twice as long as it had Gabriel. Oh well, he had lots of practice. And I'd get better with time.

All of a sudden I wasn't thinking about the efficiencies of sailing. Practice, getting better, lying in Gabriel's arms—which would never happen again—that was what I was thinking of. My body ached. Not from the work, but for him.

Enough, Blue. Enough.

The next few hours passed quickly as I made ready for my late-night visit to New Vancouver. I readied the dinghy, the same boat the two dead Runners didn't need anymore. So nice of them to loan it to me.

I checked supplies to see if I needed to steal anything, um, that is, *buy* anything. Providing I could figure out how. Come on. I was a girl. How hard could shopping be? And I spent some time with the shortwave, memorizing every nuance of Gabriel's tweaked and buffed-up model. Impressive as it was, he had put lots of gadgets on it that weren't necessary. High-grade chrome, polished brass, racing stripes. Okay, so there weren't really any racing stripes. But what is it with guys and their toys? Bigger is not always better.

I flashed on Gabriel naked in my sleeping bag. His sexiness, his size, intimidating and intriguing. Was bigger better? I guessed that remained to be seen. And as it stood, I would never find out. Sighing, I got back to the job I deemed the most important. I hadn't been on the airwaves for a few days, which by itself wasn't unusual. There wasn't a Tsunami Blue show every night. But a killer wave was coming, and I was gonna be ready for it.

I thought of Nick and Alec, with their hazel eyes and freckles sprinkled across their nose. Yeah. I'd damned well better be ready.

Lastly, I armed myself.

Gabriel had quite the arsenal of knives and weapons. You just had to know where to look.

It was like an Easter-egg hunt without the chocolate. I

actually enjoyed ripping into floorboards and prying out false ceilings. Gabriel would not have approved, but this was my boat now, and I would put it all back. If I got around to it. I hated to admit it, but I was kind of a slob. That's what happens when you live alone. Still, if I had to point fingers, Max was way worse.

I did not find guns. Salt water was hell on weapons. Salt was in the mist, the wind, the spray, everywhere. Barrels and chambers and any moving parts corroded and froze. And though handguns used to be the deadly norm, it was a world of blades now. When your life depended on it, not many wanted to risk a gun malfunction. But a blade? Well, what can I say? They always worked for me. Every time. I loaded up. I'd never been shy that way.

I was ready. Gabriel had at least until one minute after midnight to live. I say that because the festivities started at the stroke of twelve. And all bets were that he wouldn't last much longer. What the hell was the cage? And why did my heart pound and my palms sweat at the thought of Gabriel facing death?

I had to get going. I had to see for myself. As I climbed into the dinghy, I searched the water for the piranha my uncle had warned me about. But the tiny bay was calm and clear in the moonlight as only salt water can be.

I started to row, slow, exacting strokes, and fell into an easy rhythm. I'd be at the shoreline in minutes. But then, out of nowhere, the sea started to whisper.

I rowed faster. The sea whispered louder. "Not now," I said, and my voice echoed across the water.

Now, Blue, it whispered back. *Tonight.*

"No," I breathed. Not tonight. My stomach lurched and I got that sick feeling I always do when the sea wants to fuck with me. Not tonight. I hadn't broadcast, hadn't planned, hadn't warned, hadn't prepared. *I hadn't saved Gabriel.*

The sea caught my little dinghy and started to spin it slowly. I smashed an oar into the water out of frustration and it resonated like a rifle shot. The boat circled faster, and I knew enough to pull the paddles in or else they'd be lost. There was nothing I could do now but hang on.

The dinghy picked up momentum and suddenly the waters teemed with sea piranha. Hundreds, maybe thousands of them surrounded the boat, broke the surface, and, with rows of fangs gleaming in the moonlight, they snapped and bit at vacant air. As if they knew I was only inches away.

The boat spun faster. "Not fair!" I screamed. "Not fair."

The sea laughed.

I felt like Dorothy in a spinning house, like a teacup in underwater Disneyland gone insane, like a hurricane on the old Gulf Coast. A coast that didn't exist anymore. I felt sick and mad and scared all at the same time. And then I heard it. The wave would come ashore tonight, at the cage, just after midnight.

"The monster?" I whispered as I collapsed in the boat, weak from the force of the motion.

Nah, the sea said. *Just a little one, Blue. A little monster.*

Chapter Twenty

I woke up ten minutes later in the bottom of the dinghy. My eyes were greeted with the familiar sky and a bevy of stars that seemed to wink, *Welcome back.*

Much to my amazement, the little boat was beached safely on the shore, hidden even, with the oars neatly stacked alongside. Hadn't I had them stowed in the boat with me?

I stood and stepped out of the boat, checking for weapons, and yep, all accounted for, even the switchblade taped to my wrist with pink duct tape. That had been another surprise. Who would have thought that a man as dangerous-looking as Gabriel Black owned pink duct tape? The way I had been spun, I would have bet that the knife would have been dislodged. But duct tape was duct tape, pink or industrial gray. It held.

Looking to the moored sailboat, I chewed my lower lip. What to do? Row out and broadcast the impending wave? Or forget it and just get to New Vancouver and try to save the day—the night, that is—by rescuing Gabriel? Of course, after saving him, I might just turn around and kill him. Wait, hadn't we been here before?

If I did get a broadcast off, would anyone believe it? I always gave more notice. Always. Hell, I'd always had more notice. Always. "What's up with that?" I asked the sea, as if it could read my mind.

Switching it up, the sea answered.

Well, that was spooky. But I couldn't worry about it now.

If I really hurried, I could row out, broadcast, row back in, beach, walk the mile into the town, save Gabriel, kill him or not, outrun the wave, and be back at the boat before dawn. Drinking Starbucks. Hey, if I pulled this off, I deserved a little downtime. Okay, that was a plan. I pushed the dinghy back into the water.

"So, my friends, believe it or not. But as always, I beg you to believe. The wave comes at midnight or shortly thereafter. Go to high ground, New Vancouver, go to high ground. Please. This is Tsunami Blue signing off on a night when a wave is coming. I'm sorry, my friends, but please, please believe it." I held the mic to my lips and prayed as I always did when I had a broadcast like this. And then, "Please, folks. Listen. Believe. Run."

I dropped the mic and ran up and out of the boat. I knew what was most likely waiting for me in the city. The protests, the insults, the accusations. And I didn't have the time or the stomach for it tonight.

Still, as I rowed my heart out to make up precious time, I could only hope that some would listen and lives would be saved. Especially those with children.

Gabriel was right: New Vancouver was a dangerous and ugly place. Ugly because of the rotted hulks of buildings and the trash and the graffiti. I mean, I'd never minded tagging. Some of the work I'd seen in the early days after the first waves had been beautiful, artistic, hopeful, even—like my tattoo.

But now it had changed. As people lost hope and desperation set in, so too did the messages on the walls. They were full of hate and venom. There were threats, and most disturbing of all was the ugly taint of racism, creeping back like a serpent.

Then there were the ones about me.

People fear what they don't understand, Blue. Gabriel's words came to me softly, calming my nerves. A little. Even after learning of his betrayal, his association with the devil Indigo, I still held on to his words. To him. How sad was that?

I pushed Gabriel out of my mind and focused on the crowd. A crowd that intimidated me.

Through the smoke of torches and the smell of rancid oil burning in barrels, I could see the mass was easily a hundred times larger than the number of people I had seen altogether in the last ten years. They pushed, shoved, and plowed their way to wherever they were going. No one made eye contact. Unless you were targeted for theft. Or worse.

I watched two nasty-looking men eye a pretty young Uplander of about sixteen. They followed her for a block or so and I followed them, fingering a blade that I had slid down into my palm. I so did not want to get involved.

But I would.

I breathed a sigh of relief when I saw her rush into the arms of a young man who just happened to be built like a black bear. Luckily, he had two friends about the same size. The creeps backed off, but not before they made obscene gestures of masturbating behind the backs of the retreating youngsters.

I wanted to stick them. Just a little, to make them bleed. But in the forty minutes or so I'd been here, I realized I wanted to stick half the population. And as for the rest? Well, I wanted them to bathe.

The stench of human waste and filth filled my nostrils. I wanted to gag. People were ragged and filthy and, well, gross. At least with my black-on-black clothing, skull boots, pissed-off disposition, and a black eye that even the shades couldn't hide, I belonged. Kind of.

I mean, I did smell better, which set me apart. I smelled of vanilla and almonds and honey. The thought reminded me of Gabriel, which reminded me of why I was here. I moved on.

Rotting teeth, foul breath, filthy clothes—how was it possible that cows and cream and fresh vegetables came from a place like this? And potatoes? What about those spuds in Gabriel's hold? From here? Not possible. Not even.

Seamus hadn't lied: Uplanders were a lot like the Runners. At least in appearance. And as Runners mingled with the Uplanders, they mostly blended in. To a novice they might all look the same, but I could tell them apart instantly. It was the pure Runner evil showing in the eyes.

New Vancouver, which had once been a beautiful, gleaming city by the sea, was now a vipers' nest full of misfits and opportunists and worse. How had Gabriel gotten caught up in this? How?

"Tsunami Blue."

I gasped and made a critical mistake. I turned, acknowledging my name.

Relief swept over me as I saw the man was not speaking to me. It was then that I realized that my name was on the lips of the crowd everywhere. The broadcast had gotten out. *Thank you, God.*

"She lies."

Well, there you had it. Maybe I hadn't done much good.

"She's a devil. That much is for sure."

Um, no. The guy standing next to you about to steal you blind . . . now, him, the Runner, he's the devil.

"She's a witch. If I got my hands on her, I'd burn her."

How nice.

"Good idea. It ain't natural, someone seein' the future. She's unholy."

No. I'm not, I wanted to say. *Now, vampires . . .*

I kept walking.

And then, "She's never been wrong." I stopped. I recognized that voice. Didn't I?

"And she saved us. The wave would have gotten us."

Okay. I recognized both voices. And it scared me. Not for me. For them. What were Nick and Alec doing here?

"Now, you boys don't know what you're talking about," said an older man. "But we can sure educate ya. Why don't you two come with us? We'll fill ya in."

"You know her?" Nick asked, not able to hide his excitement.

"Tell us." Alec sounded equally excited.

"They call me good old Uncle Sam, boys. And I'll tell ya all about it."

I turned to see the boys talking to two men who were unshaven, unclean, and decisively unholy. I could tell by the way the older man licked his lips as he studied the boys. Uncle Sam hid his intent better, but not by much. I'd been raised in Runner camps until Seamus had stashed me on an island. I had seen this look too many times. These men were perverts. And I wanted to kill 'em.

My blood heated and I had to restrain myself from just gutting the two of them right there, leaving them to die in the filth of these streets. Just where they belonged.

I walked over and stood behind the boys.

"Gonna show them a puppy, *Uncle* Sam?" I drew out the *uncle*, long and soft, just to show him my disgust. And to show him I was onto him. Big-time.

The boys turned at the sound of my voice.

"Bambi," they said in unison.

I couldn't help it. The boys had me grinning in under a second. In under two, they both had me in a bear hug.

I wasn't used to public displays of affection. Hell, I wasn't used to displays of affection period. But I found myself hugging them back and enjoying every minute of it, even as I felt color climb into my cheeks.

When they let go, both boys were beaming. Beaming with excitement at seeing me and beaming with the excitement of thinking they had a lead on Tsunami Blue.

"Hey," Alec said. "These guys"—he hooked a thumb over his shoulder—"they know about Tsunami Blue."

"Where's Just Gabe, Bambi?" Nick asked. And then, "What happened to your eye?"

How could I tell them that Gabriel wasn't with me, had never really been? And how could I tell them about Gabriel and the cage, when I wasn't even sure what it was? All I knew for sure was that it wasn't good. Not on any level. And as for their newfound friends? That was ending. Now.

"Now, the boys and me, we're havin' a right nice conversation, girly." Sam pulled my attention away from Nick and Alec. "Why don't you just run along and find some ice for that eye of yours. Don't know what happened to ya, but"—he pulled his jacket back to reveal a knife bigger than any I had on me—"you probably deserved it. Now just shoo." He motioned at me with the back of his hand like he was batting at a fly.

I wanted to remove my sunglasses, to raise an eyebrow in warning. I wanted to show him that I indeed was Tsunami Blue. That the boys need look no further. And then? I wanted to kill him. But I kept my cool, and the shades stayed on. No sense inviting even more trouble.

The boys looked at me with wide eyes. I think they were amazed at the way Uncle Sam had talked to me. They looked around past my shoulders, clearly searching for Gabriel. Like he would put these guys in their place.

Like maybe I couldn't. Oh, but I could. Still, I looked at their young faces . . . No, it was time to move on.

If I didn't, the boys would see the ugly side of me, and I didn't want that. I'd spilled enough blood today, and the night wasn't over yet. There might be more to come.

I put my arm around each boy protectively. "Let's go, boys. I have a lot to tell you, including"—and I glared at Sam and his dirtbag friend—"how Gabriel and I met Tsunami Blue."

"What?" Nick all but screamed.

"Tell us!" Alec added, unable to keep the excitement out of his voice.

"The bitch lies." This time it was from Sam's buddy in perversion.

"She does not." Nick.

"She's no bitch." Alec.

I turned the boys around and gave them a friendly but firm push down the street. "I'll catch up, guys."

Nick looked at me with worry in his eyes.

"We shouldn't leave you," Alec said.

I gave the boys a pat on their heads. "Don't worry." I winked. "I'm the grown-up, remember?"

"A scrawny one," I heard Sam say under his breath.

That word again.

And just when I was trying to keep my temper.

I gave the boys another little nudge along with a carefree smile.

"Okay." Nick went, but not without hesitation.

"Come soon," Alec said. "Like, in a minute."

Nodding, I waved, then turned to face Creep One and Creep Two.

I was twirling a knife when I did. Fast. The silver gleamed in the light from a smoldering burn barrel. Suddenly flames played off the steel as the debris in the barrel caught fire: orange, blue, then red. More red dripped off the blade. The men screamed in pain, grabbing their throats as crimson spilled onto the dirty pavement.

I didn't slit their throats. Almost, sure, and they'd have scars, but all in all, a survivable wound. But it was the P I carved into their foreheads for the entire world to see that would ultimately be their undoing.

In this new and dangerous world where kids were more at risk than ever before, the Uplanders, at least the ones who cared about children and futures and sanity, had taken to a form of branding.

The carved P was a death sentence. It stood for *pedophile.*

I wouldn't have known about this particular brand if Gabriel had not told me. He had told me a great many things about New Vancouver, mainly not to enter the city without him. Well, he hadn't given me a choice.

As I walked away from the lowest form of humans on this blue, blue planet, I gave the men two weeks, tops, before someone took them out.

And I couldn't say I felt bad about that.

Chapter Twenty-one

I walked down the dark, damp, and dangerous streets of New Vancouver between Nick and Alec. None of us spoke. I had found out they hitched a ride to New Vancover on a supply junk. And there just wasn't enough time to lecture them properly on the dangers of that. I might have overreacted with the "what in holy hell were you two idiots thinking?" "Cage fight." They had said. Great. How was I gonna deal with that?

So for now we just shuffled in silence with a swelling, pushing crowd. With the crush of bodies ripe with filth, the air was suffocating. It was almost hard to breathe. What, I asked myself again, were the boys doing here?

The boys, just as I had feared, had seen me at my worst. Instead of walking down the street, they'd cut across it to stay closer to me. And, let's face it, to have a better look. I shook my head. Kids. Like they would do what they were told. Some things, even in a ruined and wet world, never changed.

I glanced at my moon clock, a tiny wristband that measured time by solar power, wind, and the phases of the moon. It had been on Gabriel's boat—another one of his top-quality toys. But now I figured it was mine.

With batteries so scarce and the self-wind wristwatches corroded in our new salt-ridden world, the moon clocks started to crop up. They worked best in summer, when we had sunlight for solar energy, but there was also some kind of magnetism built in and the moon pulled at the hands like it does the tides. Ingenious, really. Too bad Runners had killed the man who had invented them. Now the bands were in short supply, which was why I kept mine hidden. I'd seen men killed for far less.

The way I figured, I had an hour and twenty minutes to find the cage, figure out how to get Gabriel out of it, run far away from a wave no one believed was coming, and most important? Get Nick and Alec out of here. Before the wave did it for me.

I also had a strong feeling it wouldn't go down well with them if they knew about Gabriel's little dilemma. Okay. Not so little; he was supposed to die. And if I knew the boys—and I thought I did—they'd get right in the middle of it. I'd be damned if, should there be a body count tonight, two of them would be theirs.

"Um, Bambi?" Nick said. "You were kind of, well, awesome with those two scumbags tonight."

"Yeah, amazing. Can you teach us how to twirl knives like that? Next time Nick and I get some sicko after us, we can just kill him ourselves."

Alec sounded way too pumped on that last note. This was just what I was afraid of. The boys being, well, boys, had glamorized the bloodletting and violence. Gabriel had done well in keeping them safe and sound. And yet after ten minutes with me, they were ready to don weapons and start slicing and dicing? I didn't think so. Not on my watch. I had to turn down their adrenaline, fast.

I saw my chance and took it. A Dumpster stood off to the side, large, rusted, and—oh, I wanted to gag—smelly. But the space behind it looked private enough. I grabbed the boys by their fleece collars and yanked them behind it.

"What gives?" Nick said.

"Hey, watch the neck," Alec complained.

The crowds pressed past us, fanning out and filtering into a wide area leading to a distant stadium. Or at least, what was left of it. It had to be where the cage was; everyone seemed just a little too eager to get there. Why did I feel this was a spectator sport? A big one.

I turned to face the boys, their expressions open and honest and—this was what got me the most—innocent.

I had their full attention. Which, given that they were ten-year-olds, was a small miracle.

"First, what the holy hell are you two doing here?"

I didn't mean to sound mad, but the fear just seeped into my voice and so I had disguised it as anger.

The boys looked shocked at my tone, and then—and I didn't want this—defensive.

"Gee, don't get all mad. We just came to see the fight."

"Fight?"

"Yeah," Alec said, "the cage. It's like the biggest fight of the year. We heard about it clear in New False Bay."

The cage. A fight. To the death. *Oh, Gabriel.*

I stuck my trembling hands in my pockets and steadied my breathing. I had to get these guys out of here; I *had* to. But how? And then it came to me. Was it the right thing to do? Would it work? I had to try. But first . . .

"Look, guys." I spread my hands out in front of me. "Have either of you taken a life?"

The boys looked sheepish and shook their heads no.

"Have you ever seen anyone die?"

Again, no.

"Well, I have."

"You have?" Nick asked. "Did you kill them?"

I was silent as I thought of the two Runners who had died by my hand less than twenty-four-hours ago. And I thought of the Runner scum I'd killed when I was close to Nick and Alec's age. That death had changed my life. I didn't want it for them. I wasn't sure how the boys were being raised. But I'd bet all the Starbucks on Gabriel's boat it wasn't with Runners. These kids were too naive to survive in a Runner camp. And if they saw Gabriel die? Frustrated, I slammed my fist into the metal of the Dumpster, making the boys jump as the sound echoed around us.

Between the stench and the memories and the pain, it was all I could do not to grab the kids and shake them. *Run*, I wanted to scream at them. *Run, guys. Run away from here.* But instead I answered them.

My voice was as hard as ice and I glared at the boys.

"Don't glamorize it, kids—don't you ever. Death is death. And there's no coming back. Until you have the blood of a human being—a once living, walking, talking, human being—on your hands, and until you see someone gutted, with intestines hanging and the sea crabs feasting on their insides, you have no idea."

They looked at me like I was crazy. And maybe I was. Was this what caring about someone did to you? Made you nuts? Made you relive the most horrific death you had ever seen? I had just described finding Seamus O'Malley, my last living relative. I had thought I didn't care. But I did. Just as I cared about the boys. And damn it, I cared about Gabriel. Lord help me, I didn't want to, but there it was.

Taking off my glasses, I lowered my hood. I reached back and yanked on the band that was holding my dark mass of hair in my traditional ponytail. My hair tumbled around my shoulders. I felt better, more like myself, less like Bambi. And right now, in this dark and slimy place, I needed to be myself.

Because I was going to tell the boys that I was Tsunami Blue and a wave was coming. And they had better run.

Chapter Twenty-two

"What the hell is all the damn noise? Can't ya see we're playin' here, bitch?"

I slid my sunglasses back in place as the boys and I turned to face a giant of a man. He smelled almost as bad as the Dumpster and was certainly as ugly. The missing teeth didn't help. But on a positive note, if we got into a fight—and I had a feeling we would—he wouldn't be much of a biter.

"What is it with this town?" I asked, stepping out of the shadows and pushing the boys behind me. "Are all the women here named 'bitch,' or is it just me?"

He actually had to think about that for a moment, which gave me a clue we weren't dealing with the fastest ship in the harbor. No. He was more on the scale of a paddle-board. He was still thinking. Make that water wings.

I could see now that he had come from around an open fire pit in the alley. I hoped there weren't any more of them.

No such luck.

When his buddy came up behind him, the hairs on the nape of my neck stood up. This man was danger, wrapped in a short, thick package of sheer muscle and bone. He took one look at the three of us and hunger flared in his eyes. This man was pure evil.

The boys must have sensed it too, because they flanked

me protectively. I admired them for that. This man would chew them up and use their bones for toothpicks, and yet there they were, ready to fight alongside me. I was so proud of them. I was so afraid for them.

"Thanks, guys," I whispered.

A third man came and joined them, this one tall and so thin he looked skeletal. With sunken eyes and matted hair, he looked like a zombie from a George Romero movie. Not that I'd seen one. I'd only seen a picture of a zombie in a black-and-white glossy photo in a vintage movie store. The zombie scared me then, and this guy, who looked like he had just walked out of the same grave, scared me now.

"How about you and your little friends join us for a wager, bitch," the man with no teeth said. He pulled out a nasty-looking blade. Serrated.

"Bambi," I said.

"What?"

"Bambi. The name's Bambi. You know, like the deer."

"You mean like the pole dancer," the dangerous man said. His voice had a mean quality to it. Real mean. He licked his lips. *Great. Just great.*

I opened my fleece and pulled out the biggest knife I'd brought. They pulled out three bigger.

"What, boys?" I asked as they laughed at my blade. "Didn't anyone ever tell you that size doesn't matter?"

I twirled the knife and then, in a blink, I threw the razor-sharp blade through the air, grazing Zombie's cheek. A trail of scarlet seeped to the surface of his white flesh. So the man could bleed. Good, 'cause I'd like to make him bleed more.

The knife found its mark in Water Wings' shoulder. All the way to the hilt. His knives clattered to the ground as he howled in pain and reached to pull it out.

"Make that a life lesson, big guy. Don't pull a knife on a girl. It's just rude." Water Wings was not my first choice to knife. I had my sights set on the short, dangerous man with the dead eyes. But I knew better than to take out the brains of the group. Without leadership, the other two were unpredictable psychos, loose cannons who would charge without thinking. And they would go for the weakest targets. They would go for the boys.

I crossed my arms, tapped my foot, and waited. *Show no fear, Blue*, my Uncle Seamus had told me time and time again. *These kinds of men will respect you for it. And you will live longer.*

The dangerous man looked impressed. He shrugged and nodded our departure. Guess we could go. Still, I wasn't about to turn my back on these animals. Zombie was still holding his cheek, blood now dripping from his fingers. *Oops.* Maybe not the scrape I had thought.

"Come on, guys," I said to Nick and Alec. "Let's go." We backed up in a line, moving away from the Dumpster. Circling our way around it.

And that was when I saw her.

A small child huddled by the fire, crumpled forward in a ball. A girl? Her hair, thick and tangled, hung just inches from the open flame. She played with a long strand, sweeping it back and forth as if she wanted it to catch fire. As if she thought that might be a better alternative to hanging with these men.

Or was I just overreacting? She could be a daughter. Couldn't she? I looked at these men, filthy and evil, and I knew, just knew in my gut that this little girl shouldn't have been here.

Well, shit.

Just at that moment, she turned and looked at me. Her pale features were soft and delicate. Even through the grime, I could she how pretty she was, how tiny and petite. Petite like me. And didn't I just know how it felt to be small in a world so much bigger than you.

I shook my head. I didn't have time for this. I had a fight to catch, a wave to outrun, two kids of my own to save. A tear glistened down her cheek.

Double shit.

"Hang on, boys," I said to Nick and Alec. They stopped and looked at me in question.

"Your daughter?" I asked the man who gave us the green light, the one I feared the most.

He laughed a low, nasty, guttural laugh. "Now, what do you think, Bambi?" I hated the way he said the name. It just sounded like a rape waiting to happen.

"I think this kid shouldn't be here, that's what I think. Asshole," I added, just because I was so infuriated. She was a kid. Just a little kid.

Zombie walked up, glaring at me.

"Don't look so pissed," I said. "I could have taken an ear." Trace came to mind, and I kicked him right back out. I could handle only one bit of terror at a time.

"We're playing for her." Water Wings came from the shadows with a towel so dirty it looked black. He pressed it to his wound. Good for him. That should get a nice infection going.

"And you and Dumb and Dumber interrupted our game. Now get lost, bitch."

I turned and raised my eyebrows to the boys at the Dumb and Dumber comment. They both were trying not to laugh. Which was good. We weren't out of this yet.

"Just leave while you can, Bambi," Dangerous Man said. "Leave her to us. We'll take good care of her."

The men laughed. The little girl jumped up at the sound and dropped her blanket. I could see they had the child chained at one foot, like an animal.

I wanted to kill them. Drop all three where they stood. But I had Nick and Alec to consider. And whereas I could take Zombie and Water Wings no problem, could I do it before they hurt one of the boys? And let's face it, it was the short tank of a man that worried me. He'd fight dirty. And if he won, I didn't want to think of the aftermath.

Then I saw the cards. The men had dropped them when they decided to play with us instead.

"So, I'm just a little curious." I changed my demeanor; I was now friendly Bambi, just like the one on the pole. "What are you bad boys playing?"

"Hold 'Em," Water Wings all but growled.

Hold 'Em? Hold 'Em? I could play Texas Hold 'Em. I could play great Texas Hold 'Em.

"And the stakes?"

"The girl, of course," said Zombie. The mention of the girl was a turn-on for him. Just what I was afraid of.

"What? You interested, Bambi? I didn't think you rolled that way. Thought you had it bad for me," Dangerous Man said.

Oh, I had it bad for him. A-knife-through-his-miserable-heart bad.

"What's the buy-in?" I asked.

"What do ya got?"

I immediately thought of the moon watch. I stuck out my wrist. Flaunting and showing off a little. Okay. A lot.

He held out his. *Damn.* It was just as nice, only in blue. I liked his better. *Okay. Time to get serious.*

I reached into my fleece's inner pocket and pulled out two packets of Christmas Blend. I held the coffee in front of the men's noses and I prayed Gabriel knew what he was talking about. *It makes a good trade.* His voice played in my head and I felt a tug on my heart.

"Been a while, boys?"

The reaction was fast and loud.

"She's in."

"No limit, winner takes all."

"I'm dealing. Let's go."

"The coffee and the girl?" I asked. "Winner takes all, baby." Dangerous Guy was actually excited. He didn't look quite so murderous. Still . . .

As the men walked away to set up the game, I turned to Nick and Alec, who were speechless at the turn of events.

"Bambi," whispered Alec. "Do you even know how to play?"

"Some." I raised my glasses and winked at him with my good eye.

"What can we do?" Nick asked.

"Watch and learn," I said, lowering my glasses back in place. "And when I say game over, it's over. Understood?"

The boys nodded.

"We take the little girl and walk out of here. Okay? Just walk. Like it's no big deal."

"What makes you think you'll win?" Nick said.

Alec leaned in to hear my answer.

I smiled and thought of my days playing Texas Hold 'Em in all those Runner camps summer after summer. The games were aggressive, vocal, dangerous, and, for me, lucrative. The men lacked patience. I didn't. And I was willing to bet these guys were no different.

"I'm the best," I told the boys. "I'm the very best."

With that I turned and walked toward the fire pit to choose my place. I wanted Dangerous Guy on my right, Water Wings to my left, and Zombie right across from me so I could read every tell on his ugly face.

Oh, yeah. I knew what I was doing. It felt good to be confident again. I mean, come on. My confidence had slipped some since a Runner had washed up on my beach, burned my home, probably killed my dog, and kidnapped me.

Four players, no limit, Texas Hold 'Em.

Winner took all.

Bring it.

* * *

"What's your name, sweetheart? I said softly to the child, who had been placed in the middle of our game like the trophy she was. She stayed mute, not willing to answer. I couldn't blame her.

The men—animals, really—had been throwing their chips at her when they bet. I accused them of splashing the pot and told them to knock it off. They stopped. Still, some chips were stuck in her hair and my anger grew. No child should suffer this humiliation.

I'd bought my buy-in with Starbucks. I tossed in a third packet when I saw the chip stack Dangerous Guy, who I now knew as Tank, had in front of him.

I thought I might need a few more chips with him in the game. I was right. We were playing with casino checks; most people knew them as simply poker chips, and they were from the now-underwater Vegas casinos. Imagine my surprise when I found one with a stripper named Bambi on it. She even had her pole.

But it was the chip I was using as my card protector that amazed me the most. Mr. December, from the Thunder Down Under all-male revue, smiled up at me. The sight flipped my heart over and then back again. I decided that, win or lose, I was stealing it.

The child had been watching me with wary eyes that were the most remarkable shade of brown I had ever seen, rimmed in light gold, and the color of malt whiskey. She looked on with a scared and wary expression. Even though she was grimy, with matted hair, she looked well fed and had on nice pajamas. A gold cross hung around her neck.

Someone had taken good care of this little girl; that much was clear. I wondered, Were they still alive to miss her?

I looked at my moon band. *Shit.* Gabriel's fight was in less than thirty minutes. I was running out of time.

I looked down at my hole cards.

A seven and a nine of hearts. Any book would've told me to fold. The other players were feigning indifference, but not too well. They had something big.

Twenty-nine minutes and counting.

I had to make my move. If I made a straight or a flush, I could probably take whatever they had.

"Screw it," Zombie said. "All or nothing. I'm bored with this game." He looked at the little girl with hunger. I fought down the bile that rose in my throat as I watched him.

"I'm game. I'm in. Winner takes all," Water Wings said. Tank studied me. I knew I was going all-in. This was the hand. I could take them all down. Or lose miserably. But either way I was getting the girl. I readied a blade in my lap. The easy way was if I won. The hard way was if I lost. Call me a cheater, a sore loser, whatever, but this child, *either way*, was coming with me.

I gave Nick and Alec our prearranged sign, stroking my chin, then running two fingers under my neck as if swishing my long hair out of my face. It was a get-ready sign. Things could get messy fast.

Looking at Tank, I shoved my chips at the feet of the little girl as she sat cross-legged and pale. She knew what was going on. My heart hurt for her. "It will be over soon, sweetheart," I whispered.

"All in," I said, pushing my chips against the little girl's toes.

"Call," Tank said. Then the bastard stood, grabbed his chips, and rained them down over the child's head.

What a monster.

Chapter Twenty-three

Zombie dealt.

We all watched his every move. No one trusted anyone at this makeshift table. Tank even made him take off his ratty jacket. It was the old nothing-up-your-sleeve paranoia. The odor from Zombie's armpits almost knocked me over. I'd have to thank Tank for that. Nick and Alec, who got up to huddle around the table for the big hand, held their noses. I frowned and shook my head when Alec said, "Take a shower already."

I didn't want the boys to forget that these were dangerous men who would kill them just because they could.

I heard a small voice, a whisper so soft I almost missed it. "Good luck."

Looking up from the cards, I slid my sunglasses down on the bridge on my nose and met the gaze of the little girl. I saw fear in her eyes. And hope.

"Luck has nothing to do with it, sweetheart," I said, winking at her as I palmed the Mr. December chip. She saw me do it. I put a finger up to my lips like we had a secret, gave her a reassuring smile, and reached out to stroke her little foot. I pushed my shades back in place.

"Hey. Get your hands out of the pot until you win it." Water Wings sneered at me and jerked the chain on the little girl's foot. "And no pawing the prize"—he smiled, showing tobacco-stained gums—"until later."

"She's mine," Zombie said. "I got the hand." He reached for the chain to jerk the girl toward him.

I caught the steel links before they could cause any more damage to an already bruised and swollen ankle.

"Knock it off, you pigs," I said. I stood and slapped the table with my hand. "Hand over the key. We're unchaining her. It's not like she can get away from all of us. I mean, how old is she? Seven? Ya think you big, bad men can handle a seven-year-old?"

"Nine."

We all stopped and stared. The girl glared at all of us. "I'm nine. And I can run fast." My heart dropped. I was doing my best to get her unchained for a quick escape if the cards didn't fall the right way. Letting us all know she could run fast was so not a good thing.

Tank laughed. "Run if you can, little girl. I like to chase." He produced the key and unlocked the chain.

"*Thank you, God.*" I muttered under my breath.

The little girl put her head down and curled into a ball.

"Come on; let's do it," Water Wings urged. "Deal."

The first three cards, the flop, missed my straight draw entirely. But two hearts came. My flush draw was alive. One of the cards was a queen. I saw a tic in the jaw of Tank. Water Wings looked disappointed. Zombie looked like he was gonna jump right out of the chair and grab the girl. But I knew I almost had him beat.

The turn card, or fourth street, as some people called it, brought a blank. A card that didn't help any of us. Right now Tank had the best hand. If he won, I'd have to kill him to get the girl. Or die trying.

Now the river. My palms started to sweat and I wiped

them on my jeans. I needed dry hands to hold my blades. And it looked like I was gonna have to use them. *Damn it.*

I looked at Nick and Alec, who had slowly circled around behind me. Good. They were ready to run when I gave the word.

The last card fell.

An ace.

Water Wings looked like he might cry. Good.

Tank's hand just went down in flames, and he didn't know it. He looked smug and eyed the little girl in a way that made me want to throw up. It wasn't sexual. It was something else. He'd hurt her and enjoy every minute. How I hated the man. Zombie jumped out of his chair, flipping it over. It crashed and shattered into splinters on the cement.

He slammed down aces. "Ship it!" He tried to grab the girl from behind. She screamed, turned, kicked him in the gut, and scooted over to me.

He doubled over in pain. "You little bitch," he wheezed.

I put my arm around the child and whispered in her ear, "It's okay, honey. That's been my name all night too."

Color drained from Tank's face, replaced by a white-hot, seething anger. He'd lost. And the man didn't like losing.

I stood slowly and, as Zombie caught his breath, I laid my cards on the table in front of his nose. I'd hit my miracle card. The last card to fall, the ace that had given Zombie his set, had been the ace of hearts. Flush. Mine.

"My flush takes it down." I leaned over to Zombie and said, "You ship it."

Lifting the child off the table I hugged her. "We won, sweetie, we won." And then I whispered so softly, a whisper meant just for her. "You're safe now, little one, you're safe."

I passed her off to Nick, and he and Alec each took one of her hands in theirs. I gathered up the coffee.

Zombie, however, didn't take it that well.

"You slow-rolling bitch."

Oh, boy. Here it comes.

But I had to agree: I did slow-roll him, which entails turning your cards over dead last when you know you have won, letting an opponent think he won the pot—in this case, coffee and a kid—for as long as possible. It was a creep thing to do, and yeah, it did make me a bitch, first-class, but hey, I'd played all my life with Runners. Getting your throat slit at the table for drawing out on the river; well, now, that's something to be pissed about.

"You cheated!" he screamed. "No one calls two raises with a seven-nine, hoping to hit a flush."

"I do."

He drew a knife. But I beat him to it. In fact, I had two. It just paid to think ahead.

I sank one into his hand, pinning him to the table. He screamed in pain. I put the other to his throat. I was going to kill him, kill all of them, but not this way. Not like this. The kids had been traumatized enough for one night. And, hell, the night wasn't over. How I wished it were.

"Look, you poor loser, bad sport, asshole, whatever. I won. You lost. Get over it. And just to show you what a great player I am, in the name of sportsmanship, I'm leaving you a packet of coffee. Just one, mind you, but it's more than you deserve."

"Really?" Water Wings looked like he wanted to hug me.

"Really."

Tank was up already putting water into a bashed-up

teapot. He paused just long enough to slam a fist onto the hilt of my knife, driving it farther into Zombie's hand, just when I thought Zombie couldn't scream any louder.

"Well, boys," I said backing up slowly with the kids, so proud of Nick and Alec for remembering our exit plan, "I'd like to say it's been fun, but I'm not gonna lie: I kind of hate your town. No offense.

"And speaking of lying and hating, that Tsunami Blue chick? Well, she lies all the time."

"She does?" Water Wings looked like I'd just told him there was no Santa Claus.

"But—" One of my boys started to speak up, and I shot up a hand in warning, shaking my head at him. He backed down.

"Hate to break it to you, but yeah, she does. Like that wave tonight? No worries. If I were you I'd just sit back and enjoy your brew." I looked at Zombie, who was whimpering and trying to pull my knife out of his hand. "Looks like you're pretty much stuck here anyway."

Tank laughed and walked over to me. I kept my blade between us.

"Been nice knowin' ya, Bambi. I'll be seeing you around."

Not likely. "See ya, Tank."

I was almost past the Dumpster with all three kids when I heard Tank one more time. "If I do see you, Bambi, I'll kill you. And I'll take my time, just to do it right."

I pushed the kids out into the street, turned, and walked back to face Tank.

"You know, it's damn near impossible to make friends in this town. But if I ever see you again, I'll be sure and do the same."

How perverse were we? It sounded like we had just agreed to become pen pals. But what did it matter? I walked away, knowing the wave was coming, knowing all three would be sitting around having coffee when it came, and knowing there wasn't a chance in hell that any of them would survive.

Good fucking riddance.

Chapter Twenty-four

The kids and I sat huddled together along two huge totem poles that had toppled with the last wave. Knocked down but not destroyed, the weathered wood still bore the intricate, proud carvings of an eagle and a raven.

I felt honored to be in their company.

It gave me strength to think that if these magnificent cedars could survive a wave, a tsunami, then maybe tonight, these kids could too.

I was right in the middle of making plans to make sure that happened. But I needed a little cooperation here.

"But, Bambi," Nick protested, "you said yourself that Tsunami Blue lies, that no wave is coming."

"Yeah," Alec chimed in. "You said."

Our new little friend just sat and stared at my arm. I'd given her my fleece—the kid was so cold having only pj's on—and my full-sleeve tat was exposed. What a night to wear a tank. Now I was a walking billboard in a town where most, it would seem, thought Tsunami Blue was Satan. *Great. Just great.*

I looked at my watch. It was time to get hold of this situation with the boys. Now. They wanted to see the fight. They couldn't understand why so many people were ignoring Tsunami Blue's warning.

Frankly, neither could I. I must be losing my touch. Maybe I should try that 1-900 voice I had used on the

Runner Charlie. I touched my black eye and winced. *Yeah, Blue. 'Cause that just worked out so well.*

Gabriel was running out of time. I was running out of time. And these kids were too. They just didn't know it.

"Nick, Alec, listen to me." They must have heard something in my voice, because they both went silent. Maybe they heard the fear.

"You know when I told you that Gabriel and I met Tsunami Blue?" They nodded. The little girl continued to stare.

"Well, it's partly true."

"Partly?" It was so dark I wasn't sure which twin was talking.

"Gabriel met her." And kidnapped her. And burned her house down. And lost her kayak, and . . . *Okay, rein it in, Blue. They don't have to know that part.*

"You didn't meet her?" Who asked that? It didn't matter. At least they were paying attention.

"I didn't have to, boys. You see, I'm not . . . *They can't know who you are. They can't know. It's too dangerous . . . too dangerous. Kids talk.*

Too late, I thought. There was no other way.

"I'm not Bambi, boys."

"Huh?"

"I'm—"

"You're Tsunami Blue," a small voice said in the dark. "You're her."

"The new kid's crazy."

"Yeah, she's losin' it."

"Stop, boys, just stop." My voice had that pleading quality that sometimes bled out over the airwaves. And it gave me an idea.

"Nick, Alec, little one," I said softly. "Give me your hands. Everyone."

"Oh, man," one twin complained.

"What if someone sees us?" The other twin.

" 'Kay." The voice of our little one.

Joining hands in the dark with the intimacy only friendship could bring, we connected. The fact that it was pitch-black and I pinkie-swore to the boys that no one could see us helped too.

"Now close your eyes and listen. Listen to my voice."

"This is crazy," said Alec.

"Lame," said Nick.

"Just listen. I saved your lives once tonight, and I'm trying to do it again."

"Okay. But this is embarrassing." Twin One.

"Do we get to sing 'Kumbaya'?" Twin Two.

" 'Kay."

All three on board, a relief.

Then, before I opened my mouth, the sea blew in with the mist and wrapped around the children.

Listen, it whispered, *Listen. Listen. Listen.*

The kids shivered and got real quiet.

I took a deep breath of the cold northern winter night and looked to the stars for comfort. They were there, like always. I closed my eyes and for I moment I was home again on my beach, with Max playing in the surf. And it was time to broadcast, time for a moon bounce.

"And so, my friends," I began, "the moon is full, the sea calm, and the wave? The wave, my friends, sleeps tonight. And so can you. This is Tsunami Blue signing—"

"You really are her?" Alec broke in, and I could hear the awe in his voice.

"Yes." I squeezed his hand. "I really am."

"Wow," Nick breathed, "cool."

"Knew it," said our newest little member.

The kids couldn't see me blinking back tears. I took a moment so I could trust my voice. I had to get these kids to safety. To send them running for high ground. To send them running for their lives. But I couldn't take them myself and still save Gabriel.

First, the four of us smeared mud and dirt along my arm to cover what we could of my tattoo. The boys enjoyed Project Conceal a bit too much, and before I knew it I looked like a female mud wrestler from Vegas. *Great.*

As we worked, I had noticed only the swarms of people heading for the cage in a constant stream of ragtag, filthy bodies, pushing and shoving, fighting to get ahead of the herd.

It was only after watching a woman with a group of kids moving in the opposite direction that I noticed a much smaller group moving away from the crowd. Toward high ground.

And that was how I had found Jess, a middle-aged woman who was sweet and kind and trustworthy.

In short order, she taught me that not all Uplanders were created equal. Some were evil by nature. I guessed they just got tired of being wet. Trust me, that would piss anyone off. But there were many more who still had their humanity left.

Nick, Alec, and our little one now stood next to Jess and not next to me. She'd agreed to take them to higher ground. And—thank you, God—she was taking them now.

"Nick, Alec, take care of our little one. She's in your hands now. And, Jess, thank you." I gave the round, stout woman a hug and a packet of Starbucks. She smelled of apples and cinnamon and trust and hope. Okay, I knew there was no smell for trust and hope, but it seemed right, felt right, to entrust the Uplander woman before me with the kids. And the sea, whispering all around me now, agreed.

Jess had no idea who I really was. And the kids, who now seemed to understand the danger, had been pinkie-sworn to keep the secret. A secret that would save their lives should they encounter the wrong people. Which was likely. Which made me sick with fear. I tried not to show it.

And I had been right about the boys. They were not being raised by Runners after all. In fact they had laughed when I asked them. New False Bay held a small colony of Uplanders, a network of survivors gathered together by who else? Gabriel Black. Just who was this man, really? I was determined to find out.

But for now the kids were heading up to Grouse Mountain on a solar-powered tram. Or, in these dark winter months, more like a people-powered tram. And when Jess had pressed the packet of Starbucks back into my hand, telling me to keep it, I might need it more, I knew I had made the right decision. So why, when I watched them mesh with the crowd and fade into the night, did my heart break all over again?

I stood outside of what looked like the gates of hell and smiled. Our new "little one" had a name. *Aubrey.* A beautiful name, made even more beautiful when she put her arms around me and whispered it in my ear for the first time. Just before she said good-bye.

I had given her a high five and a kiss and a hug. *Welcome to Team Blue,* I'd said.

And then they were gone. Off to safety. At least for this wave. After all, it was just a little monster.

As I made my way toward the makeshift arena, my thoughts were of Gabriel and the task before me. I wasn't sure what that task would entail, only that it seemed daunting and dangerous and, well, most likely impossible. Still, I had to do it. I had to save Gabriel. If not for me, for the boys. Nick and Alec were devastated to learn Gabriel was nowhere to be found. And I hadn't the stomach to tell them I knew exactly where he was. I hadn't the stomach to tell them they might never see him again.

I still couldn't believe the boys had hitched a ride to New Vancouver by junk. The sketchy supply boat that made the rounds in the New San Juans. Sketchy because you never knew for sure where or when it might show. Or better yet, if it would show at all. I'd heard stories that the crew, drunk on absinthe, had lost their bearings, ended up in New Canada, and an entire family of six had starved because they hadn't gotten supplies. I had always hoped that was just a story.

The timetable might be sketchy, but the fact that sometimes Runners took over the junk was downright scary.

Gabriel would be so furious with the twins for taking such a risk. If he lived to find out.

And little Aubrey? The girl with the amazing whiskey-brown eyes? Still a mystery. But at least I knew her name. At least she was safe.

So here I was in the New World Order of Extreme Cage Fighting. At least, that was what the sign read. And, like I said, it looked like the gates of hell.

Thank God the boys hadn't come.

Giant torches lit the walkway into the old Capital Arena. Or should I say half the arena. Damaged by flood-waters, the ruins didn't look anything like an arena. No roof, missing a side, it was like everything else in New Vancouver: damaged. Inside and out.

I traveled a double-wide path that went on forever. I was flanked on either side by light and smoke and flame. The crowd roared from inside and I could smell the taint of too much booze, too much blood, too much sin. This place felt wrong, evil . . . unholy.

Vendors lined the path. Some stood beside jars of snake wine, trading and bartering for a taste of their nasty brew. Clear glass containers of varying sizes held the carcasses of some of the most dangerous snakes in the world. Their lifeless, coiled bodies fermented and rotted in the liquid. People everywhere were drinking once illegal brew, smoking once illegal weed, and chewing old meds like gum.

Some were shooting up with needles so contaminated that they risked dying from the rusted, salt-pocked metal more than the drugs.

Runners were all over.

In all this, how was I ever going to get to Gabriel? Much less get him out of here?

"Hey, you, girly. You need cleaning up real bad. How 'bout you come on over and I'll hose you off. Looks like you got something on your arm there."

I stopped midstream, my hand flying to my tattoo. Relief flooded me as I felt the thick ooze, now drying into a shield of camouflage. I got knocked hard from behind by two mean-looking women who pushed me toward the man who had shouted out to me.

"Get your scrawny ass out of the way," one woman said.

"Stupid bitch," said the other as they shoved past me.

I glared at them over my shoulder. Man, how I loved the friendly folks of New Vancouver.

"Girly, get your ass over here and let me clean you up. I've got just the hose to do it with."

I turned to face the man, ready to draw a knife if need be, only to see that he was trading what I desperately wanted to buy. Or steal. T-shirts. A long-sleeved one in particular caught my eye. I wanted it. Hell, I needed it. The mud would dry completely and flake off at some point. Yep. I needed that shirt. Now.

He was a short, stubby excuse of a guy, with a really bad comb-over. He was grabbing his crotch and making gyrating, lewd gestures, which was so not new. I rolled my eyes, drew my knife from the small of my back, and had it pressed to his penis in under a second. Needless to say the gyrating stopped.

His eyes went wide and his face paled.

"Look, Mud Girl—" he started.

"Mud Girl?" I pressed the knife in tighter. "Now is that any way to talk to a lady?"

"Sorry. Sorry. What do you want? I was only kidding."

"Of course you were." I pulled back my knife, but only by an inch. "What I want is that black tee over there, the long-sleeved one."

He paled more. "That's vintage, man. That's worth—"

"Your life?" I interrupted.

"Yours. It's yours."

He reached back and pulled it off the rusted hanger behind him and shoved it at me. He looked like he was gonna cry. Over a T-shirt? Man, he needed to get into another line of work. I grabbed it and stuffed it under my arm, not making the mistake of pulling it over my head right then and there, giving him a chance to blindside me.

"Hold out your hand." I pointed the knife at him.

"What are ya gonna do, lady?"

I smiled at the *lady* part. For a dumb-ass, he was a fast learner.

"Just hold it out."

"Don't cut me! I gave you the damn shirt, didn't I?" He fell to his knees.

I slung the shirt over my shoulder and pressed the knife under his chin. He held out his hand. It was shaking, and I couldn't blame him. I had caught a glimpse of myself in a cracked mirror strapped to a rotting post over his shoulder. Nick and Alec had painted streaks of mud on my face and forehead like war paint. My hair was a tangled, filthy mess barely contained in a ponytail. My cheek from the black eye was purple, and the shades only added to the overall psycho look.

I looked like shit.

I looked crazy-dangerous.

I did like the crazy-dangerous part, though. It seemed to be working for me. Of course, the knife helped.

I reached into my pocket and pulled out the last packet of Starbucks Christmas Blend. It was smashed and flat, but it was coffee. Damn good coffee. I dropped it in his hand. There. I could officially say I made my first trade.

He looked up, amazement flooding his face, and then joy—pure joy.

I twirled my knife, just to be a show-off. New clothes will do that to a girl. I booted him in the chest, knocking him over in the mud, and I walked away.

I was almost in and the crowd was pulling and pulsating, like a throbbing organ. I'd donned my new long-sleeved tee, which, let's face it, was so not new. In fact, it smelled. But what was I gonna do? Ask for a refund? What I was pleased about was that not only did it cover my tattoo just fine, but it had writing on the back that said, *We Leave Bite Marks.* Now I didn't need the matchbook. I had the T-shirt. Much better.

We moved as one mass, pushing our way in toward . . . what, exactly?

Then, just like that, I was in.

And that was when I saw it.

The cage.

It was a raised platform shaped like a pentagram and lined with razor wire. Huge vats of burning oil lit the stage at each point. The smells of the rancid oil and human flesh, raw and bleeding, filled my nostrils. It was the smell of death. What was this place?

I pushed through the crowd, fighting for every step. Panic was setting in. It was after midnight and Gabriel was nowhere to be seen. *Please, God,* I prayed, *let me find him.*

It was such slow going, the crowd swallowed me up at

times, and once I fell and was almost trampled. Large hands reached down and picked me up. I never even saw my savior to thank him. Incredibly loud metal music rang through my eardrums, while the air tasted hot and sour with too much sweat. Too much sin.

At last I was at the front of the cage.

It looked like a fight had just finished. They were hosing down the floors. The water ran crimson.

Suddenly the music stopped.

The crowd, knowing something I didn't, hushed. The silence, thick just with breaths being drawn, was eerie, and creeped me out. I didn't know what to expect. I didn't want to find out.

Then the drums began.

It sounded like a death march.

I looked around, but I couldn't see, I couldn't see, I couldn't—

My heart stopped. Gabriel. Bound and bloodied, he entered the cage through a hidden door. Pushed to his knees by a shirtless, scarred man, Gabriel had his hands untied and he was kicked to the side of the cage like a dog.

He wore long leather shorts already caked with dried blood. His beautiful hair, now matted and tangled, still shone blue-black under harsh lights of fire. Shirtless, scratched, and bruised, he still looked like my dark angel. An angel in trouble.

I wanted to run to him. Hold him. Cry for him. But I stood frozen. The terror crept through my bones like a ghost at midnight, gripping my heart.

Gabriel stood. His wonderful hands were clenched in rage, and the fury on his face spoke volumes. He might die tonight, but he'd go out fighting. He was battered about the face and bruised on his torso. He looked like he'd already fought.

The restless crowd chanted, "Fight, fight, fight, fight."

They stomped their feet, and soon the arena was wild with noise. Someone threw a bottle, and that started a barrage of objects thrown against the cage. Glass shattered, but nothing could penetrate the wire mesh. Gabriel was safe from the crowd.

But surely not from the huge man coming in through the opposite door.

He had to be at least six foot seven; I'd never seen anyone so tall. Dressed in the same leathers as Gabriel, barefoot and buff, he bore the most amazing tattoos I'd ever seen.

Every inch of his body was covered by scales, tattooed in iridescent blues and greens and yellows. His ears—and I couldn't help thinking about Trace—were covered in tiny scales, along with lips, everything, even toes. I strained for a closer look. The tats wove around and down, circling his body.

I could see a pattern.

Snakes. Every tattoo wove one snake into another.

A crowd favorite, Snake Man bowed, deep and low. When he raised his head, I found myself looking into serpent eyes of yellow and gold. He blinked and an opaque filter, a film really, covered his eyes. Spooky.

I had a sick feeling about this. Something told me this fight would be far from fair. Something told me things could go very wrong.

Bells rang and a man with a bullhorn came out to announce the "rules."

Head butting—good.

Eye gouging—pretty much.

Bare knuckles—of course.

Kicks to the head and spinal cord—encouraged.

Biting, chewing, swallowing. Why not?

Another bell sounded.

This was it. It would start soon. I wanted to cry.

Pushing past the last holdouts of people blocking my way I climbed onto the small platform surrounding the stage. Other people were doing it too, and I tried to blend in like an honest-to-goodness fan. My new tee helped. I was so glad my arm was covered. Flaunting my wave tattoo would have been stupid on every level.

I inched toward Gabriel, and when someone wouldn't let me pass, I showed them my knife. I had to get as close to him as possible. I wasn't about to let a snake-lovin' groupie get in the way.

I had to take care with my weapons. I was down to two blades now.

After giving Aubrey my fleece, I couldn't stow and stash all the weapons anymore. Plus I didn't have that many left; I'd used a fair number in the city. Such a warm and fuzzy place, this New Vancouver.

I still had that bright pink duct tape on my wrist holding the switchblade. It wasn't a question of whether I'd use it, but when.

Catcalls filled the air and I turned to the crowd. Men jeered. Some dropped their pants, making gross motions and sexual gestures. The women booed. I turned back to the ring.

The ring girl was parading in a circle with a sign over her head that read, *Runner vs. Cobra*. Cobra. Like I didn't see that name coming.

I looked closer at the sign bearer. A stunning girl, she wore tall platform boots in black leather that laced high on her calves. Black thong, black tank top, black belly ring; at least we liked the same color. Blonde hair tumbled over her shoulders, resting on her enormous breasts. I glanced down at my chest. Well, that didn't make me feel any better.

But there was something else about her.

What? She stopped in front of Gabriel and I wasn't

thrilled about that. She kissed him hard, pulled away, and laughed. It was then that I recognized her.

The grip on the cage turned my knuckles white. I was fantasizing about gripping her neck.

Ring Girl was the woman Gabriel had rowed away with the night of the party. The girl he'd flashed his twin dimples at. She was the woman who didn't bring him back.

She was with him the night he didn't come home.

The night I didn't get a practice session.

The night he broke my heart.

Chapter Twenty-five

I watched the blonde move away from Gabriel with hate in my heart.

She had set Gabriel up.

I watched her move and smile and wave. After she met me—and I'd make sure she did—she wouldn't be smiling anymore.

So she was working with Trace. He had to be here. He wouldn't miss Gabriel's death. Hell, he'd want to stick around just to collect the ears.

I didn't know what the man looked like, but I wanted to find out. Maybe I'd just look for a necklace made of ears.

If Gabriel died tonight and I lived, I'd find Trace and kill him. And yes, I knew there was no real logic in that—after all, Gabriel was working for the wrong side too. Still, I had business to finish with Gabriel. If Trace took away my only chance to find out why this Indigo and the entire Runner nation were looking for me now, all these years after Seamus's death, and if he took away my chance to say good-bye . . . ?

My throat closed and I willed tears to stay put. To stay hidden and secret.

Say good-bye? How?

How could I say good-bye to this man I knew well enough to fall in love with, yet not nearly as well as

I thought? He was such a dark enigma, a mystery man. Maybe I didn't know him at all.

I looked at Gabriel up there: so proud, so ready to fight, ready to defend. *I don't share.* His words floated back to me. *Well, Trace. Whoever you are*—I scanned the crowd—*I don't share either.*

The bell rang three times, and the fight was on.

There wasn't a damn thing I could do about it. It was the most helpless feeling in the entire New World.

The men began to circle each other, slowly. So slowly. Soon the speed began to change. And my heart rate increased.

Gabriel went on the offensive, rushing Cobra first. Dropping to the floor, he took out the large man's legs from under him. All six feet, seven inches of Cobra crashed on what should have been a mat, but instead was made of stainless steel. The unforgiving steel of diamond-plated metal was designed to draw more blood, make it a better spectator sport. Plus it was easier to hose off the blood.

The big man didn't get up. Blood ran over the diamond plate and pooled in little silver pockets. I was close enough to get a whiff of its coppery scent. I looked down at the spray of scarlet droplets that had splattered through the wire mesh and landed on my hands.

Blood on my hands. I couldn't deny it. My eyesight blurred as visions of all the men I'd stabbed and maimed and killed passed through my mind. I saw the Runner when I was thirteen, dead at my feet, and last I saw Seamus, whom I'd vowed not to care about, but did, lying on a beach surrounded by crimson.

My stomach twisted and a wave of nausea hit me.

The roar of the crowd brought me back to the fight at hand. A fight I wasn't in physically, yet, but a fight that was about me. If Gabriel Black hadn't hunted me, found me, hadn't kept me for a trade with Indigo, none of us would be here.

And I never would have met him.

Or the boys. Or little Aubrey. Or my Max. And I sure as hell wouldn't have Christmas Blend.

Coffee? I shook my head. Whatever happened to my priorities? I covered my eyes as Gabriel landed a particularly nasty punch. Still, coffee was important.

I chewed my bottom lip as Gabriel smashed a flat palm on Cobra's nose. I heard a sickening crunch. Gabriel and I had both done enough fighting to know that could have been a death blow. He could have sent the Cobra's nose straight into his skull, lodging it in the brain.

But he'd chosen not to. Why?

Gabriel, on top now, put a knee to Cobra's impossibly thin throat. Gagging, the man shot his tongue out, lapping and licking at the air. His long, snakelike tongue had been altered, sliced, really. Now in two parts, with a split down the middle, it forked and flailed as Cobra hissed and tried to spit.

The tongue looked every inch like a serpent's. I shivered. It gave me the creeps.

With the right amount of weight, Gabriel could crush the throat immediately. But again, he chose not to do it. Why?

It was a bad decision.

Gabriel couldn't see the scissor move behind him. But I could.

"Gabriel. Behind you!" I screamed.

Mistake. I had made a terrible mistake. Gabriel, clearly confused by my voice, paused. And it was the pause that got him.

Cobra locked his legs around Gabriel's throat. Gabriel flipped backward and landed hard on the floor. He didn't move.

I gripped the wire and shouted out his name over and over. Nothing. Nothing.

And then I saw it.

He opened an eye, just a crack. He was looking for me. I knew it. And he was playing dead. *Remember playing dead, Blue?* I hid a smile. He was so going to nail Cobra.

Cobra came in for the kill.

Gabriel got there first. He met the man with a full-on punch to the gut, then an uppercut to the ribs. I heard a crack and I knew some broke.

Cobra stumbled back, dazed and disoriented. Man, Gabriel was doing great. He was going to win this thing. He was going to live. I shouldn't have been, but I was proud. And excited. And relieved. Plus, I'd get another crack to kill him myself if I wanted to. What a win-win situation.

And that was when I saw it.

The signal. From the sidelines. Ring Girl, who I was now calling Bitch Slut Whore, was called over to a slender but well-built man in his thirties.

He pointed at me. *Oops.*

I had been so caught up in the fight, I'd failed Survival 101: Be aware of your surroundings. The man motioned to others throughout the crowd, and I felt the world close in on me. Was that Trace? Had to be. Still, he was so nondescript. Where was the ear necklace?

Now something was happening in the cage. *Shit.* I couldn't watch it all: my danger, Gabriel's danger.

And what about Ring Girl? What was she up to?

A bell sounded. Men came out of nowhere to drag Gabriel to his corner. One even punched him in the ribs.

"Hey," I shouted. "Not fair." But my voice was lost to the crowd. I wondered whether Gabriel was lost to me too. I looked behind me. Men were approaching. Fast. Now I had to get out of here. But leave Gabriel? I looked again just in time to see the guard land another blow to Gabriel's abdomen. I studied the guard. I wanted to be sure I had the right man when I killed him.

The bell again. So soon? Ring Girl had spent some time in the corner with Cobra. I didn't like it.

But I had to move. I had to get lost in here. I had to think, think. If I got nabbed, how could I help Gabriel?

As I jumped down from the stage I looked back—just in time to see Cobra bite at Gabriel, as if snapping at him like a dog might, or a snake. A stream of red smoke floated in Gabriel's face.

I froze. I knew this. Didn't I? And then . . . yes. I *knew* this. Seamus had told me the story when I was a kid. Asian mist, originating in Japan, was used by extreme boxers and wrestlers. It caused intense stinging of the eyes. And the bastard Runners had made it so much worse. Their version, now with powdered snake venom, blinded. Delivering it from a pouch that fighters hid in their mouths, they aimed at their opponents' eyes. It seared and burned and ultimately blinded. It only made sense that the snake man would be packing Asian mist, complete with snake poison. It was part of the package.

"No!" I screamed. "No."

But before I could run back to the cage to warn Gabriel, it was too late. By the time I got back I could see only what was left of the powder, as fine red mist floated around his shoulders. Gabriel dropped to his knees. Holding his hands to his eyes, he rolled over.

"Why, John?" he moaned. "Why?"

John? Gabriel knew Snake Man? Was that why Gabriel refused to go hard at him? To deliver the killing blow? I looked to Gabriel and caught my breath.

He was still. Too still.

Chapter Twenty-six

"No," I whispered. Fear paralyzed me. "No."

The thought of Gabriel Black, with those dark eyes and even darker lashes, scarred, burned, and blinded? I couldn't bear it. I couldn't.

I thought of my pirate at the helm, his dark hair blowing in the sea breeze as he scanned the horizon. I thought of him not being able to take to the sea again, to navigate by the stars, to see me. I thought, *What if . . . ?* And then, *No.* No, I wouldn't think it. I'd saved him once; I'd do it again.

And again and again and again, my heart said.

I ran back to the cage, jumped on the ledge, and grabbed the mesh with both hands. I could see Gabriel crumpled on the floor. No one was helping him. No one.

"Gabriel," I called. "Gabriel."

I saw him try to raise his head. He heard me. *Thank God.*

"Gabriel. Oh, honey, sweetie, are you all right?"

A drunken woman next to me mimicked my concern, and then: "Gabriel, can you see me? What?" She grabbed her boobs and jiggled them in an obscene way. "You can't? Too bad, baby. You don't know what you're missing." She started to laugh a loud, obnoxious laugh and gave me a hard shove.

Oh, boy. I so did not have time for this. So I decided to end it. Pronto.

"Oh, *I* see you." I punched her so hard she flew off the ledge, back into a worked-up crowd that pretty much hated her large butt landing on them. I let the crowd below take over and turned back to Gabriel. I knew I had a few precious minutes before the wrong people reached me, but I couldn't seem to move. I had to see Gabriel. I had to.

Everyone had focused on Cobra, the snake of the hour. People crowded around him, including the Ring Girl. She rubbed against him and reached up to wipe a smudge of red powder from his lips. He uncoiled his tongue and licked her hand. *Yuck.*

I struggled with what to do. I had to get in there. That much was clear. But how? I glanced back over the sea of people to check on the progress of the men who had been directed my way.

They were getting closer.

"Aw, screw it," I said to myself. "Just go for it, Blue." I tore at the pink duct tape with my teeth as I tested the mesh with my hands. I could climb better than a black bear, Seamus used to say. I had to, I'd tell him, to get away from his friends.

I opened the lethal-looking switchblade. It had a bone handle and a wicked blade. I wasn't a hundred percent sure that the bone wasn't from something other than cow; with a Runner, you just never knew.

With a quick look over my shoulder, just to check how long I'd be a free woman—oh, good, not long—I started to scale the mesh. The wire was old, ripped, and I easily found toe- and handholds all the way up.

I held the knife between my teeth as I climbed; I wished I could say I hadn't done this before. But I didn't think anyone who had known me for long had ever seen me without a knife, in all different circumstances and in all different positions. It pretty much went with the territory. *My* territory. And the old knife-between-my-teeth trick? A guy named Rambo, who the older Runners idolize, may have been famous for it, but I did it better. So I was going over the top, razor wire and all. *I'm coming, Gabriel.* I willed him to hear my thoughts, to hang on. *I'm coming.*

It took a few minutes for the people around me to notice that a crazy girl with a knife in her teeth was scaling the mesh. But when they did, news spread through the crowd fast.

By the time I was at the top, people at the bottom started to clap to a steady rhythm of, "Fall, bitch, fall, fall, bitch, fall . . ." It was just so nice to be encouraged.

When I reached the top, I ducked under the large loops of razor wire and hooked a leg over the side. I turned and faced the crowd, which I must say was really getting into their chant. They had even started the wave through the audience, which I thought was really appropriate, given, you know, the whole Tsunami Blue thing. Not that they would know it. Yet.

Still, seeing the wave running through the massive crowd was pretty impressive, I've got to say. I wanted to thank them, but it was hard to find the right words, since all they really wanted was for me to tangle up in razor wire, fall, and die a horrible death. I wanted to leave them with something, though.

So just before I hooked my leg over to the other side and started the climb down, I flipped them off with both fingers. The crowd went nuts. I was a star.

Unfortunately, I was becoming a star to the men inside the cage too. Right now, they didn't seem concerned; I was sure I wasn't the first delusional fan to scale the mesh surrounding the cage. But I was noticed. And I knew my time with Gabriel, when I reached him, would be limited. But I would reach him.

I took a lesson out of the Gabriel Black playbook and landed next to him on little cat feet.

My knife popped out of my mouth and clattered noisily on the stainless-steel floor, pretty much announcing my arrival to the entire world. The blade spun and skidded away. *Well, great. Just great.*

Of course Gabriel heard me. I think it was not only the little cat feet landing, but the drop, crash, and roll that might have tipped him off. That or the, "Ouch, my butt." And the, "Damn it, tough guy, why do I have to do all the saving?" might have clinched it.

I rolled over to him, well aware that our time together was short, maybe only a few seconds even, before someone pulled me away from him.

So I made the best use of my time I could. I put my arm around his back, stroked his hair, and said, "If we live through this, Gabriel Black, I'm next in line to kill you. You know that, right?"

"Nice to see you too, Blue," he said. "Now"—and he turned his head to face me—"get the hell out of here."

I tried not to gasp; really, I did. But his beautiful eyes were swollen shut; the skin around them was blistered and burned. I did what always comes naturally to me: I looked around for my knife. I needed to kill the man who had done this.

I pushed up from the cool steel and stripped off my new We Leave Bite Marks T-shirt. I needed something to soak up water.

I glanced at my tattoo. Still smeared with mud, it was an unrecognizable mess. I could hardly believe that I hadn't been knifed and thrown out of here yet. But then, that was never the plan. And yes, I had one. But only one.

It would come down to showing my last hand, executing my last slow roll. I would play the Tsunami Blue card. But my first concern was for Gabriel. I looked for water and found it in the corner. Right next to Snake Man.

I looked for my knife. I wanted to multitask: Get water and kill the Snake Man. Why make two trips?

"Looking for this?" The nondescript man I'd seen earlier was holding up my bone-handled blade. He was average height, but his build was strong, powerful. His cropped hair, buzzed short like the old military style, was blond. His features were all hard angles and sharp planes. He had a mean mouth and dead, dark eyes. Everything about this man said, *Stay away, or you'll be dead.* I was wrong. Up close and personal, there was nothing nondescript about this man who had to be Trace. The man was pure terror.

Gabriel pushed to sit up. He glared at the man. "Stay away from her, Trace."

"So this is her, is it, Gabriel? Your Tsunami Blue?"

Trace reached out and grabbed my arm. Reaching over, he smeared the mud clear from my shoulder. A portion of my tat showed through. He pulled off my shades and tossed them on the unforgiving steel. The glasses shattered. He grabbed my chin and looked at my eyes. The girl in the ring, taking in my tattoo, gasped, and Snake Man blinked and blinked again, as if he couldn't believe his own reptilian eyes.

I jerked away from Trace like he was nothing. I had been manhandled by Runners all my life. This was not new or unexpected. And right now I needed water. End of story. And I didn't think he would kill me. Yet. He was one of two men who had been looking for me all this time. Kill me over a bucket of water? No. I was too valuable for that.

But I was afraid for Gabriel. He had no clout, nothing to offer anyone without me. The thought felt bitter. Why should I save him? Why?

As I headed over to the water, I looked back at Trace. Before I made a bargain with the devil, I knew I had to answer that question: Why save Gabriel Black?

Because I couldn't live, couldn't breathe, couldn't exist without him somewhere in my world.

I picked up my tee and dipped it in the cool water of the bucket, glared at Snake Man, and headed back over to talk with Trace. But before I did, I pulled out what was left of my ponytail and let my hair down.

I wanted to cover my ears.

Chapter Twenty-seven

"Talk to me, Trace. I'm all ears." I was standing on my tiptoes, trying to dab Gabriel's eyes with the cool, wet T-shirt.

"Blue." Gabriel pushed the shirt away and put a hand of warning on my wrist. He was trying to convey to me that Trace was a dangerous man. Certainly not one to be made fun of. All of which I knew. But it was that show-no-fear thing that Uncle Seamus had taught me so well. Unfortunately, with Trace it wasn't working. The man didn't give a shit. Which scared me. And I was trying like hell not to show it.

But what Gabriel conveyed with a touch here, a stroke there, was that he wanted me to be careful. Careful because he couldn't protect me anymore.

And it tore up my heart.

He couldn't protect me because Gabriel Black was blind. And maybe always would be.

I hadn't been able to take my glare off John the Snake Man. He had blinded Gabriel. And he would die for that. I was working on visuals of tearing out the Snake Man's heart. Just as he had most certainly torn out mine.

"Your girlfriend has some mouth," Trace was saying.

Gabriel said nothing and just stared ahead.

"Look, Black, if it wasn't for her, you'd be gutted like a tuna up here in the cage. Hell, this crowd still wants your blood." He grinned. "You know how they feel about losers."

Trace turned and gave the crowd the loser sign while shoving Gabriel hard against the mesh. The crowd went crazy. I quickly pulled Gabriel back to my side and attempted to put myself between the two men. Gabriel tried to grab my shoulders. I knew he wanted to tuck me behind him. He wanted to keep me safe. He missed me, reached air instead, and fell to his knees. Trace roared with laughter and the noise from the crowd exploded.

Trace was a nasty man and, just like any Runner scum, ambitious. I guess that was where I came in. He who controlled the waves, or at least knew approximately when and where they would hit, ruled the world.

Well, that was the short version.

Trace had just explained the nuances of owning a "pet" like me. Sounded like a lot of fun to go live with Uncle Trace. I did the work; he used the info about waves for evil personal gain.

With me at his side he would sit at the top of the food chain as he doled out information on where to run, where to hide. He alone could decide who would live and who would die. Not to mention, he could pull the old bait-and-switch routine. Send people off to run for their lives while his crew swept in, taking everything that was left behind. Yep, Trace would know how to win friends and influence people. Umm, I'd always thought that was a funny book title.

Funny because I didn't have any friends to influence. But when I'd found the hardcover floating in the sea just after the great Seattle wave, I fished it out of the water and kept it. Just in case. Then Gabriel Black came along. Well, we all knew how that turned out.

The other turnoff for my becoming part of the Trace Runner Scum Show was the part that, if I was lucky, he wouldn't kill me in a fit of anger. I guessed he was prone to it. Oh, and he couldn't promise anything long-term on the ears. "Just one of those things," he'd said.

I looked at Gabriel and chewed my lip. I hated to admit it, but Trace was right about the crowd. We had been talking only a few minutes; still, they were getting more and more out of control. Everything imaginable was being thrown at the mesh. Including a body. *Whatever happened to a little patience, people?* Bottom line? They hadn't liked that Gabriel was still alive. They wanted blood: his and mine.

I had to work smarter. How could I get Gabriel out of this if I got killed in the process?

Trace and I struck that bargain. I talked fast, with the crowd being on the verge of a riot and all. Trace talked faster. I shut down the sarcasm and managed to get Gabriel a free pass, which just meant, in Runner terms, that Trace wouldn't kill Gabriel in front of me. Still, I had bought us some time. And in return, Trace got to know when and where the next big wave was coming. Of course, I couldn't leave his employment. Ever. Talk about job security.

I hadn't mentioned anything more about the wave coming tonight. Trace seemed to think I'd made up the warning just to get Gabriel free. Fine with me. He seemed so sure of himself and his place at the top of our New World food chain. I couldn't wait to see him wet and drowning.

Yep, no one believes me, Trace. Just keep thinking that way, 'cause—I looked at my little moon band—*the wave is coming.* It was, just like me, always late. I hoped that wouldn't be counted against me in my employee file.

Trace waved the crowd down and picked up a bullhorn. "People, I have a surprise. Be patient. I'm about to present a very special guest to you all." With a snap of his fingers the heavy metal music roared to life.

He turned to me. "I'm gonna clean you up, Tsunami Blue. Owning a bitch like you makes me top dog. And if you don't behave yourself, I'll feed you to the audience, one limb at a time." At that he walked across the ring toward the water bucket.

"Blue?"

I jumped at Gabriel's voice. I had been concentrating on how to get us the hell out of here. I turned and reached out to gently touch his eyes. He pulled back in surprise. And pain.

"Does it hurt bad?"

"Only the part where I can't see you."

My heart flipped. Why was it so hard to hate this guy?

"Blue." His voice caught. "I wish . . . I just wish you weren't here. I can't keep you safe, and there is so much I want to tell you."

"You mean about Ring Girl? Because I've got to tell you, your choice in gal pals sucks."

He shook his head at that.

"About Trace."

"What, my new employer? Do not tell me he doesn't have full benefits."

"Be serious. I'm trying to save your life."

I studied him in the harsh torchlights of the arena, and my heart tugged. His beautiful golden skin was angry and red around his eyes. The blisters looked so painful, but he hadn't complained, not once. Being blind in this New World was close to a death sentence. Most begged to get by.

"And I'm trying to save yours," I whispered.

Suddenly, without warning, the crowd erupted. Gabriel and I both jumped, and Trace came running. I helped Gabriel turn and I looked to see if I could figure out what was going on. Gabriel stood with his hand gripping my shoulder.

Trace shielded his eyes as he scanned the crowd, looking for whatever it was that was igniting a near riot. "What is that bastard doing here?" he said.

"What bastard?" I asked, looking around. Shit, they all looked like bastards to me.

"Indigo."

Trace said the name like he was spitting out something nasty and rotten. Gabriel tightened his grip on my shoulder.

"Indigo?" I asked. "As in, the guy who will stop at pretty much anything to get to me? *That* Indigo?"

Trace looked at me like I was a moron. "Like there could be more than one. You don't have to be too bright to predict waves, do you?"

Now, that was just uncalled-for. "Hey. Does that mean that he'll kill you to get to me?" I asked hopefully.

"That's the fucker," Trace said bitterly.

"Well, let's get him on over here."

Gabriel took the hit for me. How he had known it was coming was beyond me. I guess, like Gabriel had said, he knew the man. Gabriel pushed me hard and I fell on the steel floor. But that was better than taking the punch. It dropped Gabriel to his knees.

On me, it would have broken my jaw. *Stupid, Blue*, I chastised myself. *Stupid. Stupid.* Again, how could I get Gabriel out of here if got myself killed first?

A green-and-blue hand reached down to offer to pull me up. I didn't take it, just pushed up myself. Cobra bent down and looked me in the eyes with those white slits of his.

"Be very careful of Trace," he said. "If you continue on this way, you will be dead by morning. And he'll leave nothing of you behind, not even—"

"Don't tell me, Snake Man—a trace."

"And do you know the reason for that, miss?"

Miss? A polite Snake Man? I raised a questioning eyebrow.

"He eats them."

I felt the color drain from my face.

"He just doesn't like the ears."

I looked at the man, wondering if he might be lying, but no, there it was: the look of truth.

"Well." I took a breath. "Good to know."

As I turned to find Gabriel, Snake Man said, "Tell Gabriel that I'm sorry. I have few choices in these dark days."

As Trace stormed off for a better look at the approaching Indigo, I ran over to Gabriel, who had managed to stand on his own. A trickle of blood ran down a split lip. My guy sure was getting it tonight. *Wait. My guy?*

Putting my arm around him, I whispered, "You okay? I'm so sorry for the punch. And for, well, my mouth."

"Better me than you," he said as he folded his arms around me.

"Well, yeah," I said. "You do deserve it more. You know, Ring Girl and all."

Once more the crowd exploded with noise. The music blasted louder than ever, and the flames in the oil drums, doused with kerosene, shot twenty feet into the air.

Trace appeared and yanked me from Gabriel's arms, twisting my wrist until I cried out in pain. He drew a knife and ran it along Gabriel's jaw. Gabriel couldn't see the blade coming and flinched as the cold metal sliced his skin. "I would slit your throat now, Black, but you might come in handy as a trade with Indigo. Let's see what your precious Indigo thinks of you losing Tsunami Blue to me."

I looked past Gabriel's shoulder and saw the approaching entourage of Indigo and company. It looked like a traveling circus. And I swear, maybe it was just my eyes playing tricks in this smoke-filled light, but Indigo looked blue. I thought of ears and body parts on crackers and cream-of-human soup. It was time to change employers.

I wrenched away from Trace, nearly dislocating my shoulder in the process, and ran over to the mesh and snagged a bullhorn.

"Hey, Indigo, there's someone up here who wants to meet you."

Trace moved toward me with death in his eyes. It wasn't like I hadn't been warned.

"Who?" came a reply.

I had just enough time to shout into the bullhorn, "Tsunami Blue."

Chapter Twenty-eight

I yelled into the horn as loudly as possible. The entire stadium of people stopped whatever they were doing, saying whatever they were saying, and stared at the cage.

Trace had reached me. He grabbed the bullhorn out of my grip and threw it aside. But this time I was ready for him. I flattened myself on the floor just as the swing came. He swung so hard that it threw him off balance and he staggered to keep his footing.

It was then that I kicked him in the crotch.

And when I say *kicked*, let's just say it was a perfectly placed, powerful strike. I had lived with Runners most of my life. Learning to kick a two-hundred-plus-pound man in the balls and keep him down? Slam dunk.

He went down screaming, calling me names even I hadn't heard before. Who knew Trace, a cannibal and a collector of ears, had such a flair for words?

Trace stayed down long enough for Indigo's men to swarm the cage.

The men surrounded Trace, who lay moaning in a heap, holding his crotch. My brand-new employer was rolling on the floor and still swearing and—wait; tell me he was *not* crying. Because if he were, these Indigo guys would put it in the wind and he'd never, ever live it down. So not good for the New World king, or whatever he said he was going to be.

Next they swarmed me. Surrounded by Runners with blades drawn, I had no choice but to wait. I didn't have to wait long. Within minutes, the music stopped, the crowd hushed, and a large man with a bone necklace made of fingers announced, "Indigo on board."

I was so glad he didn't say, "Indigo in the house." That was so twenty years ago.

The necklace, I gotta say, disappointed me. This was Indigo's guy, and I had hoped the whole body-part thing might be left behind with Trace. I mean, come on. We live on islands. How about puka shells?

"Pay attention, Blue."

Gabriel had come up silently behind me; blind or not, he still had his stealth thing going. The Runners who had their blades trained on me had parted and led him to me. I reached out and took his hand, relieved to see him, because Indigo's men had swarmed him too and I hadn't been able to get near him.

I noticed lotion around his eyes and iodine on his wounds. His beautiful golden skin had been painted orange with the stuff. Still, I took it as a good sign that Indigo's men were looking after him. It must mean they weren't going to kill him. And if they cared enough to tend his eyes, they wouldn't let Trace and his men kill him either. So. We had a case of Runner versus Runner. Trace the Cannibal against the Blue Crew. May the best men win. Unfortunately for me, in this case there were no best men. Only homicidal, maniacal, power-hungry killers.

And the worst part of all? Gabriel was one of them. A Runner who had been sent as a delivery boy to hunt and deliver a small but lethal package. Me.

As Indigo drew nearer, some kind of horn sounded, and a flurry of banners unfurled bearing the trademark 666 with daggers. Six men walked ahead of Indigo, all

Runners, and started pounding handheld drums made of human skin. I knew the drum covering was human skin because Seamus had tried to give me one for my eleventh birthday. Plus, they just sounded different.

I pressed into Gabriel and he sensed my fear. He pulled me closer.

"What do you see?" he whispered.

"Drums. Please tell me you don't own one."

"I don't."

Thank you, God.

"What else?"

"Wolves. Five in all." On leashes hooked to harnesses, the animals looked lean, too lean. With hollowed haunches and sunken eyes, the wolves looked ready to make anyone their meal. Runners kept their animals on the edge by keeping them hungry. It made them meaner, deadlier. They were also beaten on a regular basis. It made them killers.

"Stay far away from them, Blue."

I couldn't help thinking of Max. How could he have survived these animals? Then again, in the end, he probably hadn't.

The crowd was on its feet, cheering and throwing bottles and debris.

The chanting began. "Kill, kill, kill, kill . . ."

At last Indigo stepped into the cage.

And, yup, the man was blue.

I must have gasped, because Gabriel leaned in and asked, "Is he here?"

"Yeah. You couldn't have at least warned me about the whole blue thing?"

"Don't let it throw you off. He's dangerous."

"Like Trace isn't?"

"Worse," said Gabriel. "Much worse."

Well, that gave me pause. What could possibly be worse than collecting ears and eating human flesh? "Damn it, Gabriel, you really, really need to find new friends."

"I agree."

"So this is the famed, the elusive, the amazing, the fantastical Tsunami Blue."

Indigo stood right in front of Gabriel, who had taken a protective step in front of me as the feared Runner leader approached. Wow, what a buildup. It might be hard to live up to that kind of reputation.

"Gabriel, let's have a look at our little weather vane, shall we?"

Weather vane? What a letdown. I'd really liked the fantastical part. I guess once a Runner asshole, always a Runner asshole. It didn't matter how good your vocabulary was.

Gabriel gently brought me out from behind him. He did everything by touch, caressing my skin with long fingers. He maneuvered me in front of him but kept an arm around my midriff.

Up close and personal, Indigo was an intimidating man. Long hanks of light blue hair hung to his waist, spilling out from under a crushed-velvet top hat that looked borderline ridiculous. Who wore velvet in the Pacific Northwest? His parachute pants and tie-dyed tee did little to camouflage a powerful and fit body. He looked . . . well, he looked silly. But I knew only too well to never underestimate a Runner. He might have looked like a Blue Meanie crossed with MC Hammer, but I could plainly see the promise of death in his eyes.

A glass vial filled with blood hung around his neck, capped by duct tape. I thought of rumors of Runners who drank blood, and suppressed a shudder.

He reached out and pulled me away from Gabriel, and

let me tell you, Gabriel didn't let go easily. It took a smack to his wrist with a bone club.

Trace, who was being detained by a bevy of blades, shouted, "She's mine, Indigo, you blue fucking bastard!" That hushed the crowd.

"Finders keepers," Indigo said in a voice that whispered of death. He crossed his arms and began to walk around me. Stopping, he pulled a wicked machete from one of his men and pointed it under my chin. I refused to blink.

"You have a brave one here, Gabriel," he said. He spun, swinging the machete so fast the blade blurred. He stopped just short of my neck. I still didn't blink. But I was glad that Gabriel couldn't see it. He would have overreacted. And it may have cost him his life.

Indigo motioned to one of his men to bring the bucket of water over. Within seconds the cold water was poured over my head. The mud ran from my body. My fully exposed tattoo shimmered. Indigo kicked the bucket over and jerked me up on it. I now stood precariously on the metal bucket in full view of the crowd. I shivered from the wet and cold, and my nipples hardened as I stood freezing. The surrounding men looked at me with lust and rape and death in their eyes.

Still, I knew that the time for my death, even in this wicked and unholy place, was not now. Not tonight. I had value to these men. And for once in my wet, miserable life, I believed in the value myself. And I was going to somehow, some way, parlay that into freedom.

Indigo stood in front of me and faced the crowd, spreading his arms wide. "I present to you the one, the only, the unholy Tsunami Blue." He bowed deeply, letting the crowd get a look at me.

The audience exploded. The mesh became our shield as everything imaginable was thrown at it. They screamed my name. They called me witch, devil, monster, and worse. So much worse. And when they rushed the ring, hundreds and hundreds and hundreds strong, I lost my balance and tumbled to the floor. I tried desperately to stop trembling. This time it wasn't from the cold. It was from the fear. I'd never seen so much hate in one place. I had never felt so much evil.

They fear what they don't understand, Blue.

Gabriel's words wrapped around me like an embrace, his embrace.

Armed with flamethrowers, Indigo's men beat the crowd back into submission. The effect was brutal and the air filled with screams and burning flesh. I wiped at the tears stinging my eyes and watched Indigo.

Indigo continued in a circle, dragging the blade along the stainless-steel floor. Scraping metal against metal, he circled and circled, like a great white. I knelt and sized him up too.

He wore rings made of abalone shells.

I approved. Hey, I'd wear 'em.

The human-tooth necklace, though? No. Not so much.

At least ten different knives hung from a belt similar to Gabriel's. Only the blades on Indigo's were longer. Big approval. Unless, of course, he used one on me.

White, even teeth, but not as white or as even as Gabriel's. Approval. Now I'd met two Runners who owned a toothbrush.

And so the list went. Long nails that curved. A definite no. He continued to circle, moving the blade in ever closer.

I spotted a little crystal lapel pin. Would I want it? Maybe. It would depend on the story behind it.

And then I saw the earring. It was a thick scroll of horn from a water buffalo.

I thrust my booted foot out and stopped him. "Where"—I clipped the words one by one for emphasis—"did you get that?" I pointed at his ear and felt my fear dissolve, replaced by growing rage.

Indigo moved so fast I didn't see it coming. But Gabriel, with uncanny senses, must have heard him coming at me.

He tried to lunge for me, but he couldn't see me. One of the men tripped him and he went down. Gabriel got a steel-toed boot to the kidney. As the boot started to come down on Gabriel's skull, I screamed and scrambled on all fours, trying to shield him.

"Enough." The order came from Indigo.

The boot stopped in midair.

I collected Gabriel in my arms. "Blue." He gasped.

"I'm okay," I whispered. "I'm okay."

I was yanked up by the hair. Indigo again. Gabriel was right: There was nothing nice about this man. Nothing at all.

I stood before his blueness, glaring. If I had my knife I would stab out his eyes, then take his heart—if he had one—and feed it to the vultures.

That was how much I hated this man. But first I'd disembowel him, slowly, so he lived while I did it. The same way he had done it to my uncle. In all the years I'd known him, Seamus had never taken out that water buffalo–horn earring. It had been given to him by my father, his brother, before a woman came between them and my father had to choose. That woman had been my mother. Seamus had loved her first.

And Seamus had died protecting me. Even under torture, he hadn't revealed to Indigo where I was hidden. He had died doing something honorable for once in his unhappy, miserable life. He had died saving Lilly's daughter.

I hurt all over. Not only physically, but deep within my soul.

"I expected more from you, Tsunami Blue."

"I expected a better hat from you, Indigo."

"Your eyes are remarkable, but the rest"—he gave a wave of his hand—"scrawny. And you're a muddy mess."

"You look like a Smurf. Only not cute. In fact, you give the color blue a bad name."

I got a smack for that. He could beat me around all he wanted, but I knew he wouldn't kill me. He wouldn't hurt me too badly. He needed me to tell him about the waves. All I had to do was bide my time and stay alive.

But me being me, I just couldn't keep my mouth shut. Plus my hatred for Indigo ran so deep I almost didn't care about the beatings. I would stay alive no matter what. Just to kill him. For me. For Gabriel. For Seamus. I felt the rage surge again.

"Too bad you're not pink. You could have gotten a job as the tooth fairy instead of an asshole."

"Chemical poisoning, bitch. You think I want to be blue? And if you don't watch that mouth, your new color will be red. From all the blood." He grabbed my forearm and nicked my pale flesh with his blade. A crimson line formed and droplets of blood dripped on the steel.

Gabriel leaned against the mesh and shook his head. I knew he was heartsick. I knew he wanted me to shut my mouth and survive. Try, at the very least. Indigo hit me again, and the crowd roared. But I'd been hit before. Many times. I was tough. Hardened. I had Seamus to thank for that. He had taught me how to survive. I'd heal.

It was Gabriel I was worried about. They had seen his loyalty to me. He complicated things. I knew the feeling. He complicated things for me too.

The sea whispered. *Coming, coming, coming, Blue. Be ready.*

"It's about time," I said. Indigo looked at me and shrugged.

I looked at my moon watch. The wave should have hit a half hour ago. But really, what did it matter? It was coming. People would die. I only hoped it wasn't me.

Or my dark angel.

Chapter Twenty-nine

Murmurs rippled through the crowd. Someone off the streets had come in shouting that water was receding near what used to be Stanley Park. Totem poles, long submerged, poked their heads out of the water for the first time in a decade. Little by little the beautifully carved cedar totem poles bearing the images of a raven and beaver, the orca and eagle, regained their place in the New Vancouver skyline.

But not for long.

The sea was merely taking a deep breath. This temporary reprieve signaled awful devastation to come.

I'm coming, the water whispered. *Run*, *Blue*, *run*.

My mind raced as I thought of all the different scenarios.

Gabriel and I could drown in here.

Right now.

Together.

But no. I refused to let him drown until we had an official date. Or at least a few more practice sessions. Besides, who wanted to die with all these morons who had refused to listen, chanted for me to fall to my death, and watched me get pummeled by a Smurf? Not the kind of crowd I wished to spend my last moments on earth with.

We could run but would most likely get trampled by the panic of the crowd. Some might make it. But with

Gabriel's blindness and my bruised ribs, we'd most likely be the bodies others walked out on.

"Stay put. I'll be back to make you bleed." Oh, good, like he hadn't already. Indigo pointed his machete at me, then turned and walked toward a group of his Runners who were holding Trace. Or trying to. It looked like the balance was shifting. Trace met him halfway.

Oblivious to the rising level of voices, shouts, and noise, Trace and Indigo started to make an uneasy peace between them. It seemed each faction had about the same number of players. And unless they didn't want both sides butchering one another, they would have to learn to share. Me. *Great.*

They argued over who got to use me first, and I don't mean in a wave-reading capacity.

I didn't think I was their type. Scrawny and a ballbuster. But that was Runners for ya. Just not too picky.

"The Gastown steam clock is showing. Gastown is coming back," someone shouted.

"Let's go. The place is full of antiques and jewelry and gold."

Oh, my. The jingle played in my mind: *Antiques and jewelry and gold, oh, my. Antiques and jewelry and gold . . .*

Gold? I didn't think so. But wasn't that just like human nature to think there was free treasure when the fires went out and the floodwaters receded? When something was left unguarded, abandoned, stranded?

There was no gold in Gastown unless you counted a ruined pocket watch or ring. The gold was a myth, an urban legend started by the Runners years ago when the infrastructure first went down. The tale was designed to keep people in and around New Vancouver, to keep the port alive and thriving for the Runner ships that now ruled the sea. I should know: Seamus was one of the first who put it in the wind. With human nature being what it is, no matter how much our world crumbled, how much of it when to pure shit, gold was gold. And people would always want it. No, tonight there would be no gold found in New Vancouver. Tonight there would be only death.

"Blue," Gabriel whispered, "is something happening?"

I took his hand in mine. The Runners were still arguing over me.

Holding Gabriel's hand, I placed it over my heart.

"Yes," I whispered.

"Wave?"

His fingers splayed and the warmth of his touch on my breast brought tears to my eyes. There was no denying it: I had missed him.

Missed loving him.

And now to end like this?

That's rich, Blue. In love with a Runner scum.

Uncle Seamus, once again in my mind. And he was right: I was in love with a Runner, this Runner. And always would be.

I looked at Gabriel, and even with his swollen eyes and battered face, he couldn't have looked more beautiful.

Gabriel hung his head, clearly miserable that there was nothing he could do. He pulled me into his arms.

I risked the reprisal from the Kings of Pain, and clung to him for the first time since he had disappeared. I realized now that it wasn't his fault. He had no say in the matter. No control. I knew what that was like. What my childhood was like.

He'd been caught in a trap, a setup, and now a death sentence. And Tsunami Blue—me—should have known better than to get us caught in her own wave. What a big help I was turning out to be.

I pushed away before we got caught in each other's arms. It would only hasten Gabriel's death. Something I just couldn't bear.

"Where is the wave, exactly?" Gabriel asked, his voice strong, steady. I could tell he was thinking things through too, looking for options, for a way out, for a way to live. "Please tell me it's not as far as New False Bay." His voice broke. "The boys."

I grabbed his hands in mine, "No, no, Gabriel. The boys are safe. The wave is here in New Vancouver, now." I just couldn't get into the fact that the boys were here too. What good purpose could it serve to worry Gabriel now? And I hadn't lied: The boys were safe; I was sure of it.

"I can't see. I'm too weak. I can't stop it."

I kissed his hands, his swollen knuckles, his broken nails. "No one can, Gabriel."

"You don't understand. I *need* my eyes. I can—"

"Break it up, you two." Wolf Man approached us. He was having a hell of a time holding the wolves. I thought of the elephants in Sri Lanka who ran from the water long before anyone had a clue. If he didn't release the animals soon, they'd turn on him.

"Trace and Indigo made a decision," Wolf Man said, like a little kid who couldn't wait to tell a secret. "Guess they'll be sharing you."

Sharing me? They were supposed to fight over me, and kill each other in the process. Simple. *Well, shit.*

"What?" I stood up slowly. "Are they going to saw me in half?"

"Nope. A little threesome, as I understand. Trace has something special planned, I 'ear.'" He motioned to my ear and laughed at his joke.

I, on the other hand, didn't.

He'd been holding the leashes with two hands. He switched to one to grab his crotch, pumping forward and back. Like I'd never seen that before.

Still, it was a dangerous thing to do. The wolves worked

as a pack, and the alpha, a huge black animal, led the way. He felt it in the leash, the weakness. All the animals needed was a spark. They got it from Gabriel. His fury was almost tangible.

He couldn't see, but he took a gamble and swung, making a miraculous, brutal connection with Wolf Man. The brute went down with a thud.

"Tell the bastards," Gabriel said in a voice that could cut steel, "that I don't share."

The black wolf broke first, turned on its handler and attacked. Wolf Man's throat was torn out in thirty seconds. Four others followed suit.

It was just the chaos we needed.

The attacking wolves and subsequent body count threw a block for us.

I'm here, Blue, the sea whispered to me. *I've arrived.*

I looked for the bullhorn. Thank God it was where I had left it.

"So, don't believe me, assholes? Well, have a look." I dropped the bullhorn and passed the torch above my arm, illuminating the wave tattoo. Cobalt and aqua and turquoise danced in the light of the flames.

"Believe!" I screamed.

I watched as the crowd went from anger, to hate, to insanity. And I watched the water rush in and sweep around their legs. The wave was here.

"Satan," someone yelled. The masses were on their feet, panicked and rushing the cage.

"Witch," another chimed in. Bodies pushed and slammed against the wire.

"Whore," another yelled. Well, now, *that* was beyond insulting.

Hundreds of people climbed the mesh, just as I had a short time ago.

I grabbed the torch and Gabriel's hand and we ran for the back entrance that Snake had come through. The cage would be a death trap in a matter of minutes.

Trace's and Indigo's men tried to stop us. That lasted about two seconds. They jumped to "every man for himself" pretty damn quick. A world record, I was thinking. Runners—go figure.

I could hear Trace and Indigo swearing, screaming futile orders that were being ignored. How I prayed they would both drown. More and more screams filled the arena as the water, so strong now, swept in. In the crush of madness drums of burning oil overturned as people ran and pushed and trampled. Flames spread, first to the stage and then to bodies.

As the water rushed in, we ran out.

Out to the grassy knoll that went *up* and *up* and *up*.

Blessed up.

Gabriel tripped. "Blue, I'm slowing us down. I can't see. I—"

"No. We can do this," I shouted. I stopped and grabbed his swollen and battered hand. I could see what he couldn't. Lions Gate Bridge. Reaching high into the night sky, with the tower at 364 feet, it would be a safe haven. If we could reach it in time, and we could climb—

You can reach it, Blue. You can. Run, run, run. The sea, whispering, like always.

"We're running," I said back. I knelt and helped Gabriel to his feet. I ran like the old days, when I was back on the beach with Max. And Gabriel, so strong, so brave, ran with me. And I was by his side for every stumble, every fall.

I told Gabriel I would not leave him.

I told him I didn't care if he couldn't see; I had always looked better in the dark.

I told him to get new friends, get Max back, build my kayak.

I told him to live for Nick and Alec.

I told him to live for me.

And last, I told him I loved him. Even if he was a Runner and a delivery boy and a dark angel who had made some bad choices. Nothing a twelve-step program couldn't fix.

But the sea, unrelenting, once again caught up.

We were engulfed by salt water; the sea tore my hand from Gabriel's grip and we were separated by foam and water and crashing debris.

The sound was deafening. Still I screamed for him. And I heard him scream for me.

"Damn it, you owe me," I shouted at the sea. "You've taken my family. Please. Don't take him too."

I felt myself lifted on the water, up and up. I stopped tumbling and I could swim; I could breathe; I could reach out to hang on to the steel girder that appeared before me. I slammed into the metal beam. My ribs screamed in protest. But I hung on. And all the while the sea laughed.

Gabriel was delivered to me moments later.

His strong arms held me and we found ourselves balanced precariously on the steel beam. Clinging to Gabriel, I watched the water as it tumbled and swept bodies of the dead on to final unknown resting places. And when I saw Ring Girl's lifeless body battered by debris, I gripped Gabriel harder, knowing it could have been me.

The sea whispered to me: *A gift, Blue. A gift.* An amber float appeared. Such a small token for so much pain, for so much death . . . I let it slip away.

The once beautiful and famous Lions Gate Bridge was now a corroded and rusted skeleton of itself. Still, the bridge held strong, though it groaned and swayed as the water battered its base. I watched the water rise, while all along the sea whispered, *A little monster, Blue, just big enough to tickle your toes.*

When the wave crested, just below my boots, and water started to slink back into the night, Gabriel finally dozed off in my arms. Fighting the cold and the wet and fog, he trembled in his sleep, and I heard him call my name. I talked with the sea, pleaded with it. "If you want to bring a gift, please, please, please bring me my boat."

Moments later, the sea, the monster that had taken so much from me, finally gave something back. The sleek black-hulled sailboat rocked in the now receding waters just off to our left.

I looked at the sailboat I'd come to love, waiting for us, and I still could not believe it. I'd never asked the sea for so much. I'd never dreamed it would deliver.

We made our descent and scrambled aboard. As we sailed out of the inlet, I knew that New Vancouver was now New New Vancouver. I sighed and shook my head. Another coastline had changed, another city lost.

Chapter Thirty

Gabriel slept soundly in the V-berth of his sailboat.

Which was really my boat.

But I'd given it back to him, so once again, it was his boat. Whatever. Bottom line? I was a really bad pirate. I had buyer's remorse. That is, pirate's remorse. Okay. I'd just call it what it was—guilt.

After all, no one looked better on this boat than Gabriel Black.

Exhaustion had set in, total and complete. I didn't think one of my waves could wake him up.

This time it was my turn to strip him naked and tuck him in. I loved it. Loved him.

I crawled in next to him, snuggling against the side less bruised. Believe me, it was hard to choose. His beautiful body, now stained with iodine, had more cuts, scrapes, and bruises than healthy skin. Still, the golden color fought to shine through the battered areas, once again reminding me that Gabriel wasn't originally from around here.

So many unanswered questions. All that we had been through and yet so many secrets. For both of us.

Tonight we sailed north, deep into the heart of the New Canadian Gulf Islands. These islands were wild and remote. There was a rawness, a stillness about them that I loved. Craggy cliffs surrounded us. There were deep, clear bays, and even a magnificent waterfall. I felt hidden and safe here, for the first time in days.

We had tied up to a rotting piling that held up the remnants of an abandoned dock. The dock stopped at the mouth of the waterfall and the path that wove beside it. I was grateful for the constant rush of water from the waterfall. Grateful because I could hear the message the sea was whispering in it.

We were running out of time.

At some point we would make our way back to New False Bay. A place I swore I'd never go back to. But to help escort the boys and Aubrey home, back to the safe haven of the familiar bay, I would suck it up and go. After all, I'd do anything for those kids. And both of us couldn't wait to get back to them.

For now they were still tucked safely away on Grouse Mountain. I had told Gabriel that his little band of two had grown to three, and Aubrey was her name. And didn't I just love him all the more when he flashed his twin dimples and simply said, "Good. I can't wait to meet her."

The waters around what was once New Vancouver had been almost impossible to navigate. The sea, still angry, had filled with giant swallowing swells. The sea had also filled with Runner ships. All looking for us. For me. Unfortunately, two of the ships we sighted belonged to Trace and Indigo. I should have known they were just too stubborn to die. *Damn it anyway.*

Gabriel moaned in his sleep and I put my hand on his heart, calming him. I brushed his long black hair from his shoulders and kissed his neck. I couldn't see his eyes, but I knew they were swollen, the flesh around them angry and red. How I wanted this man. With or without sight, legs or no legs, arms or no arms, I'd take him anyway I could. I'd just take him, my pirate with the golden skin; take him and sail and sail and sail. Away from Runners, and ruined cities. Away from filth and violence and unhappy souls. Just away.

But of course that wasn't possible.

Gabriel had a family in the boys. And Bacon. And maybe little Aubrey. And I was crazy about them too.

That's why I couldn't stay. In this bed, on this boat, in his life.

I was a danger to them all. I was Tsunami Blue. The wave girl everyone wanted to use for their own gain.

It wasn't over.

My thoughts turned to Indigo and Trace, such evil men in a lawless world. How could I risk bringing that into the innocent lives of children? Of Nick and Alec? Of Aubrey?

Arriving under a blanket of stars last night, we had both been so exhausted, so physically and mentally beaten up, that we had simply collapsed the moment the boat sailed into this tiny bay.

And the second night was already upon us.

I wished time would just stop. Just end at this moment with Gabriel Black in my arms, and the stars, always familiar, winking, watching, smiling. Time could just take a holiday and leave us in the safety of this bay, this blessed sanctuary.

The bay was pictured on a creased and frayed postcard Gabriel had pinned next to a picture of me at age five, sitting in the Thai sun. Both, it seemed, were destinations for him.

He had never been here, he said, had always wanted to find it, to experience it. And now, after all these years of searching, searching for this place, searching for me, he couldn't see any of it. Couldn't see me.

Gabriel Black was still blind.

As I caressed his back, he moaned and rolled, taking me in his arms. I went to him willingly, wanting this, wanting him.

All of him.

Because time wouldn't stop. Men like Trace and Indigo wouldn't stop. The waves, huge and monstrous, wouldn't stop.

And time, of course, would never—could never—stop.

The sea was living in the waterfall now, whispering to me throughout the night: *Coming, coming, coming, Blue. A wave like no other.*

I slipped out of his arms and off the bunk, padding out to the cabin, and climbed out into the cockpit. I couldn't put it off any longer. I thought of Nick and Alec, of our mystery girl, Aubrey. I thought of Bacon and pictured Max, waiting for me on the shores of New San Juan. And last I saw the children, the thousands I knew in my heart were out there, waiting, waiting for Tsunami Blue to tell them, *Sleep, sleep now, little ones; the wave tonight does too.*

But it wouldn't for long.

We had two days. At best. The message had been tapping on the hull, had been sprinkled in the evening rain, had shown up—when I cried alone while Gabriel slept—in my tears.

Coming, coming, coming.

So I now had a fairly good idea when. But where? Where?

I had to have a conversation with the sea. And I would have to go to the waterfall to do it.

I had the time frame when the wave would come. Now all I needed was the place. I had to broadcast soon. Or there would be no one left on our blue, blue planet to broadcast to.

I huddled on a rock under the falls and listened. The winter night chilled me. The message in the water chilled me more.

The wave would peak at New Seattle. What was left of

the city would be underwater completely. So would the New San Juans, including as far up as New False Bay and farther. And it would roll on and on and on.

A monster like no other.

We might not be safe even this far north. Was anywhere safe?

I couldn't stop it. What good was it to know what was coming? I couldn't stop the death. Stop the bodies that would float up afterward, their stark, unseeing eyes accusing me.

If you knew, if you know so much, why couldn't you stop it? Why? How many times had I been asked that question?

I put my head on my knees and cried.

"Blue?"

I heard his voice, soft, like silk against bare skin on a summer's day. It floated through the air and wrapped around me like a lover, offering me warmth. Protection. Peace.

And how I needed that. How I needed him.

"Gabriel?"

"I'm over here."

I watched him walk the path, his hands against the rocks for guidance, working toward me, toward my voice. He had on jeans, the fly not even fully zipped, the metal button undone. He had dressed in a hurry and set out to find me.

It was in his steps, in the way he moved—blind. Gabriel was still blind. Right? I watched him struggle for his footing, search for handholds. Yes. Still blind.

Tears tumbled down my cheeks. I tried to wipe them away. I didn't care that he couldn't see. Hell, I could see enough for both of us. And yet in this world, there was so much I didn't want to see anymore, didn't want to see ever again. I went to him, held him, kissed him. And yet the tears would not stop.

I cried for the souls that would be lost in a matter of days; I cried for Max and Seamus, for my mother and father and Finn. And I cried for us—for Gabriel, for me, for the us that would never be. I cried hardest for the kids.

"Oh, Blue. Please don't. Don't cry."

We slid together down on the rocks, the spray of the waterfall misting over us, the cold of the shale pressing beneath our bodies. Gabriel was on top of me now and I clung to him. I wouldn't let him go, fearing I might lose him if I did. I couldn't breathe without him; I couldn't live; I couldn't go on.

He moved against me, opening my legs to him. The low pull in my belly flared, and I was damp with need and wanting. I wrapped my legs around him, pulling him into me, moving against him, finding a rhythm I didn't know I had.

Gabriel moaned and whispered, "Not like this, not here. Please. I might hurt you. I—"

I kissed him. It was hard and bruising and real. Real because I loved him so much, real because it might have been the last time for this, for the two of us.

Coming, Blue, the waterfall whispered, *coming, coming* . . .

I pushed back from Gabriel and sat up, stripping off my fleece, my tank, my pink bra. I couldn't get them off fast enough, couldn't get to him fast enough.

"Blue"—Gabriel held out his hand—"what are you doing?"

I took his hand and placed it on my bare breast. He stroked and gently squeezed until my nipples were tender and sore with need. And when he put his lips over my nipple, pulling and tugging, I gasped. I didn't know . . . didn't know it could be like this, could be like this with him.

Gabriel responded by stripping off his own fleece. I helped with his thermal and the two of us were flesh on flesh.

"I didn't want it to be like this, didn't want to scare you, hurt you."

"You could never hurt me, Gabriel. Never. I love you, love you." And we were lost in a kiss.

As we broke from the kiss, I reached up and touched his red and swollen eyes. "Does this hurt?" I asked as I traced the angry welts. We were going to make love. For the first time. And it broke my heart that he would not be able to see me. To see how much I loved him.

"No. Not much now." He sighed. "Sometimes I think I see shadows or a flicker of light, but then nothing. I'm sorry. How I want to see you. I want to see the amazing blue of your eyes"—he kissed my lips—"to see that blush that makes them the color of the ocean"—he kissed my neck—"to see your beautiful, perfect body"—he kissed my nipples, one, then the other. I gasped.

When Gabriel came to me, our bodies melting into each other, I knew I was ready. I'd been ready my whole life. Ready for him. For the man I loved.

"This might hurt," he whispered. "I'll try to be gentle, to hold back, to—"

"Never hold back, Gabriel. Not from me, please. Not ever."

And then I said, "I won't break, tough guy. You've seen me in action, remember?"

Gabriel laughed, and when I rose to meet him, when he entered me for the first time, my breath caught and my heart beat a rapid tattoo: *I love you, I love you, I love you.*

Tears fell. Heartbeats pounded. Pain and joy and blood all mingling for the first time, for my first time. And I wasn't sorry, wasn't sorry, not ever sorry.

The feeling built and built and built until at last we climaxed together, both of us screaming each other's name until our voices became harsh, then soft, then whispers.

"I love you, tough guy," I said.

And then Gabriel said those words to me, those words I hadn't heard since I was five and sitting on a Thai beach in my mother's arms.

"I love you, Blue."

Chapter Thirty-one

"Are you sore?" Gabriel had come up behind me and smoothed my hair.

"No." *Yes*. But a good yes.

Heat warmed my cheeks.

He kissed me. "Liar," he said.

He had sat with me most of the morning, listening to my broadcasts. I had hit it hard, every hour on the hour. I spilled every detail, telling people to head far north, stay out of New Seattle, go upland, go up, up, up.

Taking a break, I crossed my legs and put my feet up. I had my badass boots on, and what I wouldn't have given to have Max here barking at them. But even if Max were alive, I couldn't save him now. I might die too. I'd try not to think about it; I couldn't afford the emotional toll. I'd cry later. That much I knew.

Holding coffee in my hand, I looked at Gabriel. He'd been thoughtful all morning, quiet.

I tried to lighten the mood.

"Where to, tough guy? The Bahamas?"

He looked at me through unseeing eyes.

"Blue, we have to go."

"I know." I sighed, thinking he meant leaving here. I was sad too. I'd never forget this place. I shifted in my chair and felt the wonderful twinge of discomfort.

Wonderful because it served as a reminder of him, of us. Yes, I would never forget this place, for all my life.

"We go to New Seattle."

I couldn't have been more surprised than if he had said the North Pole.

"You're kidding."

"I'm not," he said.

"Gabriel, it's death in waiting."

"It's a chance I have to take."

"Why?"

"Because"—and he ran his hand through his hair—"because I can stop it."

"Gabriel"—I was out of my chair now and kneeling at his side—"you can't. You can't. No one can."

He looked at me now, really looked. I gasped and touched his eyes. "You can see," I said as a tear tumbled down my cheek. "You can see?"

He took my hand and kissed it. "I can. Just barely."

"But how? When?" I could hardly contain my excitement. I felt overwhelmed. Teary. And that was just annoying. These tears had to stop. Still, I was so happy I wanted to cry.

"Off and on all morning. I didn't want to tell you in case it was like before."

"Before?"

"Like when the shadows came, then went."

"I was so scared. The snake poison—"

"I think I may have John to thank."

"John? Snake Man John?"

"Yes. John. It could not have been the real thing, the real mist. If it were, I would never see again."

"You knew this for certain?"

"I did."

"And you didn't tell me?"

"I didn't want to worry you."

I punched him in the arm.

"Hey. Ow." He rubbed his arm.

"Get over it, tough guy, 'cause next time—and there had better not be a next time, by the way—but next time, worry me." I started to rub his arm for him. Not that I'd hit him that hard. But it was just so damn nice to touch him. I stopped and put my arms around him. And damn it all, I started to cry. Again.

He folded his arms around me and shook his head. "Your logic, Blue." He kissed me. The kiss was long, powerful, perfect. He pulled away.

"And it's because I can see that I have to go to New Seattle. I need you to come with me."

I didn't know what to say. *Great, you got your sight back, but lost your mind*? I wasn't sure I liked that trade.

"Blue"—he took my hand in his—"I'm not a Runner."

"You are. You have the tattoo to prove it. Just show it to anyone and they'll tell you."

"Be serious."

I gave him a look.

"You know how you always said I wasn't from around here?"

"Yeah," I said slowly. "So you're not the boy next door. What are you? A tourist?"

"I've traveled extensively. Sailing to places all around the globe. I sailed up from way south. It was hot—tropical even."

"Tropical?" I asked in amazement. I thought of the magazines Uncle Seamus had stashed under his bunk, the ones with white beaches and azure waters. I did, however, try to block out the pics of the naked centerfolds. And then I remembered Thailand and the beaches of Phuket just before the wave. I gasped. He had traveled around the world, right?

"Thailand? I said. "Have you been to Phuket?"

His eyes said it all, even red and swollen; I could plainly read the sadness there.

"Many years ago."

"Were you"—my voice dropped to a whisper, my throat closed, and I fought back the sting of more tears—"were you there? Were you there when the wave . . ." I couldn't say any more.

"I was."

I swayed and dropped back into the chair. I put my head in my hands as the memory of that fateful day slammed into me. Christmas day on the beach in Phuket in 2004 was the day when the sea had first called my name. It was the day the sea had taken everyone I had ever loved away from me.

It was now Gabriel's turn to kneel before me. He took my hand in his and reached out to lift my chin, forcing me to meet his gaze.

"I'm so sorry."

"About?" I pulled away from him, not knowing if I wanted to hear the answer or not. I didn't want pity. I didn't want . . . Hell, I didn't know what I wanted.

"I couldn't stop it," he said gently as he brushed back a strand of my hair.

I swore I could feel the color drain from my face. I felt dizzy, sick. All I could do was stare.

"I was there, on holiday with my uncle," he continued. "I was twelve. And I didn't know"—his voice broke—"I didn't know the wave was coming. If I had I would have saved them. I would have saved them all."

I could hear the agony in his voice, the regret. Still, I couldn't believe it. I needed more of this story.

"How could a twelve-year-old stop a wave, a tsunami like that? How?" I didn't believe him, couldn't believe him. If I did I'd have to live with the reality that my family could have been saved, along with thousands and thousands of others. Saved by this very man kneeling before me.

He pushed away from the chair and stood. Running a hand through his dark hair, shoving it away from his face, he started to pace.

"I watched the media like everyone else. I watched you at five years old being heralded as the Angel of the Beach. I watched as they followed you with cameras and stuck microphones in your face. I kept watching you. You were so small and yet so brave, never crying, always silent, staring with those amazing blue eyes, and I could see your pain. So much so that I started to feel it, to live with it. And it tore me up inside."

"Why?" I whispered.

"Because I could have stopped it. All of it."

Exasperated, he ran both hands through his hair and shook his head.

"I watched you board the plane, flying off to an undisclosed location. The media had finally been forced to give you a break. But not before they captured it."

"Captured what?" I asked.

"That single tear." He reached over my head into an open cupboard that I thought had just held candles and soap. Pushing aside the contents he put pressure on a small strip of teak. The board sprang up. There it was. A secret compartment. One that I had apparently missed. *Damn.* He pulled out a newspaper clipping locked tight in a Ziploc bag. He handed it to me.

Gabriel had saved only the picture. There I stood on the steps of a private plane looking toward the water, looking out to the sea that now held my family. And there it was: the tear. The first one I had shed in public. Gabriel's voice jolted me back.

"The media wasn't allowed to know where you were going. They lost you that day. And so did I."

He knelt before me and gathered me in his arms. "I've spent a lifetime looking for you. At first it was about the waves. About stopping them once and for all. Your talent lets you know when and where they are coming. And my talent? I can stop them. But now that I've found you, it's about so much more. It's about you. And me. Together. I can't ever let you go."

I pulled away from him. I could see the hurt in his eyes. He thought I was rejecting him. And maybe I was. Did he want me for the same reason all the others did? Did he want me only because I could predict waves? And could he really stop them? I stood up and pushed past him. It was my turn to pace.

"So you what, Gabriel? Smoke peyote and dance with rattlesnakes between your teeth? Does this stop the waves?"

The dark gaze turned to midnight. And even through the swelling and redness I saw the anger in his eyes.

And that just pushed a button of my own. Now both of us were pissed. *Great.* That always worked out so well.

"Look, Magic Man." Boy, did that ever get a look. "Can I take just a minute here and first thank God, as you should, that you can see again?"

Raw emotion caught hold of my heart as I thought of his beautiful eyes so dark, so hard to read, such a big part of who he was, of his mystery and soul, that just the thought of Gabriel never seeing again . . . ? Unbearable. I had refused to think about it before, not knowing if I could be strong enough for him. And me.

"I am grateful, Blue." He stood. "You can't possibly know how much."

"Why? Because you can read tea leaves? Or scattered bones in the sand? Or how about this? Conjure up the wave gods that kick ass and the waves just stop and it's all good?"

"I'm grateful because I can see you, Blue."

That gave me pause. But was I being used? I felt so defensive, and so damned confused, I just had to take one more swipe. And it was a good one. I mean, come on, stop waves? In all my years of searching, of reading and begging Seamus for answers, I had never heard of anyone who had a power like mine. When had I stopped believing that it was possible? When had I become so jaded? And if this was true, where had he been all these years that humanity had been battered and bruised and dying? Where had he been for my family?

Why not stop waves, whispered the sea through the hull. *Why not, Blue?*

I ignored the whispers of logic and let my ragged emotions run wild. I went for the low blow. "If you can stop waves, why not stop the one that killed my family?" Tears sprang to my eyes. "If you could see it, if you were there, why not stop it? Why?"

He slammed his fist on the teak wall next to my head in frustration. I jumped out of fear, and saw the disappointment in his eyes. It broke my heart. It was only an old habit, an old reaction left over from the days of Seamus and Runner camps. I had nothing to fear from this man. If I knew anything I knew that.

But was the Runner Gabriel back? Where was my Gabriel, the one I had given myself to so totally?

He turned from me. "I tried," I heard him say. "God help me, Blue, I tried."

I watched his shoulders slump and heard the sigh. And then, "I need you, Blue. I'm lost without you."

I put my hand on his shoulder and turned him toward me. "Need me for what?" I said. "To stop waves?" I held my breath, not wanting to hear the answer. Did he want me for the same reason as all the others who had come before? Did he want me because I was a freak?

He reached for me, and my breaking heart pushed me to reach back. I let him hold me. And that was when I heard it. The whisper in my ear.

"I need you because I love you. Because I don't want to live without you. The fact that you can predict waves is just a bonus."

And then he kissed me.

The shortwave radio crackled to life. Static filled the air, and a young voice, timid and soft, tried to fight its way through the static and interference.

"Tsunami Blue? Are you there?" For a moment the tiny voice faded, then came in loud and clear. "This is Aubrey."

"And me, Alec."

"And Nick."

Gabriel broke from our kiss and got to the mic before I did. "Guys, where are you? Tell me you're still north. Tell me you're still on the mountain."

"We're home, Just Gabe. We're at New False Bay." It was one of the boys—which one I couldn't be sure. I watched the color drain from Gabriel's face, and I was pretty sure I was just as pale. The boys and Aubrey were right in the path of the wave.

Gabriel gripped the mic so hard his knuckles turned white. "Why didn't you stay put?" he said. I could see he was trying like hell to keep the fury out of his voice, to disguise the fear. It wasn't working.

"What's wrong?" Nick asked. Or was it Alec? It didn't matter. What mattered was that Gabriel's fear had bled over the airwaves to the kids. And I had to stop it before they became terrified. I gently took the mic from his hands. He had been gripping it so tightly his knuckles were white.

"Hey, guys, it's Blue." I made my voice sound as light and upbeat as possible. "Just Gabe is a bit surprised, that's all. We thought you were in New Vancouver." I bit my lip. How should I ask the next question? I had to be delicate. "Have you been listening in?" I held my breath.

"Yeah. We heard about—" They cut out. And then, "the wave." And then, "scared."

Gabriel shook his head at me, and I read the raw fear in his eyes. He knew what I did: The kids were directly in the path of the biggest wave our planet had ever known. How could we possibly get to them in time?

Gabriel gripped my shoulders and turned me to face him. "I can stop it, Blue. Believe me. But we've got to leave now."

I gave a sharp nod and got back on the air. I told the kids to be strong, not to be afraid, that we were coming for them. We just had to make one little stop along the way. I kinda left out the part that the "little stop" would be New Seattle, where Gabriel Black, my maybe Runner turned cage fighter, aka fallen angel, all-around tough guy, and father of Max, was going to stop the biggest tsunami known to mankind. But lastly? I told them how much we loved them.

I watched as Gabriel crumpled to the bench, his head in his hands. He looked up. "They're my family, Blue. I have to save them. We have to."

"I know."

"They've been with me a long time, since I found them in that tree. Their dad," his voice broke, "was my best friend. When the wave came, I couldn't save him, but damn it, I saved his sons.

I nodded, unable to speak.

"They're my sons now. Mine."

I dropped the mic to the floor, grabbed Gabriel by his thermal, and pulled him up. I stood on tiptoe and pulled him down into a crushing kiss. He responded by kissing me back, fierce and hard. Gabriel the warrior was back.

I pulled away first. "Okay. It's official," I said. "We just had our first fight."

Gabriel raised a dark eyebrow. "Our first?"

"Yes. Our first as, well, you know, a couple." I felt the all too familiar heat climb into my cheeks.

"Okay," he said cautiously. "A couple."

"And we just kissed and made up."

"We made up?" He sounded hopeful.

"We made up. Now let's go stop a wave, tough guy."

Thick clouds had moved over the moon, and Gabriel and I welcomed the cover of darkness. We sailed south toward New Seattle. Our spinnaker with the 666 symbol was lost in the night sky, blending into the inky darkness. But I could hear the whispers of the sea echoing against the sails, bouncing a warning off the stretched and stiff canvas.

Hurry. Hurry. HURRY.

Gabriel's sight had continued to improve, and just like always he moved across the deck like the seasoned pro he was. He moved like a pirate.

Like a Runner.

But he wasn't, right? I tried to sort it out. My head said yes, he could be. My heart said no way. But for now the question was not up for discussion. We had other, bigger distractions.

Trace had found us.

We had sailed at breakneck speed. The wind had been at our backs and the sea had calmed, sending us smooth, flat waters. We had buried the rail and made good time. Good, but apparently not good enough.

We spotted Trace and his crew on the horizon at daybreak just a few nautical miles from the shores of New San Juan. There could be no mistaking the boat. The rails were lined with human skulls, and a bloody and beaten corpse was hanging from the bowsprit. *Oh, joy.*

"We still have the lead," said Gabriel as he lowered his binoculars.

"Maybe they haven't seen us," I said. But even I didn't believe the hope in my voice.

I heard the crackle of the shortwave filter up through the open hatch as it came to life downstairs. I bit my lower lip and wiped my clammy hands on my jeans. Fear had once again invaded my chest, kicking my heartbeat into high gear.

"Now, who could that be? A telemarketer?" I said, trying to kick some smart-ass into my voice. It wasn't working.

We set the wheel and both ran down to the hold. We knew it wasn't the kids; we had told them to stay off the air. It was safer for them that way. After all, you never knew who might be listening in.

The radio snapped to life and through the static was the all too familiar voice of Trace. He sounded as wicked and evil as ever.

"I assume you have my cargo, Black. Don't deny it, because of course you do. You are either delivering her to that bastard Indigo, or you're keeping her for yourself. No matter. You are dead, and she is mine. See you soon."

The radio faded to silence.

Then it crackled to life once more. "Oh. By the way, I have a special place reserved for your head on my rail. And I have a special place reserved for Blue. *In. My. Bed.*"

He drew out the last three words, and the menace in his voice spoke volumes.

Gabriel grabbed the mic. His voice seethed with rage. "You never listen, Trace. *I. Don't. Fucking. Share. Ever.*" And then, "But if the price is right and you can catch us in that derelict dump you call a boat, I might consider a trade."

"Aw, what? You not in love anymore?" Trace laughed.

"Let's just say the scrawny bitch is getting on my nerves." Gabriel threw the mic to the floor.

I knew if I could see myself that my mouth would be hanging open. Scrawny bitch? Getting on his nerves? If the price is right?

"Um, Gabriel? Scrawny bitch here has a few questions?"

"Just trust me on this, Blue. Follow me."

I followed him back up the ladder to the deck. I shook my head in disbelief. *If you can catch us?* Like Trace needed another reason to chase us? Damned male testosterone. Although I must say, I did heartily agree about the *asshole* part.

Once back on top I watched the Runner ship getting closer and closer. This was so not good. I thought we had the fast boat.

"Um, Gabriel?"

"Yeah?"

"They're gaining on us."

"That's the plan."

Plan? That was the plan? I folded my arms around my waist and started to count to ten to calm myself. I didn't make it past three.

"I don't like your plan."

"Trust me. It will work."

Okay. "Um, so we get caught and what? You lose your head and I—"

"You stay with me." He dropped the line he was holding, walked across the deck, took me in his arms, and kissed me. He pulled away and looked me in the eyes with that dark look of his. "You will always stay with me."

We slowed our pace to a crawl. Our sails slackened and the boom swung loosely back and forth. We bobbed precariously close to the shore of New San Juan. We were now rowing distance from the beach where so much of my life had played out. This was the beach where I had been kidnapped by Gabriel, where I had watched my uncle die, where I had last seen Max.

Max.

My heart squeezed painfully and I couldn't help but scan the shore for him.

"Don't put yourself through this, Blue. He's not there." Gabriel had came up behind and wrapped his arms around me. I blinked back tears.

"You ready?"

I nodded. It was time to take care of Trace. No way could we sail into New Seattle with him glued to our tail. And if we didn't make it to New Seattle in time to stop the wave, the kids would die. New False Bay was in the wave's path too.

And that just wasn't an option.

That left us with only one solution. Trace and the Runner scum who traveled with him would have to . . . have to . . . I stumbled over the thought. They would all have to die.

"Showtime." Gabriel pushed me against the mast and tied my arms behind me using a knot a two-year-old could get out of.

I had been used for a lot of things in my life. But this was the first time I had ever been bait. And if it ended like this, with me being fed to a Runner like chum to a shark, I was truly going to be pissed.

Gabriel went below to arm himself.

Trace's boat slowly approached our starboard side. It was still a way off, but I could see Trace pacing like the madman he was. I could hear him swearing across the water.

I counted five of them on board. That left us down by three. *Shit.*

Gabriel appeared on deck with a bottle of absinthe in his hand and a bowie knife in the other.

I knitted my brows and frowned. Was this really a good time to drink? He pulled the cork out with his teeth, spit it on the deck, and paused to take a swig. A very big swig. Very piratelike, I had to say. But still . . .

"Um, Gabriel—"

He held up a hand. "Not now, Blue."

"But—" I got the look. The dark one that turned my Gabriel into killer/murderer Gabriel. *Shit.* Now I wanted to take a swig.

He walked over and pulled a red bandanna out of his pocket.

"Open up."

I narrowed my eyes. "You are not going to gag me, Gabriel Black."

"I am."

"You're not."

He shoved it in my mouth. "Just play along. Can you do that for five minutes?"

I sighed and nodded. The bandanna tasted like dry, scratchy oatmeal, but it smelled of almonds and honey and sunshine. I didn't know what amazed me the most, the fact that I was agreeing to keep my mouth shut for five minutes, or that Gabriel, a supposed Runner scum, did laundry.

We watched as Trace's boat neared. I could smell rotting flesh and it was all I could do not to gag. Gabriel stood next to me with his knife to my throat. He held up the bottle of absinthe in clear view, and I could see Trace's crew lick their lips. All but one.

John the Snake Man was standing next to Trace. His hands were bound, and crimson now mixed with the greens and blues of his tattooed scales. The crimson, of course, was blood. I was glad to note, however, that the man still had his ears.

I could see the tic in Gabriel's jaw as he caught sight of John.

"Gabriel. Looks like you got tired of running," said Trace. His men had steered the boat alongside ours and secured a line. We were rafted together now. All his men had to do was step aboard.

"Well, what are you going to do, Trace? Your boat always was faster."

Was not, I thought.

"Besides, I'm tired of the girl." Gabriel ran his knife along my jugular. He looked at me and gave me a wink only I could see. "She never stops running her mouth."

Nice.

"I'll make good use of her mouth."

Yuck. I saw Gabriel's fist close tight on his blade with that comment.

"I see the Snake Man has pissed you off," Gabe called.

Trace laughed and punched John in the gut. The blow took him to his knees. "You might say that I was disappointed when I found the mist lacked a certain blinding element."

"What are we gonna do here, Trace?" Gabriel held up his bottle for the crew to see. And the crew, upon seeing the green fairy, started to get mighty restless. "Are we making a deal and drinking on it, or what?"

"Are you in position for making a deal?"

Gabriel pressed the blade to my throat. "I believe I am."

Trace narrowed his eyes and licked his lips nervously. "You would kill her?"

"I would."

That gave him pause.

"I told you. I'm sick of her and the cat-and-mouse

game that comes with her. Make it worth my while and we all get out of here alive." Gabriel took another swig.

"What do you want?"

"I want out," Gabriel said.

"Out?"

"Out of this with my life. I want my ship and I want the gold you have stashed under the fourth skull on the starboard side."

Trace didn't deny it. And why would he? If Gabriel said it was there, it would be. Runners were notorious for not keeping secrets.

"Indigo will hunt you."

"That's my problem. And for the record, I'm sick of the blue bastard."

Trace laughed. "That makes two of us, my man. That makes two of us. Okay. Deal. Send the bitch over."

I did an eye roll, and I was pretty sure Gabriel would have too. But that was not his style. He was more of a knife-to-the-throat kind of guy.

Gabriel laughed and played the blade along my neck. "Nice try, Trace. But here is what we are going to do. Throw the gold over. In fact, you—you with the bone in your nose, go get it."

Trace clenched his jaw, clearly hating Gabriel for ordering his men around. Still, he gave a sharp nod, and moments later the burlap bag of gold landed at my feet.

"Now your men can come over for a celebratory drink. And then I set sail. With Blue."

"Wait a minute, Black." Trace pointed his knife. "If you think I'm just going to let you sail off with her—"

"Leave a man on board with me. Hell, leave two men on board. Your choice. They can set the sails, and when we are forty feet from shore I'll dump them in the water. You can fish them out."

What? Dump me in the water?

"You can fish, right, Trace?"

"And if I don't agree?"

"Then I slit her throat now and take my chances."

Trace sighed and fingered his blade. He wasn't sold and he wasn't happy. In frustration he kicked John, who still had not gotten up from the last blow.

"Okay," he said at last. "Let's do it."

The men cheered as Gabriel held up the absinthe. They came over the railing.

And then the cheering stopped.

Everything from that point on was a blur.

Gabriel knifed the first Runner to step foot on his deck. Limb, gut, heart, throat—the Runner ritual, and Gabriel was deadly efficient at it. Just that quickly, the man with the bone in his nose was dead.

I spit out the bandanna, slid my hands from knots that weren't cinched, and caught the bowie Gabriel tossed at me in midair.

Two more Runners came at Gabriel, but they didn't have a prayer. Gabriel had abandoned his blades for a small repeating crossbow he had stowed under a pile of fenders. The two men were riddled with arrows in seconds. Screams filled the air, and blood, red and slick and smelling of copper, coated the deck. I had never seen the weapon, only heard of its existence. Leave it to Gabriel to have one.

And now there were two: Trace and John.

I went for Trace and so did Gabriel. But before I could reach him, he kicked John overboard, and with bound hands and feet it was a death sentence.

Gabriel froze and watched as the blue-green body hit the water. It was all the opportunity Trace needed. He was coming at Gabriel.

"Look out!" I screamed. Gabriel flattened on the deck just as the fillet knife sliced though the air. It would have taken out his throat. Gabriel looked frantically toward the water where John had disappeared, and I realized that his concentration was gone.

And that would get him killed.

I didn't think. I just reacted. I pulled off my boots, stripped off my fleece, and shouted to Gabriel, "I've got him; I've got John."

Gabriel rolled to his side, catching Trace in the legs with a vicious kick. Trace landed a few feet away. Gabriel looked at me. *Damn him.* Didn't he just have that questioning raised-eyebrow thing going on? Who had time for that shit?

"I can swim. I'll get Snake Man, and you kill Trace. Got it?"

Well, he had to get it. Because I had my knife in my mouth and dived over the side before he could react.

The water was take-your-breath-away cold. Reaching up to grab my blade, I broke the surface, gasping. The cold had knocked the air from my lungs. I wouldn't last long in these waters; no one would. I took a deep breath and dived back under the water.

I knew where John had gone in, but in the few moments that had passed there were currents and tide action and— I saw him. I saw him. Only a few feet before me, he wasn't moving. *Damn.* I swam alongside him, cutting ropes from his feet, then his wrists. I tucked him under my arm in a neck hold and kicked with all my might, pushing for the surface. I aimed for daylight and air and life.

Seconds later we burst to the surface—just as Gabriel and Trace tumbled overboard.

What had just happened? Now all four of us were in the water? Unbelievable.

Let's play, Blue. Let's play, the sea whispered.

"Let's not," I said as I treaded water.

Ready? whispered the sea.

I wasn't, but the swells hit us anyway. Hard, fast, and furious, they tumbled us over and over and over until we were spit out onto the rocks and sand and debris.

We were sprawled out on the beach like salmon fillets drying in the sun.

Gabriel and John didn't move. They could not be dead. They just could not.

Trace was up on his feet. He carried a piece of driftwood in his hand like a club. And he was coming right for me.

I scooted backward on my butt, scrambling on all fours like a crab, but he reached me quickly and had his boot at my throat.

"You are a shitload of work, Tsunami Blue," he said as he ground his boot into my neck. "And I'm not sure that you're worth it. But the way I see it, you'll do your job just as well with or without an ear." He knelt and, with his knee on my chest, he pulled a knife from the small of his back. The blade looked sharp enough to cut silk. "Let this be a lesson."

He put more pressure on my chest, and now I could hardly breathe. "Gabriel will kill you," I said in a gasp.

Trace laughed. "Gabriel is dead, sweetheart. They both are."

"No . . ." My voice was weak, and stars were starting to form from lack of oxygen.

He leaned over me. "Oh, yes," he hissed.

Trace fisted my hair in his hand and brought the blade down just under my earlobe.

"You sick fuck," I wheezed.

"You got that right."

I saw a flash, a blur really, of rich colors. Gold and white and black twirled together and flew before my eyes. Trace went airborne, screaming. I heard growling, thunderous and frightening. What was happening? What—? I pushed up and saw stars. My vision blurred. I put my head between my legs to keep from passing out. The feeling passed in seconds. My vision cleared, only to be clouded again from tears.

Max.

It was Max.

My Max.

I was sobbing now, calling my dog's name, calling for him to stop. To come.

He was doing what he always had. He was protecting me.

Standing right behind him, leaning on each other for support, were John and Gabriel.

I cried harder.

My Max and my Gabriel were alive. Alive!

I was on my feet, calling my dog's name. Max stopped and looked first at me, then at Gabriel. Gabriel pointed and Max ran to me, knocking me over. We tumbled and tangled and rolled. He licked and barked and hit me with a tail that refused to stop wagging. He was matted and filthy and oh, so beautiful.

For the first time in I didn't know how long, I laughed. I cried tears of real joy.

I was so involved with Max that when Gabriel told me a few moments later that John the Snake Man had taken Trace's life I dropped to the sand on weak knees. And I sure as hell was glad I didn't see that before John delivered the killing blow, he had sliced off Trace's ears and tossed them to the circling gulls above.

The lights of New Seattle beckoned in the distance. Standing out in the ink of night, they twinkled and waved, looking friendly and harmless.

Not so.

The lights were huge fires, lit on platforms that stood hundreds of feet in the air. The Runner fires. Fire from hell was more like it.

New Seattle held the largest contingency of Runners in the northern hemisphere. After the last big wave, they had sailed into the city, set up base, and never left. It had pretty much ruined my underwater shopping adventures. And even though I had prayed that most would be gone, frightened off by my message of impending doom and all, it was unrealistic to think there would be none left behind. There were always disbelievers in the bunch. And there were the opportunists. The ones who would risk anything, even their own lives, for the old finders-keepers game. That applied to anything left behind. Including women and children.

We had sailed from New San Juan with the wind and sea pushing us along at an unbelievable speed. It was like nature knew what lay ahead and was forcing us forward before we changed our minds. But forward to what? I had to wonder. Life? Or death?

We had said good-bye to John. For now. Using Trace's boat, which was now his boat, minus the rotting body and skulls, John had sailed to New False Bay.

The Snake Man, it seemed, was our new babysitter.

And no one was more shocked about that than I was.

But, boy, were the twins revved up. When we had raised them on the shortwave, they had insisted on putting Aubrey on for introductions. She was excited to see all his colors.

The boys knew him. Turns out John the Snake Man, had been a friend who had visited New False Bay often. Gabriel trusted him. And me? Well, I had saved his life, so he owed me. But when the kids didn't sound scared anymore, when they knew John was on the way to take them as far north as possible, I decided we were even.

Because even Tsunami Blue hadn't been able to take their fears away.

John had been a friend of Gabriel's in another life before being captured and hauled away to perform in Trace's cage of terror. He'd been born with the spooky film over his eyes. A birth defect. A freak of nature. And didn't I know how that felt. But the tattoos and piercings and the rest had been done by the Runners. Then they had split his tongue.

All against his will.

And I thought my childhood was hard.

But for me it was saying good-bye to Max—again—that was the hardest. I had gotten my best friend back, but as I watched him run along the deck and bark his good-bye, I broke down all over again. Logic dictated that it was the best move to take Max to the kids and Bacon and safety. But my emotions said differently.

I wiped my eyes.

"Thinking about Max?" Gabriel reached out and smoothed my hair. "I'm so glad you got him back."

I managed a smile and nodded.

A huge flash of flames shot high into the night sky.

"The fires of hell are burning bright tonight," I said.

I stood with Gabriel, and as we sailed into New Seattle, I braced for the same old insanity that only this many Runners could conjure.

But tonight was different. There was more chaos than ever. More insanity.

The Runners were moving out.

There was panic in the air. We could see the flurry of frantic activity. Like a mass of killer bees, the Runners swarmed. Men raced across platforms, carrying supplies. They hung from scaffolding, using pulleys and weights to haul cargo down to the waiting ships. They shouted, swore, fought, and killed. I watched as a man slipped, snapping his leg. As he lay screaming in agony, a Runner kicked him off the platform. Another put an arrow in him halfway down. He was still screaming when he hit the water. A crippled Runner was a dead Runner. It was just the way of the world. Their twisted world, that is.

We sailed on, blending easily into the insanity all around us. What was one more ship in the midst of hundreds? We passed the shark pens and a fierce chill swept along my spine. The pens were legendary. As were the great whites held captive in them. It was once thought that the sharks couldn't survive in captivity. But leave it to the Runners to figure out a way.

They kept the sharks well fed.

To keep my fear at bay, I sat in the cockpit huddled under a blanket and watched Gabriel at the wheel. And I talked. And talked. And, well, basically, I drove Gabriel crazy.

"So you're not a Runner, but you pretended to be a Runner and then you got a tattoo. Doesn't that make you a Runner?"

"Blue." He leaned down where I now sat and kissed me. "I am *not* a Runner. I never was a Runner. I only pretended to be a Runner to find you. If I could find you, then together we could do so much good. We could stop these monster waves, stop this insane destruction, save lives. We could try to give humanity a chance." He sighed and ran his hand through his hair. "There were thousands of Runners looking for you, Blue. Thousands."

"Thousands?" My voice squeaked.

He nodded. "They had better resources. More manpower. So I joined."

"And that doesn't make you a Runner?"

"It makes me a *pretend* Runner. Pretend." He swung the wheel and the sails responded, filling with the night wind.

I thought for a moment. "And when you found me? When you gave me Max? Why?"

"I couldn't get you out safely. They were closing in. All the factions. Trace, Indigo, all getting close. So I took them in another direction. That other direction lasted five years," he said bitterly. "I left you Max just before I convinced them to go south."

"Ah, south." I thought of his sun-kissed skin. "And when I found you? When you almost died?"

"They had found you and were coming for you in the morning. I tried to beat them to it. The sea was rough, too rough." He shifted his hands and gripped the wheel. "I almost didn't make it in time to save you."

I watched the tension in his body build as he relived that night. I stood and shared my blanket with him. "But you did make it, tough guy, you did."

"So. How 'bout I change the subject?" I said after a moment. "I have a few more questions."

He looked skeptical.

"How does this thing work?"

"This thing?" he asked.

"Yeah. You know, the whole, stoppin'-the-wave thing." I twirled my finger in the air.

"It's complicated." He looked wary, like he always did when he didn't know what was gonna come out of my mouth.

"So let me see if I can wrap my mind around this."

"Let's not."

"Crystals?" I said, ignoring him.

"No."

"Meditation?"

"No."

"Chanting?"

Sigh. "No."

"Incense and peppermint?"

"Not funny."

"What?"

"Never mind."

"I've got it. Parsley, sage, rosemary, and thyme."

"Damn it, Blue."

I shut up. The shark pens were too close. He might give 'em a snack. Me.

We sailed through the city that had once been so green and lush, so unbelievably beautiful on a summer's day. It now lay in ruins, like every other major city in the world.

We passed Seattle's famous landmark, the Space Needle—actually, just the needle. That was all that remained for human eyes. Everything else was underwater.

Stick a needle in your eye, the sea whispered at me.

It was then, at that moment, that I knew the exact location the wave would come in. The sea, with its taunting game had just pinpointed it for me.

Do you know how to thread a needle, Blue?

I knew without looking that all the color had drained from my face. I thought I might be sick.

And of course Gabriel noticed.

"You okay?" he asked.

"No, not really. But I will be. If you can really do what you say you can. Because now I know exactly where the wave will crest. Exactly." I fought back the nausea while the sea laughed and taunted. *Needle in a haystack, Blue. Needle in a haystack.*

"The wave?" Gabriel asked.

"There," I said as we sailed past. "The wave crests there."

Gabriel squinted into the dark at the famous, now partially submerged Seattle Space Needle. "The Needle, then?"

"The Needle." He didn't ask me again. He believed me.

And it was time I believed him. Completely.

We sailed among the rooftops of Pike Place Market. I had been there only once as a kid. I remembered the noise and the people and colors and smells and food. But mostly, I remembered the fish.

I remembered the boys at the fish market throwing salmon through the air for their customers to catch if they dared. The kings were slippery and a worker was always there as backup should the customer miss. The customers missed a lot.

I loved it. So sure was I that those fish, the king salmon, could fly, I told Seamus. It was the first time he called me stupid. But now, knowing he had suffered and died without giving me up, that in the end he had protected me, took the sting out of the memory. It took the sting out of a lot of memories.

Gabriel tied the boat to an old sign advertising Starbucks Pike Place Blend. If Christmas Blend traded like gold, the Pike Place Blend would be platinum.

"We wait here," he said. "It's a good vantage point. I can watch the water."

I went below. I didn't want to care anymore. I was with either a madman or a miracle worker. Either way I didn't think we'd live to see the morning. And for the first time I started to grieve for my future. For Gabriel's future. A future that held the promise of us.

I woke to footsteps above deck. Loud voices echoed in the night. Swearing, laughter, and one oh, so familiar voice. Indigo. *Damn it.* I'd so much rather die in a wave.

The hatch flew open and a nasty-looking Runner, ripe with alcohol and weed, climbed down.

"I found the bitch!" he said, revealing teeth he'd filed into wicked points.

I turned to run. Yeah. Like that was gonna work. So much room in a sailboat.

He grabbed me and twisted the butter knife out of my hand, almost breaking my wrist. I was hauled up by my hair and tossed at Indigo's feet. When I looked up, he was embracing Gabriel.

Gabriel pulled away and thumped Indigo on the back with a hearty slap. "I knew I'd find you here. Thought you'd be pleased with my little present." He nudged me with his boot. "All that's missing is the bow."

I thought I was going to be sick.

Both men looked down at me like so much garbage.

Indigo, still wearing his stupid hat, spit on me and laughed. I thought I saw Gabriel flinch. No. I was wrong. He was smiling.

I. Would. Not. Cry.

"She looks like shit, Gabriel. All black and blue and purple. Please tell me this is my work."

Gabriel thumped Indigo on the back. "It is."

Indigo probed at me with his boot. "Did you nail her? Break her in for me? Tell me our little wave rat is a good ride."

I. Would. Not. Cry.

"Naw." Gabriel looked at me like I was dirt under his boot. "She's too damn scrawny for me. Look at her, she's a fucking toothpick. What fun is that?"

Indigo's eyes narrowed. "Do you not want to share her? Is that it? Because she may be a little shit, but she's gorgeous." He reached down and captured my chin. "Just look at those eyes."

"Suit yourself. I'm done with her."

I do not share. How many times had I heard that? How many? Was everything about this man a lie? *Not possible*, my heart said. *Not even*.

"You're a good man, Gabriel, one of my favorites. I should be pissed at you for leaving the cage without even a proper good-bye. But since you saved my little weather vane here along with your own sorry ass, I can forgive the slight. I just wish I'd been there sooner to help you out with that bastard Trace. But I heard in the wind that you took care of him just fine." He laughed a wicked, mean laugh. "And that idiot thought he was having me for dinner."

Chapter Thirty-two

Indigo had given Gabriel "last rights" with me. It was another twisted and sick Runner ritual: giving the captor one romp with his captive before she was handed over to the next in line.

I sat cross-legged on the V-berth. My hands were bound and I stared up through the hatch where the twins had first appeared. If I closed my eyes, I could see their hazel almond-shaped eyes, their shaggy heads, their wide-eyed look of innocence. It was that look, fixed forever in my mind, that haunted me the most. Gabriel cared about the kids—hell, he loved the kids. And he loved me. If I died this night at Runner hands, that was just what I would choose to believe. That was what I had to believe to keep on breathing.

The hatch swung open, and Gabriel stepped down into the cabin. He brought the smell of fresh sea air that mingled with the scent that was uniquely Gabriel Black. It was like an embrace from an old friend. The wind blew in behind him, sending his duster flapping around his leather boots. Midnight hair whipped around his shoulders, and his scowl was back. He looked like he had the morning after I found him, when I had held a knife to his throat. He looked dangerous and dark and threatening all over again. But I wasn't afraid. I couldn't be afraid of him. I loved him.

He slammed the hatch closed and threw the bolt. He came to me and swept me off the berth and into his arms. He carried me into the main cabin, away from prying eyes, and set me down. He pinned me against the teakwood wall and kissed me. It was hard and bruising and desperate. He kissed me like he never wanted to stop. He kissed me like I was his and his alone. He kissed me like he was saying good-bye. Tears spilled down my cheeks at the thought. And finally, he kissed me like he loved me.

He broke from the kiss and untied my hands. He kissed my wrists where red, angry welts started to rise. Cupping my face in his hands, he looked into my eyes. I saw worry and fear reflected in his gaze, but I saw something else too: a raw, fierce determination.

"I will be back for you. You know this, right?"

I hesitated.

He put his hands on my shoulders and gently shook me. "Right?" he said again.

I nodded, unable to find my voice.

"You will survive. Right?"

I nodded again.

"Damn it, Blue, say it. I need to hear you say it."

"I will."

"Will what?"

"Survive."

"Until?"

"Until you come for me." I couldn't believe my own voice. I sounded scared, weak, defeated. And Gabriel could hear it too. But he had it wrong. I wasn't afraid for me. I was afraid for him. How was he going to get past the entire Runner nation and live? How?

He put his forehead to mine and whispered, "Where's my Tsunami Blue? The one who swears and kicks and spins knives?"

"And throws a mean rock," I added. That got me a smile.

"Where is the woman who will fight for Max and Nick and Alec and—"

"Aubrey," I finished the sentence for him. I reached up and looped my arms around his neck. "She's right here, tough guy. Come back for me. Or I'll come lookin' for you." I punched him in the arm. And for the first time ever, I punched him like a girl. I couldn't bear to put another mark on his already bruised body.

A fist pounded at the hatch and my heartbeat kicked into overdrive.

"Time's up, lover boy. We're all getting under way. We got a fuckin' wave to outrun."

Gabriel pulled away. He reached out and mussed my hair, then tore my thermal and retied my hands.

And before he delivered me to the lions, he said the only words I needed to hear: "I love you."

I climbed onto Indigo's boat and was immediately thrown on the deck face-first. I pushed up, frantically brushing my hair from my eyes so I could watch the tall silhouette of Gabriel Black fade as we were pulled away from his boat by the currents.

He was watching me.

At that moment I knew I might never see him again.

It hurt like hell.

Good-bye, the sea said, lapping against the hull. *Good-bye, good-bye, good-bye.*

So there was my answer. The sea knew. This was good-bye.

There would be nothing left for me in this wet, fucked-up world without Gabriel and his little band of kids in it. And Max. Nothing. So I did what anyone in my position would do: I set out to make a plan. I'd forgo the pie charts and spreadsheets and five-year goals. I figured

I had a five-minute, three-step goal. One, stay alive, at least for a while. Two, get the Runners to hang a bit longer. And three, wait for Gabriel to save me. Or else I'd save him. Again. *Oops.* That was four.

But deep down in my gut, I knew Gabriel could not save me. If he truly could stop waves, there would be no time to come back for me. I could only pray that he would save himself. Save himself for the little family who depended on him so. Save himself for Max.

And I thought I knew how to buy him time to make it happen.

Runners were predictable, greedy bastards. That was why they were still here. Still sacking and hoarding and looting. They couldn't bear to leave anything behind. Greed was what drove them. Greed would kill them. Greed would take them straight to hell. The only problem with my plan was that I might have to go to hell with them.

I thought of the blood I'd spilled. And maybe, just maybe I deserved the same fate too. But not Gabriel. Not the kids. Not Max.

It was time to put my plan in action. And it had to start with His Blueness, Indigo.

I struggled to my feet, gaining balance against the rail. I tried to smooth my long and knotted hair with my tied hands. And when that didn't work, I went for the obvious: I tore my thermal down farther, revealing cleavage. I turned to find Indigo.

"So you think you're a pretty smart bitch, don't you, Tsunami Blue?"

A tall, thin Runner with a 666 tattooed on his forehead sneered at me. He drew his knife. I wanted to knee him in the balls, stomp on his face, and kick him in the ribs. I could do it in under ten seconds. But I had a new four-step plan. And number one was staying alive. So those . . . what should I call them? Shenanigans seemed like a good Irish word. Those shenanigans of the old days had to stop. *Damn it anyway.*

He pushed his blade closer to my eye.

"Look at them pretty, pretty baby blues," he said. "I wouldn't mind having one for a little souvenir." The man grinned.

I wasn't worried about losing an eye. I'd use the knee-drop-and-stomp thing first. But damn it—another Runner who didn't use a toothbrush. That in itself was torture.

"Please do not ruin my four-step plan." I sighed, shaking my head. He only brought the knife closer and shoved me to my knees. *Well, shit.* There went my advantage.

The man went to his knees right in front of me. His blade dropped from his fingers and he toppled over. On me. Blood splattered everywhere: in my hair, in my eyes, on my clothes.

Indigo appeared over us with a wicked-looking blade that dripped blood. He had just slit the man's throat.

"No one," he screamed, "and I mean no one, goes near her. Understood?"

He stepped over the body. A man ran to heave it overboard, and got a blade to the throat instead.

"The body stays. No need to waste perfectly good meat for the whites," said Indigo.

He reached down and cut the rope from my wrists and offered me a hand up. I didn't take it, but chose instead to stand up on my own.

"You're a stubborn one, that's for sure. I can't wait to get you trained my way. It will be fun." He reached over and wiped his bloody blade on my pants.

I slowly breathed in the midnight air, so crisp and clean. It calmed my pounding heart and soothed my frayed and raw nerves. I had to hold it together just a while longer.

The wave would be on time tonight. The sea, knowing that I would be joining it soon, had promised.

I rolled my shoulders and stood straighter. I looked Indigo in the eyes and remembered all the reasons I wanted to kill him. And before this night was through, I would. With that thought in mind, I felt surprisingly better.

"So, sometimes"—I wiped the blood from my lips—"I get the timing off." I heard the sea laugh.

Indigo looked at my breasts, reaching out to grab and squeeze. "My timing's never off," he said.

"Sorry." I swatted his hand away in a teasing gesture that looked a lot like flirting. He seemed to enjoy it, blood dripping from me and all. I wanted to throw up. All over his clown pants. It was all I could do not to.

I proceeded to convince him that I had it all wrong. I talked fast while pressing up against him using what cleavage I had to distract. I even batted my baby blues.

Oh, sure, I had said, *the wave is coming, of course. Am I ever wrong? But not for hours. You have plenty of time to keep looting and hoarding. Why would I lie? Do you think I have a death wish? And why not throw in a little absinthe drinking too?* Sure, I'd join him. My stomach had rolled at the thought. But if it hadn't been for the sea, I would not have been able to pull it off. The sea, loving a game, calmed, and sent gentle soothing laps to brush the hull. The rhythm was hypnotic, cryptic. And only I could read the message hidden there. *I'm coming. I'm coming. I'm coming.*

But it worked. In the end, it was that greed thing, after all. Human nature. At the very least, Runner nature. They turned the boat around for one last run at a supply station.

Phase one of my plan was a success. I had survived long enough to lie and manipulate and bend the truth my way. I played their wicked game and I was winning. Hell—I would win.

Instead of sailing away from the wave, we were right in its path. And all of us would die. Nothing like taking someone with you.

I heard it before anyone else.

The water had started to recede.

Indigo heard it second. "What the—" Indigo sounded hysterical. "The bitch lied. The fucking bitch lied."

He turned and hit me. Hard. I went down, landing on the teak deck next to the lifeless eyes of a dead man. The 666 that had been inked into his forehead glared at me. I turned away from him.

Down on the deck, with my cheek near the hull, I heard the sea whispering, *I'm here, Blue. I'm here.*

The chaos on board started. Running. Screams. Crying.

Indigo came back my way and landed a kick in my ribs. Damn, but I was tired of being a human punching bag.

"Get up. Save us, you stupid bitch."

"I can't."

Indigo dropped to his knees and lifted my head by grabbing my hair. "I said, save us."

I closed my eyes and faked a blackout. I mean, why not? I was done talking to this man. Done.

"I don't want to die," Indigo screamed.

Get over it and die like a man.

"Shit, the water. Where's it going?" a Runner screamed.

Out, Einstein.

"Is that a wave?" asked another.

A big-ass one.

"We're going to die."

Yep, pretty much. That was the beauty of a plan: When it worked, it really worked. I had led them into the wave and now, if I were going to die, I would take all these Runner scum with me. Straight to hell.

I thought of Gabriel. The man who thought he could stop waves. I prayed that he could. I mean, why not?

I could talk to the ocean. Predict waves. Why couldn't he be the yin to my yang? *Wait. What?* Did that ever sound corny. Man, impending death sure messed with your head.

Our boat, caught by the force of the receding waters, spun and spun. I tried to get up and grabbed for the railings. The shark pen was just yards in front of us. The receding water tore and ripped like it had arms, destroying the sea cage.

In an instant the sharks, the whites, were free.

There were so many of them.

Our boat, jolted by confused tides and swells, sent the body on deck flying into the water. A shark leaped in midair, its eyes rolling back into its head as its jaws unhinged. The creature caught the body and half the man was gone before my eyes.

I rolled back on the deck, sick. What a sight to take to the watery grave with you. *Shit. Isn't anything easy?*

I heard the sea whispering, *Coming, coming.*

"You're already here," I said. "And you're off to a hell of a start, I've got to say."

Gabriel, the sea whispered. *Gabriel, Gabriel, Gabriel.*

"What about Gabriel?" I said. My heartbeat raced as I waited for an answer.

Gabriel. Here, the sea whispered. And then it laughed.

No. No! He could not be here. He needed to be at the Needle. He needed to stop this wave and get the hell out of here and live. He could not be caught up in this. If he tried to save me and tangle with the Runners, the wave would finish the job and take him too. I needed him to live. To take care of the kids and Max and— No. Just no. I did not want him to die. I wanted—no, I needed him to live. I wanted to die knowing that the best, most beautiful thing that ever happened to me would live on. Live on to watch three kids grow into wonderful adults. Live on to run with Max on the beach. Live on to drink Christmas Blend. I needed him to live.

I reached for the railing to hoist myself up. And that was when I saw it.

Tsunami.

Still a good distance away, the wave rose and rose and rose. Moonlight, streaming through dark clouds, highlighted the curl and color, the foam and mist.

It was beautiful. It was terrifying. It was the end.

And one thing was perfectly clear: Anything in its way would not, could not survive.

I focused. Gabriel and his sleek black sailboat were right in its path.

I couldn't help it: I started to cry. Not for me, but for him. For my beautiful dark angel I had found on my beach on a moonlit night. I wanted him to live. He had to. He just had to.

Yes, the sea whispered, *yes*, *Tsunami Blue*.

My hair was yanked, and my head and neck were pulled back at an impossible angle.

"You die tonight, Blue. As do I. But not before you feel what real pain is." Indigo held a blade at my throat.

I rolled my eyes. "Real pain"? He obviously had no idea what I had been through in the last few days.

The wave suddenly roared as the water rushed forward now, faster and faster. The sound rang in my ears, straining my eardrums to the breaking point.

Indigo couldn't keep his footing. The fact that Gabriel had appeared behind him and driven a fillet knife all the way through him didn't help. I knew this because Indigo had let me drop, and when I turned, no one was more astonished than I was to see Gabriel Black on board.

"Remember, you bastard? I don't share," Gabriel said with ice in his voice. "Not Blue. Not ever."

Wow. He had just saved my life. All three minutes of it.

He lifted Indigo into the air with the knife still embedded. Gabriel personally fed him to a great white, with Indigo screaming all the way.

"Blue"—Gabriel tossed me a knife—"behind you."

I caught the knife in the air. It felt smooth, familiar. It fit my hand perfectly. My bowie. I turned, twirling my blade like old times. The Runner stopped short. My blade was bigger. He turned and ran down the deck. I smiled down at my knife. A girl and her knife. Now that was what I was talking about.

"We gotta get out of here," Gabriel said as he swung me up over his shoulder. Again.

The sea had become Gabriel's new best friend. Kind of like Max. Which explained how Gabriel got on Indigo's boat. Just in time to save me.

The sea whispered, and Gabriel heard.

The sea protected us, and before I could say *tsunami*, the sea delivered us to the Space Needle, with only moments to spare.

We climbed into the interior of the Needle and ran up the little stairway to the top as fast as we could. Stepping through a large crack in the Needle's tip, we found ourselves standing on a little ledge facing the deadliest wave in our blue planet's history.

So we were either going to die together in a few minutes because my guy was nuts, or I would be pleasantly surprised and we would live happily ever after.

Gabriel tossed off his duster and stripped off his shirt. Wave or no wave, I was just enjoying the view when he took out a knife and turned to me.

"Do not tell me you need a blood sacrifice, Gabriel Black. Because I don't think I have a drop left."

"Blue, calm down. I just want you to hold this for me."

"Oh."

"And I need you to be real quiet." He put a slender finger to his lips. "Okay?"

"'Kay," I said, borrowing from Aubrey.

And then he kissed me. Who knew we had the time?

Gabriel spread his arms out in front of him, his golden and bruised skin now damp with the salt mist. He murmured words foreign to me. His concentration was such that I ceased to exist, as did the entire world around him. It was freezing and well past midnight, but the heat radiating from his body warmed me to the point where I stripped off my torn thermal.

His golden skin turned white as sea salt dried against it. And still the heat grew. The wave had paused like a rearing horse, and the sight was so unbelievable that my breath caught and tears stung my eyes.

I thought of my mother and father, and lastly, but mostly, of Finnegan. I whispered his name on the wind, and the wave, monstrous yet so beautiful, shimmered just like my tattoo did when it was wet. I fell to my knees as my brother's name appeared in the mist. And just like that the monster tsunami was gone, folding back into the sea from where it had come. Gabriel had somehow turned it away.

Good-bye, the sea whispered to me. *Good-bye, good-bye, good-bye.*

Gabriel dropped to his knees, exhausted, and I rushed to embrace him, crying.

"I know, Blue, I know. I saw it too."

"Do you think it was a message?"

He leaned against the steel, holding me in his arms. "Or a good-bye," he whispered, and kissed the top of my head.

They found us in each other's arms a day later. Hungry, battered, bruised, half-naked, we were quite the sight.

Gabriel had a reason to be half-naked.

I, on the other hand, did not.

But luckily, Aubrey was below deck when John anchored, launched a dinghy, and brought us home. Unfortunately, Nick and Alec were topside.

Home was a sleek black sailboat that would, if Gabriel got his way, belong to both of us. And time would tell if our little whiskey-brown-eyed Aubrey would remain with us. But for now she was part of our family. We loved her already.

Nick and Alec and Aubrey were thrilled to spend a little more time with John, and had hitched a ride back home to New False Bay. After all, he had a real pirate ship. And dogs, namely Max and Bacon, were allowed on board. And it seemed, according to the boys, that the new kid, Aubrey, turned out to be a lot of fun. Hanging with us? Not so much. They said something about "old" people.

They lost some future pancakes on that one.

Sailing away from New Seattle the next morning, with Starbucks in my hand and a wonderful new soreness in my body, I saw a shark.

It was blue.

"Don't ask," Gabriel said. I didn't. But I did feel sorry for the shark. I just hoped he ate the hat too.

Epilogue

New San Juan Island
Six months later

"And so, my friends, I come to you today with news of a different sort. News that's been in the wind, and I'm here to set you straight. It's true. A little tsunami is heading our way."

I paused for effect, just for fun.

"Actually, my way. And"—I couldn't help but smile, remembering Gabriel's reaction, the soft tears and kisses—"Gabriel's too. Yep. We are going to have a baby, folks.

"I'm so thrilled and proud and honored to share this news with you. Together we can build a safe, sane, waveless world for all our children.

"This is Tsunami Blue signing off on another of many, many, many smooth-sailing days."

I put down the mic and touched my belly and smiled. I'd been doing a lot of that these days. I watched Nick and Alec playing in the surf with Max. I watched our Aubrey—Aubie, as we had come to call her—draw pictures in the sand. She had considerably more talent than I. We continued to search for her family, putting out messages in the wind and on the air. But word had it they had last been seen in New Vancouver, trying to reach high ground. So for now, she was ours. Maybe forever. And should that be the case, it was more than all right with all of us.

My heart swelled at the sight of my new wonderful

family. A tear slipped down my cheek. I'd been doing a lot of that lately too.

"Blue? You okay?"

Startled, I turned and saw Gabriel, my pirate, my dark angel, my husband, at the door. And he was in trouble again.

"Fudge, Gabriel, do not sneak up on a pregnant woman that way."

He walked over, took me in his arms, and kissed the tear away.

"Happy tears?"

"Yeah."

" 'Fudge'?"

I walked over and pointed to the nearly empty pickle jar. I'd really been working hard at it.

"Damn right," I said proudly. Then, "Damn it! I mean, darn right, darn it." I socked him in the arm for laughing.

Gabriel reached into his pocket and put two twenties in the pickle jar for me.

He gathered me into his arms once again. "I love you. Keep up the good work." He released me and rubbed his arm. Smiling, he said, "Don't ever change, Blue. Don't ever change."

"An exceptional literary debut." —John Charles, reviewer, *The Chicago Tribune* and *Booklist* on *The Battle Sylph*

The Shattered Sylph

L. J. McDonald

SHATTERED

Kidnapped by slavers, Lizzie Petrule was dragged in chains across the Great Sea to the corrupt empire of Meridal. There, beneath a floating citadel and an ocean of golden sand, lies a pleasure den for gladiators—and a prison for the maidens forced to slake their carnal thirst.

Despite impossible odds, against imponderable magic, three men have vowed Lizzie's return: Justin, her suitor; Leon, her father; and Ril, the shape-shifting but war-weary battler. Together, this broken band can save her, but only with a word that must remain unsaid, a foe that is a friend, and a betrayal that is, at heart, an act of love.

"Wonderful, innovative and fresh. Don't miss this fantastic story." —#1 *New York Times* Bestselling Author Christine Feehan on *The Batle Sylph*

ISBN 13: 978-0-8439-6323-6